Adventure Vixen

Welcome sisters of the light!

This Vixen guidebook has powers as yet unknown to you.

It is invaluable in the success of being a Vixen.

Use it wisely and guard its secrets with your life.

THE VIXEN'S SECRET HANDBOOK SERIES
Book 1

Adventure Vixen

By

KM Chapman

Kaycee Energy
Publishing

Adventure Vixen

THE VIXEN'S SECRET HANDBOOK SERIES

This book is a work of fiction. Names, characters, incidents and dialogue are either the product of the author's imagination or are used fictitiously. Any resemblance to actual persons, living or dead, businesses, companies or events is entirely coincidental.

This book contains content that is not suitable for young readers 17 and under.

ISBN: 978-0-6481111-4-6
Editing: www.thewriterssurgeon.com
Cover Artist: Simone Design
Publisher: Kaycee Energy Publishing

This paperback edition published by Kaycee Energy Publishing.

www.karinachapman.com/books

Preface

The information contained within these pages is for the eyes of Vixens only. We cannot give away the secrets of the Vixens, so be alert and guard these words with care, sisters! Read on and take delight in the awakening of your own inner Vixen. Draw her into the light. Have fun, be playful and light-hearted. Share around the delights of your mystical Vixen love!

BUT do not share the most sacred of all ... "The Vixen's Secret Handbook" Shh! Don't even utter the words aloud as yet, make sure you are alone first! Read on, dear sisters and willing purveyors of the path of Vixendom, as your lives will be changed forever ...

IF YOU DARE!

The Vixen's Secret Handbook

Vixen Coven Commandments

- Everyone's time is valuable, so do not waste a moment on anything or anyone unworthy of receiving the wondrous gift of a Vixen's precious time and attention.

- At all times, Vixens remain respectful, kind and mindful of others' feelings. Vixens are not rude to unwanted Marks either online or in person. Even if you are horrified or revolted at what you hear or see, remain outwardly calm and extract yourself from the situation with grace and kindness, for it costs nothing to be kind to others, and this is the Vixen way.

- When in play mode, ensure each Mark chosen meets one of the major 'unsuitability' points previously determined by each Vixen. This is to prevent a Vixen's heart from being affected negatively, and to help her to stay conscious of the fact she is currently in Vixen play mode, not marriage mode.

- Thou shalt not knowingly play with or ensnare any man who is married or in a monogamous relationship. Such underhanded behaviour is beneath the Vixen. (Failure to adhere to this rule will result in more headaches, heartaches, and issues than it is worth, so stay vigilant on your dates.)

- Never covet or play with another Vixen's established Mark. Vixens are not in competition with each other, rather a supportive sisterhood taking a break from the rollercoaster of emotions that traditional relationships ca/n be. There are many more potential Marks available than there are Vixens, so if you come to realise another Vixen has already ensnared a Mark, step down.

- Know ye well the Vixen's Secret Handbook! Yes, it will enable you to protect your heart for a while, and indulge in light-hearted play and adventure ... but there will come a time when these lessons and dates will serve you well.

- When the Vixen life no longer suits your needs, do not be afraid of this revelation, instead recognise this change within, and see if your inner light is strong enough to withstand the search for the true love and connection we all yearn for at some stage of our lives.

- Be prepared, oh Vixens, that this living Book will morph as needed, so constant consultation of its pages is recommended, even if you transition into hunting a love-match

Adventure Vixen

Hello Singledom

Dammit! What the hell am I doing back here?

In total disgust I shake my head in disbelief at the unexpected situation I find myself dropped into. Another break-up to deal with—this time caused by the infidelity of a guy I was so sure I could trust completely. How could I let this happen again? Wasn't I watching out for the tell-tale signs? Was I too complacent with my pair of rose-coloured glasses? The enormity of the emotional turmoil, total upheaval and an apparently lonely path into the future looms darkly in front of me.

Oh, for God's sake! I wipe my tear stained face in frustration. If anyone was nearby right now, I'd ask them to slap some sense into me. How will I tackle being single this time round, I wonder?

What is the best way to survive and thrive after the unexpected demise of a relationship? Should I wallow in self-pity, miserably stuffing my face with chocolate bars in unattractive food-stained pyjamas, with several empty wine bottles on the floor? Crying myself into an alcohol-addled sleep with melted chocolate stuck on my sateen sheets? Should I continue to cry, complain and whine to anyone who would listen? Yuck!

Or should I contemplate the unthinkable ... the, dare I say, daring or *marvellous*? Forget his stupid ass name as fast as possible, kick the dust off my sparkling wedges and move on to living life to the fullest?

These questions reverberate around my brain once I come to after having received the sudden, shocking news. I have unexpectedly been thrust back into singledom again. This is so not where I expected to be at this stage of my life.

My heart quakes in fear of the unknown. In hindsight I do not understand how I was caught so unaware. Change is the only certainty in life—along with the old cliché of death and taxes. I am now a single woman past forty! What the hell? My rational mind knows that age is only the amount of years that I've been on the planet in this life—nothing to freak out about at all. Not a disease like the anti-age cures in magazines and advertising everywhere leads us to believe!

Of course, a few kilograms less on the scale *would* make me happier. OK, OK. I could lose close to fifteen kilos, but nobody is perfect! Why can I easily put on four kilos in a week-long holiday, yet working it off takes me at least four months of sweating in the gym? A few years ago, this would not have been a not a problem at all.

I could carry on picking faults with myself until the cows come home, but what is the point of berating myself further? There is no real reason to complain—I have been doing pretty damn well for myself for over forty-years.

In the mirror I can see my hazel eyes steadily regaining more of their normal twinkle. Almost the same pretty face I'm fortunate enough to have been born with, stares back. There are faint laughter lines around my eyes, but no other big differences. I dare my reflection to contradict me.

Luckily, I still look much younger than my age—this fact is going to help a lot in my quest for change and adventure.

Hang on. That was not what my question was in the slightest. My original question was how to best survive and then *thrive* after a relationship bust-up? I want to leave the past behind me where it belongs.

My goal is to waste no time in regretting what was, but to instead live in this moment NOW. To enjoy each new moment of my life! I want to move forward as fast as I can this time. My life needs to be filled with new experiences, exuberance and laughter. How do I do this? I close my eyes and relax, breathing deeply, mentally throwing my question out to the universe.

Slipping into a meditative state, I wait for an answer from within. Minutes tick by. Finally, from the depths of my memories, it resurfaces. I suddenly remember … *the Book!*

A few years ago, I had a strange encounter with a mysterious woman at a psychic fair where I was shopping for some Goddess cards. Approaching me from behind, she grabbed my hand and spun me around to face her before I could register what was happening. Her dark eyes locked onto mine, looking into my soul in an unsettling way. She nodded her head at me, large gold hoops on her ears bobbing wildly beneath dark curls.

"It's YOU. I knew it was! I felt you coming closer this past week, and now you are here!"

Bewildered, I stared back. I was speechless; I did not know how to respond to this bizarre declaration from a stranger.

Laughing delightedly at my expression, she motioned for me to wait. I wasn't sure I could move my limbs even if I wanted to. What did she mean? Who was she? For that matter, who did she think I was? That's as far as my mind got before she reappeared in front of me clutching what seemed to be a cruddy old second-hand book.

Pressing it into my hands, she clutched both the book and my hands tightly for a long moment. I peered past her long red fingernails to the book pressed into my palms, trying to see what it was that this weird woman wanted me to have. The book started to emit a soft golden glow and grew warmer in my hands. Shocked, I almost dropped it. Glancing back at her face, I saw it soften from an intense probing expression to a satisfied grin.

"I knew it! I knew it was yours!" She crowed excitedly as she pulled me closer and lowered her voice. "I know this is completely unexpected, but this book has been waiting for you. It has been handed down from generation to generation for many years, and now it is yours. The signs never lie. I knew its new owner would appear today to claim it and lead the next generation of Vixens to the light!"

A quick glance around told me that the friends I came with were nowhere in sight, and no-one else seemed to notice this bizarre event unfolding beneath their noses. What was she talking about? I played along with this strange woman—my curiosity was too strong, and I had to find out more.

"What is this book—did I really see it glow? And how do you know I'm its owner?"

Her breath tickled my ear as she leaned closer.

"This is the *Vixen's Secret Handbook*, and it possesses many powers, my dear. In the right hands, this book can be used to lead women from darkness to light. You will know when to use it; but be careful how you use its power."

Intrigued, I strained to catch her words against the intrusive background noise of the fair. Speaking quickly, she explained the uses, dangers, and consequences of using the book. She even confirmed that I *did* indeed see a glow emanate from the book. She explained the book's origin hundreds of years earlier, and the enchantment which still enables the book to glow in approval or warning. It transforms itself as each generation of Vixen ownership changes. She was certain that it now belonged to me.

Just as she issued a final warning to me stressing the importance of my position and the book's power, music blared loudly over the speakers, startling me. I looked around distractedly for a moment.

When I looked back again the woman had vanished. Confused, I searched the crowd, but could see no sign of her. Did that really happen? I looked down at my hands, almost expecting them to be empty. To my surprise my fingers were clenched around a small, tatty, leather-bound book. I had completely forgotten about this amazing book since then, seeing that I'd been in a long, committed relationship.

The Book might, however, be the answer to my prayers now. When long-term relationships end, we experience a mourning period. Lost future dreams hit us hard as they sail out the window, never to be realised. The gaping black empty hole of tomorrow appears to be the only thing left.

No new dreams to look forward to yet. We have been neglected, cheated on or deceived. Perhaps we just fell out of love. These things can make us crazy - filling us with red hot rage one moment, transforming us into a sobbing emotional wreck the next.

I spent so much time creating future celebrations in my mind—birthdays, Christmases and holidays. Being half of the 'perfect couple' who appeared to be deliriously in love, I was the envy of others. That's what is most upsetting to me—the lost illusion of that rosy future!

Maybe it was a total fantasy dreamed up in my head, like Cinderella who gets her prince and lives happily ever after! Was I being honest with myself? Or was I torturing myself with delusional visions that would never materialise? Would these imagined events ever have happened if I was still with my ex? The definition of madness is to keep expecting different results from the same action. I will need to change something or end up crazy!

I hold on to hope. I've been thrust into Singledom before. As time passes, the power and strength of my pain will diminish. At the beginning of a new single life, it is normal to think that thriving ever again is impossible. Even just surviving the break-up is damned hard to be optimistic about ... except perhaps the vision I picture in my mind of smashing a fist into the face of my ex!

Beware, any well-intentioned person who even *dares* to suggest that I should start dating others too early after a bust-up. The inclination to launch at them with a wild scream to scratch their eyes out is hard to resist. While they gaze at their injuries in bewilderment and disbelief, I will reassure them:

"Don't worry! Time heals all wounds — I'm sure you will be just fine!" Oops. Too strong a reaction? You get my drift, though. Oh, I thought of one even worse one. Hideously insensitive even! How about:

"Don't worry dear, you will find someone else." Tactlessly suggested by some patronising nitwit who thinks in her own deluded way that she is helping me by voicing this insensitive sentence. Such platitudes drive me to drink!

Some people I know sit in the safe, gilded cage of a convenient marriage that wouldn't make financial sense to jeopardise. The best I can do when they try to sympathise, is count to ten backwards and walk away, lest I be inclined to smash my fist into their inconsiderate thick skulls!

Lucky for me I always have my girlfriends to remind me of my awesomeness! Thank God for friends who will answer their phones when I call at two in the morning, drunk and teary because I 'miss that stupid arsehole'. They remind me of the reason I am single — and help me to maintain my sanity.

As I see it, I can choose to hold onto all my negative emotions and the pain caused by this life event within forever, dwell on the past and on what may have been.
Or I can choose to let these emotions go ... and be free to move forward to new adventures.

I imagine the relief gained from pessimistic thoughts and past dramas dissolving into nothingness. Ahead of me I see the shining bright light of all the things possible and attainable now. Immediately my body and spirit feel lighter, uplifted and joyous as the weight of the heavy energy in my soul dissolves.

I'll choose option number two please! I don't think this will be easy though—nothing is at first. I won't revisit my break-up day ever again in my head. Once in real life is quite enough, thank you — so on to a new journey and positive thoughts!

Seated in comfort, I continue to meditate. Hours pass. Focussing on regaining my joy and inner peace, I move forward from the past. I try to stay conscious and present in each moment, to not be dragged back into the fading quicksand of negative shit. This path is not for the faint-hearted, but the rewards are great.

Staying conscious in each moment can be difficult at first, but it becomes easier with time. I banish from my mind any unwanted obstructive thoughts and focus on the wonder that will become my new life, with the help of *the Book*. I want to bloom in a different way and find a new direction and excitement. I will grow gratitude for the abundance surrounding me daily, instead of becoming blind to new wonders by being stuck in the past, reliving past sorrows and refusing to bloom.

"But wait!" I hear you exclaim. "You were going to tell us about Vixens ... when are you getting to that?"

Alright. Fair call! I'm almost at that point ... be patient, oh eager ones! Once freed of all previous burdens, you can sprint forward as fast as possible towards a new life and the merriment of being a Vixen! I must admit, the mental transformation can take some effort; nothing worthwhile in life is easy!

I feel a lot calmer after meditating, and my heavy heart has lifted. Thank God! I reach for my Goddess cards to confirm what I feel and ask for a card to jump from the pack as I shuffle. It only takes a few seconds before my request is granted. Aeracura flies from the deck flipping face up on the floor. As I pick up the card to read it, I give thanks with a grin.

Aeracura: Blossoming

You are just getting started, so have patience with yourself and the process, and do not give up. You are like a flower bud who is ripe and ready to open and grow. Don't try to rush this process, as it's part of your beautiful path. Enjoy learning new knowledge and skills. Take your time to gather new ideas. Soon enough you will get the unmistakable signal that it's time to put your learning into action. Have Patience. Keep the faith.

Well. The universe can't be clearer than that. Reassured by the cards I feel a rush of excitement at my new life path. Hence ... the transformation into a new life, new adventures and the fun and frolicking of Vixendom!

You still want to find out what the hell Vixendom is, don't you? Well come with me on a journey of wonder and discovery and I shall tell you. First, let me check what the dictionary says about the word Vixen.

Vixen—*noun* 1. A female fox. 2. A fierce or spiteful woman.

Hmm. No. That will not do. I believe I will need to replace the poor description above with a much better version of my own, more befitting of a Vixen.

> Vixen—*noun* 1. A fierce and passionate woman: strong and relentless in the pursuit of her goals.
>
> 2. A playful and powerful being, possessing the ability to drive any man worthy of her attention wild with her mystical powers.

Oh yes. This is a kick arse description! Maybe I need to contact Wikipedia or Encyclopaedia Britannia? There is a definite need to amend this definition.

Imagine what any man would say when confronted by a lovely vixen lazing languidly on her luxurious lounge, luring him into her lair. How could he resist? Well, I think I'd like to find out. So, in the spirit of research for all women, I am going to embark on the mysterious and adventuresome journey of Vixendom. Here I go!

Ladder in position, I reach up into the far recesses of my closet; blindly feeling for what I know is still there, hidden until the right moment in time arrives to emerge and be rediscovered. My fingers at last feel the tattered edge of the small leather-bound book. I smile in satisfaction. The book seems to have a life of its own and emits a bright glow as my hand grasps it firmly. Blowing off the dust, I see the front inscription sparkle and shimmer invitingly as I stroke my finger across the title.

The mystical book shivers and springs open at my touch, long hidden and unused. I feel it move excitedly against my fingers, willing me to read it. There is no turning back now.

Essential Criteria for Mark Selection:

- Hot, sexy and single

- Treats women well and with respect

- Playful with a naughty sense of humour

- High level of emotional intelligence

- Quick witted with a curious mind

- Interested in exploring fantasy play

- Out of your social circle

- Likes to have fun

- Willingness to be ensnared

*Note: You may think emotional intelligence would not be needed and that fun is a given, but remember vixens are smart, playful and mystical—dumb men are far too easy to access and will not be able to hold your attention or appreciate your vixenly ways.

Adventure Vixen

Transformation

Bursting with excitement, I plunge in! I am nervous and petrified of the unknown, but the overwhelming anticipation of change and new adventure is spurring me on. The book has stirred something inside me that's been long dormant. The sudden pressing need in a forgotten region of my soul reminds me again of what I used to want. The energy gained from my cards and the Book's words thrusts me forward into an unknown, yet somehow familiar, arena.

Where does a Vixen, who is trying to recall how to be one, go to find men who are unsuitable for a serious relationship? There is only one possibility in this technological age … online dating sites are the best thing ever for women! We can shop for any type of suitable or unsuitable man online, checking out the wares clinically, as if we're at the supermarket doing our grocery shopping. We can shamelessly go for visual appeal first. Stop to read the list of ingredients only if the outside wrapping is appealing enough and pop the item straight into our carts if it seems tasty enough—a delightful delicacy to be enjoyed at our leisure!

You may wonder why a Vixen would want an unsuitable man. Well, Vixens are not looking for stable long-term monotony, oops, I mean monogamy! So, I will choose only unsuitable men who are not relationship hunting. No sweet boys, no cute broken-hearted men, no sports fanatics OR genuine long-term relationship seekers need apply here. Strictly disposable models only!

Apart from the bootylicious hot man criteria which, let's face it girls, is a given; a Vixen's hunt is also for emotional intelligence and humour. She seeks only the playfulness and delight of beddable, delicious men, so she may entice them to her lair, bedazzling them with her sophisticated charm and wit. A Vixen must choose with wisdom, for only the most privileged of intelligent and sexy men will be allowed the exquisite pleasure of her acquaintance.

Satisfaction and delight wash through me. A Vixen looking for adventure and fun with gorgeous men is something I can relate to. The idea entices me, my excitement building as I realise what an excellent idea this is. How entertaining being a mature Vixen who knows exactly what she wants, would be.

I logon eagerly and my adventure begins! OK. I'm logged in. Online. Now what? Oh, of course—Google to the rescue! What the heck did everyone do before the invention of Google? Typing in 'most popular dating sites,' I hit enter.

Oodles of sites crowd my screen. Beckoning and alluring, wanting me to click on their link with promises of love, matches made in heaven and finding Mr Right. Well, I'm just looking for a Mr Right Now or possibly a few of them ... Which one is the website for that? Mwaaahahaahaaahahaaa!

I narrow my choices down to the free sites. No point in paying to go into the supermarket of lust before getting to view the goodies on offer! I settle on one website to check out. Hmmm ... Create a profile name. What, right this minute? Now I am stumped! Surely that's a pretty important thing to decide on, isn't it? How will I decide what to call myself? I don't want anything embarrassing—no sickly-sweet nicknames, no obvious raunchy sex goddess name, no real first name with a number attached to the end. What to do? Think, damn you, think! I am an intelligent woman ... why don't I know what the hell I'm doing?

All of a sudden, the best possible profile name comes to me as clear as a lightning bolt. Are you ready? I'm quite proud of myself for this one. It's: 'A Trixen Vixen' Yes, I think that's the ONE! Not too silly, sexy or stupid, no real name and not too long. The A in front of 'Trixen Vixen' is a special touch, seeing that's what my name starts with.

Oh. It's occurred to me I am forgetting something quite important. Apologies for taking this long to introduce myself. Let's start with my first name, Arleia. Hi. That's all I can tell you right now; if my words are read by those in the darkness, who knows what may happen. It's a delight to meet any prospective sister Vixen! Welcome, please join me on my adventure!

The screen beckons again. 'Create Your Profile.' What the hell am I going to write on here? Choosing my profile name gave me cold sweats and made me scoff down the last three Tim Tams in the packet without even realising that I ate them. How am I going to start my blurb? For inspiration, I open another window to check out what other women have written on this site. There's a ridiculous number who like to cook and watch movies on the couch, or love watching sports all day with their man. Some like beach walks, others list shopping as their only hobby. My lip curls in distaste. That's not the vibe I want my profile to project as a Vixen!

Hmm ... perhaps my profile needs to be something like this:

Profile Name: ATrixenVixen

Female: 41

Laughter and fun are what I love, and I am an upbeat, positive person. I can be a bit crazy in a good way and am always honest ... quirky, funny, open and spiritual ... with a naughty sense of humour. My love of life and nature is strong, and I'm grateful for each day I'm here and every new experience gained.

My family and friends are important to me, and I treat them all with great love, respect and consideration. Communication is the key to intimacy of souls ... To travel, discover new things or new places and being adventurous is what I love!

I think I'm happy with this initial version, but will men read anything I write on here? Or will they only be checking out my cool Vixen-like photo with the hint of cleavage beckoning? A great picture draws them in, according to the handbook.

Location Sydney | New South Wales | Australia

Seeking Criteria Members within 15km.

Casual Dating with a male.

What I'm looking for: Open and honest is most important! A guy who loves to laugh and enjoys life, is a little naughty, appreciates the little things and likes to show his woman how much he cares. I'm not into football, cricket or watching any sport on TV. I'd rather be out living and loving life than having life pass me by from the couch.

Details Ethnicity: White (Caucasian)

Relationship Status: Single

Religion: Spiritual / New Age

Children: Don't have any

Drinking Habits: Socially

Hair Colour: Blonde

Eye Colour: Hazel

Height: 5'6" / 167cm

Sign of the Zodiac: Gemini

Interests: Going Out, Health and Fitness, Movies, Reading, Travel, Meditation, Tarot Cards

There! That's my first attempt at a profile completed. Now for a picture or two to add—no point in wasting time creating a profile if you are not going to add an image of yourself! Of course, I want to put the right one up on show—I'm going to use a smiling headshot I think. Possibly with a dash of cleavage showing. Just a hint, though!

I'm amazed at how many raunchy photos women choose to display on their profiles. Now it's fine if you are looking for the type of man who is an easy lay, and more on the Neanderthal level of intelligence, but he is not our target, Vixens! Our targets might view the flesh displaying pictures and appreciate them, but do they then want to chat with you? Engage in playful banter and match wits? Unlikely.

They'd be thinking you are out for sex and be happy to oblige, but that's about all you are going to get, which is usually disappointing. Too easy to draw men with flesh! Also, to target these men is beneath the code and ways of the Vixen. Vixens need inviting, understated shots. Photos which hint at what your assets are, rather than showing you naked on display for the world to ogle!

The men worth hunting tend to be more interested in something left to the imagination—much more enticing and mysterious! The majority of guys who contact flesh displaying women are the 'looking for a fuck' guys, which is not the type of Mark we will put time into hunting or teasing ... No challenge for us with those losers!

I was talking to a male friend last week, who made the comment that he has been to many strip clubs over the years. He is of the opinion that the strippers are much more alluring and interesting while they're still wearing some of their clothes, because a hint of seduction and lace engage his sense of imagination more. Once all their provocative garments are off, he loses interest. As he said, "It's just a naked chick, no mystery!"

OK. Pictures are chosen. Showing a suggestive glimpse of my cleavage, but not too revealing. A gorgeous sexy smile; a hint of naughtiness in the sparkle of my eyes. Inviting potential Marks to investigate further. Yippee! I'm done!

Getting that blurb and picture organised took forever. Who would have thought that I'd need to put so much time, thought and effort into creating an online profile? These men better take the time to read my profile after the angst and effort I put into crafting my masterpiece!

I don't know about you, but I don't own a handy plethora of perfect photos for profile constructions sitting on my computer. Instead, I've had to spend the last hour modelling in different contorted positions to snap the angle I am after. Yes, a whole hour of posing, checking, deleting, cringing and laughing at a few ridiculous or horrifying shots. Be prepared girls — you will need to put the effort in! Don't be surprised either when you're forced to take at least twenty-or thirty-awful photos to obtain the one amazing shot of you.

Right, back to the task at hand now. Profile written? Check! Pictures uploaded? Check! I'm ready to jump into the online dating world. Watch out all you lush hot men, here I come!

Oh. Hang on. An 'age preference' must be set now. This will be exciting! My last boyfriend was a lot younger than me, so I should first try checking out the guys closer to my own years on earth for a change. When I think about looking at men my own age, I realise it's been quite a few years since I did! Here goes, I will put my age preference for the forty-to forty-five range ... Now let's examine the results.

Oh. Oh dear. Ewwww. *Really?* No way. What the hell happened to the men who are my peers? Why do most of them appear as if they are closer to my father's generation than to mine? Let me recheck my settings; it's my first time here, and I might be getting the age setting thing wrong. Oh no! That WAS correct!

Holy crap. I'm going to rethink my age preferences! I'm not too discouraged; there are still some real hotties among the men in this range, but it's unfortunate that they are much thinner on the ground; and many now are rather thin on top!

Now I suppose you think I am exaggerating but take a glance yourself and you will agree with me. My dad is about twenty-five years older than me, and still looking pretty good, but some of these forty-something year old guys are now looking closer in age to my father! How is it possible that most of these men appear to be middle-aged or completely decrepit? Do they not care about themselves anymore? Or are they all victims of circumstance?

I imagine what their lives have been like for them to look so much older than their years. From a carefree happy youth to the responsibility of a wife, kids, mortgage and work, they have become unrecognisable. Receding hairlines, rounded beer-baby bellies and hair sprouting from unfamiliar orifices, coupled with the stresses of life have all aged these men prematurely. Let this be a lesson to all, Vixens! Be mindful at all times of YOU. Take care of yourself, cherish and admire what you see. Be kind and considerate and show yourself love, for loving you first is the only way you will receive love back. Find the spark inside yourself and draw it out. You deserve only the best. Believe this and feel the truth deep within yourself—because it will resonate with your soul.

This is the difference between you, and those who are still unconscious and unaware of their own inner light. You are ready. This is why you are still reading. Why you want to know what was in the book that was given to me many years ago by the mysterious woman.

A Vixen wants to amuse and enjoy herself by the impish enticement of hot intelligent men to appreciate her charms and her company. They must compliment her and be dazzled by her as she flits through and touches their lives in ways they can never imagine, like a beautiful butterfly; appreciated but not held or restrained (unless, of course, you agree to a bit of restraining in the bedroom). Mwaaahaaahaahaa!

Vixens aim to move forward with only a positive impression left in their wake.

Sooo ... What do you think? Are you in? It's sounding like a pretty damned good idea so far, I think! You can guess what I'm going to say now ... it's back to the younger hot men for me!

Optional Criteria Suggestions for Mark Selection:

- Broad-minded and open to new things

- Meets your age requirement: five-to-fifteen years younger than you

- Possesses a member worthy of your attention

- Nicely built body and face which is attractive to you

- Meets the minimum height requirement determined by you

Adventure Vixen

Fishing

Right! New ages for my search, let's try men between the ages of twenty-eight and forty. That should give me a better selection. Oohhhhh, yes. There are way more sexy men in this range. This is what I'm looking for—beddable men unsuitable for a long-term relationship, but oh so suitable for the fun a Vixen's got in mind.

Let's start fishing, I say! Ok. Laptop? Check! Age setting reset. Check! Comfy couch and clothes? Yes! Drinks and snacks within reach? Check! Let the fishing begin. Mwaaahahaahaaa!

Did I forget to mention the evil Vixen laugh? It's reserved for when you find a suitable Mark to entice and is only to be used when in Vixen mode. Practise your laugh before you go fishing for unsuitable men to put you in the Vixen mood ready for distraction and action!

Hey now. During the short time I've been chatting to you, there have been another three contact requests! Wow. Is hunting online for men really this easy? Hang on, I'm not going to jump ahead of myself here! The most important things I'm looking at first are profile pictures and ages. No being sucked into the excitement of settling for the very first request. I will circle patiently like a hungry shark and only swoop in when my prey looks really tasty.

Hmm ... Contact request number one. Age: 47 FAIL! Picture: Long plaited hair and tattoos, reflective glasses. Ermmm... NO. Make it a double no! A HELL NO, even! FAIL! I am only interested in a traditionally hot guy, ranging upwards to the stereotypical smoking hot Chippendale-type dancer with cut abs glistening and bulging biceps bouncing becomingly before ...

Oh. Err. Sorry. I got carried away imagining those rippling muscles! Once I started visualising bulging biceps and the like I got distracted. I may even have started drooling. Only a little.

Bring on number two! Age: 33. Phew! PASS! Picture: Stylish dark hair, cute smile, straight white teeth, worthy of further investigation. PASS! OK. Scroll down ... down ... to my next most important criteria—height.

Now, I am aware that it's super shallow. I've told myself this a million times before. I have even participated in several in-depth discussions with my friends about acceptable height levels for dates. There's no doing shorter for me. I can't. My man needs to be at least three inches taller than me. Short men do not attract me or turn me on at all. I'm 5ft 6" tall, so my minimum requirement is 5ft 9". I *will* only consider a couple of inches taller than me if he is sexy as hell, built like a bodybuilder and he can dance like a professional stripper!

Focus, Vixen! Height check'… 5ft 10". Acceptable; may even be promising. Next check—the profile description: "It's hard to write about myself, but here goes: I'm a normal guy... blah ... like walks on the beach … dog is best friend ... watch DVDs ... quiet nights in … blah go the Sydney Swans … love football …"

Oh dear. BORING! This won't do. My eyes can't even bear to read any further down. It doesn't matter what he is looking for, because I'm sure as hell not looking for him! OK. That's two out of the three that failed the initial tests. Let me check the third and last one and find out if he is any closer to what I'm hunting for. Hang on. No way!

Now another two more men have joined the queue. The speed of requests flying my way amazes me. This is easier than I thought. I hope I find more suitable possible Marks this time!

OK, let's check out contestant number three. Age: 34 PASS! Picture: Cute with a cheeky smile, warm brown eyes, quite handsome. PASS! Right, straight for the height ... 6ft 3" PASS! Wow, this one may be worth investigating further! Hmmm ...

"Hi There I am Krystian. Bit about myself easy goin'. honest I am genuine ambitious able to hold a good conversation, single got separated last year, new to dating sites, hard worker, love kids got two of my own, live in northern suburbs, got my own house, my hobbies be doin' my garden up and my place up, I am fit, for relaxin' time I spend it in my spa a lot, also love animals.

Location 27km outside Sydney | New South Wales | Australia

Seeking Criteria Members anywhere in New South Wales.

Relationship with a female or Casual Dating with a female. Between 25 and 48 years of age.

What I'm Looking For: Honest and easy goin', drama free, fun adventures, sumbody who wonts to enjoy good life, party a bit. Have a drink, relax, watch DVD, likes me for me, likes animals, good food, is not a control freak

Details Ethnicity: Other

Relationship Status: Single

Religion: Christian/Catholic

Hair Colour: Black

Eye Colour: Hazel

Height Over: 6'3" / 190cm

Body Type: Fit

Spoken Languages: English, Polish

Children: Have and don't live with

Drinking Habits: Socially

Pets: Yes a dog

Interests: UFC, family, gardening, Game of Thrones, Spartacus. serious relaxation, arts, animals, cultures, history, Cars and Motoring Cooking, Gaming Going Out, Health and Fitness Movies, Music, Reading, Sports, Travel, Photos

Now this guy holds promise. Easy going, honest, genuine sounding, with his own huge spa with added pictures to prove he loves spending time lazing in the water. I am partial to a frothing hot tub, there's an extra bonus point for Krystian right now! Wow. I can't believe I read a whole profile this time. Hmmm ... maybe I can be the easy going, drama free, adventurous someone you are looking for... Mwaaahahaahaaahahaaa!

Now girls, remember there always needs to be a large enough element of unsuitability with each guy you choose, to ensure that you will NOT fall for them. If you come across the perfect sounding man for you with every single quality you require AND he is drop dead gorgeous ... RUN AS FAST AS YOU CAN IN THE OPPOSITE DIRECTION! Make sure that you first bookmark/save/add him in your hot list or do whatever you need to do so that you can find him later... should you choose to! You never know when you might change your mind and decide that you want to settle down and tame your Vixen ways.

OK. On to the unsuitability criteria for contestant number three. Did you spot what makes him a perfect fit for my 'hot but unsuitable' category? His spelling and punctuation are *terrible*! I cannot stand poor punctuation and spelling—even in this case where English may be a second language!

The second unsuitable thing is that he is twenty-seven kilometres away from me. I know this does not sound a substantial distance. Considering Sydney distances his, place is not out in the boondocks. However, his suburb is one I would never choose to live in. He also owns a dog. Now I don't mind dogs, but I am more of a cat lover. No feline will be impressed with any canine near them, so there's the third unsuitable criteria!

Wow, I think we have found a winner! A suitable specimen at last ... Here goes: YOU ADDED KRYSTIAN TO YOUR CONTACT LIST! Good Lord, they even make an announcement flash across the screen. OMG. It took me this long to find one well qualified guy to add to my list of contacts. Let's hope he doesn't fuck up by breaking one of the Vixen rules straight away! Oh damn, I am going to need to replenish my drink and snacks. I head to the kitchen to restock my supplies, and flop back on my comfortable couch.

Hee hee hee ... oops I mean Mwaaahahaahaaahahaaa, my first contact!

Chortling to myself, I stare at the lone 'Krystian' contact on my list. I'm going for the big snappers ... back to the outstanding requests awaiting my attention. I need a lot more than only one on my list to choose from! Whoa. This is hilarious! Four new ones have appeared. Can they somehow spot fresh meat on the site? How can I be this popular? Of course, it's flattering and a pretty big ego boost. I am an attractive woman, so I shouldn't be surprised. But I still am. The speed with which these men want to make contact with me surprises me. Did I logon at the busiest time of the day for traffic on dating sites?

A flattering current picture of myself with a hint of cleavage showing, a mischievous smile and a sparkle in my eye seems to be working very well. Yay! I'm way ahead of the other women on here who have posted weird, super serious, photoshopped or strained expression photos. A picture speaks a thousand words, and if you appear playful, happy and enjoyable to be with, more guys are going to want to check you out further and may even read your whole profile. You can draw more Marks to you with an amazing image, which is much faster than having to do a search yourself.

If a man sends you a contact request, you know he is already interested in you to a degree. You can check out his picture, read his profile and decide if he passes the first few Vixen tests and wield your delete finger if he doesn't. We don't want to waste too much of our time on men we are not attracted to!

Within an hour I receive another nine requests, as well as several flirts and shout outs. Boy, I am going to need to investigate this site further—what the heck is a shout out? Is that for impolite people who can't be bothered with the regular standard contact me request bit? I'm going to ignore those for now, enough is already going on without being shouted at!

After weeding through and rejecting most requests, I manage to add a total of four possible Marks to start my adventure with. I'm quite proud of myself. I didn't think online dating would be this easy to get started with. Dating via the internet has been available for a long time and I have experienced this kind of hook-up before, but it's been many years since then and I thought I'd forgotten how. My manhunt memory that was long dormant is seeping back into my consciousness now. I remember how much fun it can be to be daring and adventurous, to jump out of my comfort zone that I reside in daily. *To be nervous, excited, or fearful.* To be able to acknowledge this and still choose to be courageous and move forward is not for the faint-hearted!

Neither is being a Vixen. You see, Vixens are not about the end result, it's about the chase - the engaging mental challenge of wit and humour. The teasing and banter between two people attracted to each other having fun and enjoying the flirting game.

However, to me, if a guy starts off by calling me honey, hun, babe, darling, sweetie or any other inappropriate endearment right from the start, I'm like, 'Yeah, right ... See you later and no thanks, idiot!' I mean, dude. Are you serious? I'm not your anything in the first two seconds of conversation. Such forwardness shows low levels of emotional intelligence where women are concerned.

Intelligent guys will always come up with something more interesting to say than, "Hey hun!" The more I chat online to different men, the more this becomes apparent, believe me! Don't be fooled by the hot outer packages, girls—it's an unfortunate truth that many men possess only air between their ears. Their brains have taken up permanent residence in their crotches, so be mindful of these arousal-inspiring, delicious looking delights in the supermarket of lust.

Whenever I come across one, I'm reminded of the Book's words about the Cream Puff Man. This man seems to be able to attract us like an enticing, mouth-watering, chocolate-dipped cream puff. He makes us want to throw caution to the wind and take a big cream-squirting bite out of him! Unfortunately, only once you bite into Cream Puff Man, do you realise that the appetising treat is all a sham. There is *never* enough cream inside the puff. He is anywhere nearly as tasty as it first appeared, or as yummy as you were expecting! Stay away from these time-wasting cream puffs—you will find yourself bored out of your skull, fighting off his sticky fingers or even be in the midst of bad sex with him before he even remembers your name.

Oh dear. I've spent so long talking to you that I forgot that I'm online! Oooooh, and here are three messages from my new list of contacts that I need to reply to—the beauty of computers!

"Hi there ☺ Sorry … I was away from the computer! How are you tonight?"

Now, this will be a perfect message to post to all three. A little cut and paste magic and hey, presto... Three answers in the flash of a key and click of the mouse... Complete with a smiley face! A smiley face says a couple of things:

1. You are a happy type of person (not a drama queen who is annoyed at having to answer when busy).

2. You are pleased to get a message from him.

However, if you feel compelled to interject at least fifteen different emoji into any of your sentences, you will give off a confusing vibe! You may appear to be desperate or needy, even psychotic or crazy in some way—who would contort so many expressions in one sentence?

Now don't get me wrong here, emoticons are cool tools to use. They do help to convey the emotions or vibe of the conversation in addition to words and should be used when chatting to Marks. It is overkill that we want to avoid!

There's something I should mention to you that is quite important if you are interested in being a bona fide Vixen. You possess an open curiousness or feel an inner stirring. I strived to arouse this within you by my first words, so that you would recognise that *it is YOU* that I am speaking to and inviting to read on.

Dimly lit souls do not deserve to gain knowledge of the *Vixen's Secret Handbook*, or to discover the pleasures of being a Vixen. They are instead relegated to a life of ignorance and dullness of routine and repetition. They are prevented from stepping into the light because they have forgotten the excitement of extreme consciousness, of being a strong sensual woman. Of being desired, worshipped or celebrated and appreciated. They console themselves instead with the fact that they are good wives, mothers, daughters or friends.

These women sacrifice the spark of light inside of them wanting to be seen. Afraid of change, they prefer to cover and dull their inner light with such things as shopping, house chores, kids or even alcohol. They take children to sporting events and attend civilised gatherings with mundane other couples of the same social circle and standing. They participate in repetitive conversations about the weather, sport, recipes and other people—rather than discussing their own secret wishes, hopes and dreams.

You know this to be true from within, as many times you yourself have also covered up your spark, the real magic which is you. Society's beliefs, and the 'should' installed in us all from childhood can be deafening. These rules bind us, control us and limit us. They tell us what we should be doing, wearing, thinking, being, buying or watching. They silence the internal whisperings within us of faraway dreams and delights we could be experiencing instead.

The so-called real world we get caught up in stops us from remembering who we are. A Vixen is a goddess, enchantress, lover, dreamer, woman, powerful spirit, eternal light.

It's easy to be distracted by the materialism of this world, then one day find ourselves in the cliché of a gilded cage of our own making. Beauty and wealth surround us, created by us because it was once so deeply desired by us.

However, deep within our souls is a quiet yearning. It can be heard if we listen with intent. Only those whom are brave and courageous can break the bonds of our mundane daily existence and rediscover the truth about ourselves. We ARE the shining light, and to awaken from a deep slumber can be an amazing and wondrous, yet scary thing!

So, Vixens, read on if you dare, and I will lead you down the path of freedom and Vixendom, of playfulness and fun. Discover what your heart truly desires, the magic of Vixendom.

However, you are going to have to wait a moment, I fear. I need to refill my drink and restock with some chocolate before I can continue!

Krystian: Hi there pretty lady

ATrixenVixen: Hi there! Sorry I was away from the computer. How are you?

Krystian: All the better for talking to you! My name is Krystian.

ATrixenVixen: Hi Krystian, lovely to meet you! I'm Arleia.

Krystian: Osome pic Arleia.

ATrixenVixen: Thanks ...Yours are not too bad either.

Krystian: I'm olways happy to get a compliment from a prety lady, such as yourself.

ATrixenVixen: Oh... erm ... cool! So what are you looking for here Krystian?

Krystian: You! Lol ... Depends on what I find.

ATrixenVixen: Good answer there Lol ... same here.

Wow. I may want to meet this dude—so far! He is polite, respectful, complimentary but not too pushy or over the top. He also meets one of my major unsuitability criteria—he's a terrible speller! Mwaaahahaahaaahahaaa!

So far so good ... it seems like it's worth continuing the conversation.

Krystian: So ... what are you up to this weekend Arleia?

ATrixenVixen: Hmmm ... Good question! I have a couple of things on with friends. What about you?

Remember Vixens, even if your weekend is yawningly empty and you need to resort to pencilling in things like 'wash my hair' and 'take the dog for a walk' to pretend that you enjoy some sort of life, don't let this on to your Mark! We want him to think we are popular and busy, and that he would be lucky if we decided to make time in our busy schedules for him. Even for a coffee!

Krystian: I also have a few things on.

ATrixenVixen: Cool ... well I think I am free on Thursday night. Is that easier?

Krystian: That'd be fantastic! Want to catch-up for a drink?

ATrixenVixen: What kind of drink are you thinking?

Krystian: Whatever the sexy lady would like ;)

ATrixenVixen: Oh ... err ... Think we better make it an alcoholic drink! I may need some alcohol to stop my flaming cheeks if you keep complimenting me like that, lol!

Krystian: LOL. What is there not to compliment?

ATrixenVixen: Oh stop it! LOL ... you will make me blush!

Krystian: You will need to stop looking so cute then.

Oh yes, he's playing back with me. I like that! There's another tick for Krystian in my Mark suitability box. But now that we are going to meet, I need to make an excuse to end the conversation once the time and date is set. It's better to talk in person with the guy instead of wasting further time online, once they qualify as a Mark to meet and they have passed the first Vixen tests! Plus ... two other Marks are awaiting my reply!

ATrixenVixen: Hahahaaaa! So what time do you think, and where's a good place somewhere between us?

Do you like how I redirect the conversation straight back to the task at hand?

ATrixenVixen: What about the English pub near you on the corner of Main and West Streets. Say at 6.30pm?

Krystian: Cool I know where you mean!

ATrixenVixen: Excellent ... I look forward to meeting you then Krystian ;)

Krystian: Sounds great prety lady

We swap phone numbers and it's done. I can't help but chortle in glee to myself. My first Mark in my newly chosen field of Vixendom! MWAAAHAhaaahahahaaaa!

I hope I'm choosing wisely. I am following the code and have a good feeling about this guy! Plus ... amongst the many pictures of Krystian on his profile I drooled over was his wicked looking eight person heated outdoor spa. Complete with flashing lights, pop up speakers and a built-in stereo. Yippee, we have a winner! Who doesn't like a good hot tub session?! Bonus points awarded to Krystian before we even meet. But of course, they will only count if he passes the next Vixen test; the first meeting.

A mischievous smile of satisfaction crosses my mouth, as I applaud myself in congratulations on arranging my first rendezvous! I even jump up and perform a little victory dance. Now *that* is something no-one else should ever see! Oh, this is going to be such fun!

I stop as something important occurs to me. The Book! I need to review its words before this date, as I'm a bit rusty. The Vixen in me has not been awakened in many years, and I need as much help and energy as I can get. I see a glow appear beside my bed. It's as if the book knows what I need and is beckoning me to absorb its energy, to cast off the shackles of my past. To weave the tapestry of the Vixen. To grow and rediscover my powers once again.

Acceptable Emoticon Use Test

Emoticons are an excellent tool for gauging the tone of a message, and excellent for conveying many different moods in almost every situation. They can be a fabulous flirting tool when used in the correct manner, or they can be very off putting when used inappropriately.

When conversing online remember the following guidelines:

Each post should contain no more than three different emoticons (unless something hilarious happens that needs over-exagg4eration as a response in emoticons). In regular conversation if you use emoticons in three posts in a row you MUST have the next two 'emoticon free' (T

here needs to be a balance maintained).

When a lewd, surprising or rude, suggestive comment is made by the potential Mark, the appropriate response is not a wink. That would suggest you are easy to get or seduce, which Vixens are not.

The correct response is the 'shocked' or 'crying with laughter' emoticons, which suggests that you may be offended by his forwardness and he better rein it in before you delete him.

Even if you are thinking to yourself, 'Take me now, you delicious hunk!' you can't make this decision until you meet in person. Some men are not who they appear to be, so for safety's sake err on the side of caution.

When all a potential Mark can do is send single word replies with emoticons (no actual sentence typing to you) then he and his conversation will be as boring in person, no matter how delicious he appears ... he is a Cream Puff Man.

If the potential Mark persists in the following actions:

× Overtly lewd sexual suggestions

× Pushing you to meet him in the next hour from now

× Engaging in overuse or improper use of emoticons

FAIL: Delete unsuitable Mark immediately from your contact list. You can also choose to wait until he is offline so he is less aware of the fact that you have deleted him, but end your conversation with such an unsuitable Mark as fast as possible with the excuse of a sudden phone call or unexpected arrival of a friend.

A Vixen's time is precious, and we do not want to waste our valuable commodity on any Mark that does not prove himself worthy of our attention and general Vixenly awesomeness.

Adventure Vixen

Supermarket Rules

Now, remember two other messages popped up which I started to reply to? Don't worry Vixens, I am prepared for this. With a smidge more of the old cut and paste magic both other Marks now know my name and receive the same message which is: Be right back ... phone call! Sorry! (For those of you uninitiated in the acronym world of chatting online, I could have used 'BRB' that means 'be right back', but I feel that's too lazy in a first conversation.)

On occasion girls, you need to buy yourself a little time! It may not always be the case that your slow reply is because of chatting to other Marks. You may be a slow typist, or trying to do some work between chatting, and not always be available to reply to their messages straight away. Even if you are a super-fast typing champion, most likely they are not! If you type replies too fast at first, your quick reply may be construed as being desperate, needy or crazy, none of which we want.

So make sure that you give your hottie enough time to think and respond before firing off another three messages. With men in general, we can be sure the first thing that pops into their heads is often not advisable to put on the screen unless you are already engaging in an X-rated conversation with them! They need time to come up with something witty or interesting and not sex related to capture your attention, or at least act relatively normal.

Right! Damn, I'm good at getting side-tracked. But letting you in on the secrets of the Vixen handbook is important, don't you think? Of course, it's just as crucial to answer them in a timely manner as well. A slow reply can be understood to mean that you are not interested in the conversation or him. So unless you pre-warn the prospective Mark that you are at work and cannot always reply, or provide some other reason, he may become restless and give up.

Also, when you are speaking to anyone in person, you can feel whether the chat flows well or not, and the same happens when you are online. However, what is more difficult to convey to others is your sense of humour, wit and fabulousness without the use of body language, facial expressions or tone of voice.

If you do manage a good flowing conversation which makes you laugh several times, chances are that your banter will be the same in person. It may be worth meeting up with him to check him out over a drink ... but always make sure you prepare an 'out' though!

OK, who can I find on here next? Clapping my hands in excited anticipation, I draw my attention back to the screen. "Sorry, I didn't mean to take so long!" I double reply to both waiting Marks. Flexing my fingers, I settle in for a good chat session to decide my next move. After two hours of vigorous typing, two soft drinks, a packet of salt and vinegar rice crackers and an hour long talk over the phone, I manage to find out a few important things.

Mark #2: Mitch Age: 43 Height: 5ft 10" Brown hair, cute smile, quite young looking in his picture for his years, good sense of humour and wit. He seems to possess a high enough level of intelligence, works in the corporate arena and even has a couple of hobbies which are not sport related.

Unsuitability criteria? His age is above what I'm looking for and also, he's NEVER had a long-term relationship in his whole forty-three years on the planet. That's either a total fluke and he has not met the right woman yet, or all the women who ventured to date him found fault and bailed long before the relationship could be referred to as long-term. Bingo! There's appointment number two lined up for Friday night next week!

Now, I can hear what you are thinking ... forty-three? That's out of my preferred age bracket! I do realise this, but perhaps I still need to check out the occasional guy around my age to find out if I'm missing something. Plus, his age is an excellent first reason in the unsuitability criteria selection! Mwaaahahaahaaahahaaa!

The third candidate does not pass in all areas to progress forward on to my list of potentials. His stats are promising at first— a thirty-two-year-old French Canadian with a hot, chocolate body. He is playful, with a model-like face and plump kissable lips ... and extremely keen! So, what the heck happened? Let me tell you. The conversation was sailing along with ease until:

AJ: So, sexy lady ...

ATrixenVixen: Yeessss?

AJ: Do you want to know one thing that turns me on a lot?

ATrixenVixen: LOL well why not. If you are sharing.

AJ: I love it when a woman rims me.

ATrixenVixen: Oh you do, hey?

Hold it right there. RIMMING? When a woman rims you? What the hell is that? Oh Lord, thank you for technology and the wisdom of Google ... a quick search and I will understand what he is talking about! I buy myself a little time so I can do research. Maybe I always need to be prepared with Google open and at the ready !

Rimming ... Hmmm here we are! Ok, the act of running your tongue around the edge of ... OHH! For the love of God! Are you serious? I don't know about this. Would I want to allow my tongue that close to a stranger's hairy arse? I think not! Yikes!

All sorts of thoughts run through my head in a simultaneous kaleidoscope. What if his arse smells bad?

Does he do a special butt washing ceremony first? Are women supposed to just like or ignore the possible unpleasant stench of his bum? Why would this be the first thing he would tell me? What the fuck is with this dude?

I don't think I've ever found myself in a regular social encounter where, without warning someone threw in the unusual sentence of, "By the way, I do rather enjoy rimming! It's quite delightful to receive, don't you think?" This just doesn't happen! Oh wait. It just did.

I don't want to sound uncool in my response, nor do I want to take him up on his unique offer, especially not if that is the first thing he mentions! Apart from the fact that he is being exceptionally pushy in wanting to come over to my place for the first meeting, which of course is against the Vixen's rules! The second option he gives me is to meet with him in the car park of a local oval for a chat first before heading to my place once I determine that he is to be trusted with my address. Are you kidding me? *A car park?* My lip curls in disgust. If you are the type of guy who can't even be bothered meeting me in a cosy bar for a drink and take the time to get to know me in a comfortable setting first, then you can piss off!

A 'FAIL' for sure! Wow. To my surprise, AJ has managed to dig himself even deeper into the putrid hole he has created, and into the ditch of deletion with this sparkling gem:

AJ: I do, yes baby. I would come into your bedroom, lay face down on your bed with my arse in the air. You would come over to me, kneel on the bed beside me ... bend over towards me, your hands on my arse cheeks, pulling them apart ready for your tongue to rim my arsehole.

ATrixenVixen: Ohh! Gee that's forward. Hmm ... I don't take instructions or demands well!

AJ: You would do it for me babe.

ATrixenVixen: I think you may be mistaken there! LOL

AJ: Meet me and find out babe.

ATrixenVixen: You know ... I think I will decline this one ... But I do appreciate such an appealing offer!

Now I could have been much ruder in my refusal, especially since I was gagging at the thought, but Vixens are not rude or judgemental! We accept that everyone has their own things that turn them on, and whatever they want to do is fine. Just don't include Vixens in your perverted world before checking that rimming is indeed our thing.

Good manners are not a lot to ask of someone, and you would prefer that you are also afforded the same courtesy. You will be immensely glad you did ... even if your written response is far from your first reaction! So, you can imagine why he did not make my meeting or dating criteria. Too damn pushy!

Sex talk with a dominant fetish twist in the first five-minutes.

His expectations were ridiculous and it's so obvious that he is only after sex, not the enjoyment of the playing.

Would not agree to rendezvous in a neutral acceptable location.

Fail, fail and fail again on so many levels ... Mwaaahahaahaaahahaaa!

Delete and block, I say! I glance around me and realise that all that remains is a few crumbs from my long-forgotten snacks, and an empty glass drained of every drop of liquid, and I sigh in happiness to myself. What an excellent start! Two good potential dates set, not too much wasted time and an evening which flew by.

Without the infusion of extra knowledge from the Book it would have taken at least double the time. Energised by its guidance and golden light of approval, I feel an inner glow. I have chosen well. Empowered by the thought, I'm excited at the prospect of the unknown. Bring it on!

Recognition of Supermarket Duds

Types of men in the supermarket of lust are varied. Some have a very short use-by date, some appear delicious but taste foul, while others are so boring that it's preferable to watch paint dry. Here are a few of the types of men to watch out for and avoid:

- Cream Puff Man - Looks delicious but empty inside—no conversation, relies on good looks alone

- Sweet Pie Man - Likes to share a piece of himself with each girl he meets

- Glazed Doughnut Boy - Delicious and satisfying but come and gone too fast before you get a good taste

- Mud Cake Man - Appears tasty but will weigh you down with his stodginess

- Chocolate Chip Brownie Dude - Dark-skinned dessert hiding a secret inside that's not always good

x   *Frosting Laden Cup Cake Boy - Too sickly sweet on the outside, covering a plain, boring stale lump of man*

Adventure Vixen

Krystian

The week passes by in a blur of work, phone calls, coffee dates with friends and chores. Thursday flashes by, and soon it is time to leave the office and prepare for my tryst with Krystian! I rush to arrive home in time to jump through the shower. Dammit! I'm running late. Not horrendously as yet, but enough to give myself a stern talking to, to try and move a bit faster. A final glance at the Book which is glowing in golden approval, a spritz of perfume and I'm out the door! I should only be a few minutes late, as long as the traffic is OK, of course.

What was I thinking? I slam straight into a wall of cars that is the usual delightful afternoon peak-hour traffic which still has not cleared. Perhaps I should have considered this in my calculations as to how long the drive would take. Oops! I start to weave my way through a myriad of back streets as best I can to avoid the onslaught of traffic and manage to arrive at my destination only a mere fifteen-minutes behind schedule. A stellar performance, if I may say so myself!

Of course, I let him know that I am running late. He meets me outside the quaint English style pub we chose for our date. Krystian is wearing a checked shirt, jeans and sneakers, which compliment his big smile and twinkling eyes. I'm instantly enveloped by his big friendly hello hug.

"Lovely to meet you, Miss Arleia!"

I step back slightly and look up to take all of Krystian in. His broad shoulders, well-built body and smile are the exact image of his pictures. He also smells delicious ... phew! He has passed the essential scent check test! For me it is an essential 'must do' when I meet a new man. If I get the chance early in the date to inhale my intended Mark's scent, I take it.

I'm always as discreet as possible - I don't want to remind him of a sniffer dog at the airport looking for drugs! We all own a natural scent specific to us. We can't inhale our own scent, but we pick up the scent of others. Some men emit an organic odour I just can't abide. When

I am not attracted to the scent of a guy, it is never a good sign!

This is why Vixens sneak in the sniff test as soon as possible—usually in the initial 'hello, it's delightful to meet you!' hug stage. If I don't like the smell of my Mark, I may put my prearranged Vixen escape plan into place much earlier than anticipated. I know this sounds harsh, but it is true. If I don't like the natural scent of a guy, the chances are strong that I will not be as into him in the bedroom either, no matter how witty or attractive he may appear! So I advise you to pay serious attention the next time you hug a member of the opposite sex. Take note of his unique fragrance and ask yourself whether it is an appealing aroma. It's a lot more in depth than the aftershave or cologne they choose to wear. Their natural essence is what you want to identify and examine.

Many years ago, I met this incredible, gorgeous, hot guy from Pakistan. This guy was spectacular and reminded me of a hot young Antonio Banderas. Suave with smouldering dark eyes and an incredible sexy smile. Even thinking about him now brings a smile to my face! He was super intelligent, amazingly attractive, rich, kind, funny, considerate, desirable, and a good friend all rolled into one delicious package. When he stepped fresh from the shower, he smelt divine. However, as soon as his natural odour snuck back, I was not as attracted to him. Even though I wanted to be! Indeed, after a day of work or horse riding which was his passion, his natural aroma made my lip curl and nose crinkle; and not in a good way! I was devastated to realise that we do need to listen to our basic animal instincts regarding scent and attraction. Think about any animal's behaviour. The first thing they all do is to sniff each other in an intimate and thorough manner. It seems to work for them. This initial testing should be the principle followed by us.

Krystian and I chat as we walk towards the pub. He steps forward to open the heavy wooden door for me. Impressive! I like this so far! He leads me over to the bar, and, as per my request, orders a glass of champagne.

I glance around the interior of the pub. Decorated in an old cosy English pub style, it features elaborate stained-glass windows and a rich wooden interior. Beautiful roaring flames in the open fireplace beckon us to sit closer to its warmth. I become mesmerised by the flickering tendrils from its glowing logs licking upwards towards the chimney.

Krystian recaptures my attention as he hands me a glass of champagne and leads me away from the fire and over to one of the cosy red leather booths. We slide in and end up sitting at right angles from each other. I swivel my knees around towards him so that I can observe him better.

"So, Miss Arleia! It is lovely to meet you." His eye smile at me along with his cheeky grin.

"Yes indeed, Master Krystian, it is," I reply with a stupid matching grin.

Sucking in a deep breath, I take a couple of large sips of my champagne. As the warm feel of the alcohol invades my system, I realise there had been no time to eat anything in my rush. Quite OK with me, as I rather appreciate a bit of Dutch courage with a first date!

Krystian is funny and charming ... I hope I am too! Three flutes of champagne later I am feeling relaxed and happy, as is he. The only thing I find disconcerting is that he often talks without looking me in the eye. Perhaps he is shy. My eyes can be pretty mesmerising, so I can't blame the poor guy for not being able to stare into them for a long time! Mwaaahahaahaaahahaaa!

By this time, I'm quite convinced that he is not some sort of psychopath, stalker or weirdo. I agree to go back to his place nearby for a drink and to check out his spa.

Krystian is courteous in welcoming me into his home. He invites me to sit down on the black leather couch while he gets us a drink. I realise that he lit a few candles on his way to fetch us drinks from the kitchen. Awwww, how cute, I think, stifling a smile.

"Do you have any music we can listen to, Krystian?" I raise my voice to reach him in the kitchen. The black leather lounge is the feature along with a couple of bookcases, all giving the room a bachelor pad feel. On the walls there are posters of favourite movies, swords and war memorabilia. I wonder how long it took him to tidy up his house, in the hope that I would agree to come back to his place tonight for a visit.

A small, white furry dog launches itself at me in a friendly and enthusiastic way ... Yikes! The little Maltese cross wags his tail at a furious speed in greeting, licking any part of me he can reach until Krystian comes back into the room bearing drinks.

"Baxy! Leave Miss Arleia alone!" he admonishes the over-excited dog.

"It's OK, he's such a cutie ... must take after his owner!" Smiling, I take one of the drinks from his hand. He winks at me.

"Hahaaaa! Of course he does! Come on, Miss Arleia, come check out my spa. I will even put the lights on and give you a show!"

We make our way out to the back of the house where there is a long half-enclosed veranda with the large bubbling hot tub down the far end. The frothing water and rising steam beckon me towards the edge to dip my fingers in. Warm and steaming, it is set at the ultimate temperature for pleasure. Krystian walks over to the spa and leans over, turning on the lights. The swirling water turns green, then red, purple and blue, making the water in the spa almost appear magical.

"So, do you want to take a dip in the spa, Miss Arleia? There is nothing better or more relaxing than hot bubbling water at the end of a long workday!"

Krystian is slyly enticing me, so I stall for time to think. I did come half prepared with a fitted black silky tank top and lace edged cute black knickers, which would be suitable hot tub wear. But there's no way I am getting naked in a hot tub at this point, especially not in one equipped with bright flashing lights!

A good Vixen is always prepared, hence the right choice of clothing knowing there is even a slight chance I would end up wet later! The only thing I forgot to pack is a spare pair of knickers! How remiss of me! You never know when you may need them.

Another drink or two and I will join him in the spa, I decide. But I must do something immensely important first. I need to see whether he can pass the next test or not ... the kiss!

I can't stress enough how imperative it is that a Mark must be a skilful kisser. It will determine whether you want to go out with the guy again or not. I'm looking forward to testing out Krystian's kissing skills!

Natural Smell Test

Upon meeting your Mark for the first time, you need to conduct the Vixen smell test. We are all either attracted or repelled by each other's natural scent. Why waste time with a guy if you are not attracted to the smell of his body, and cringe while holding your breath whenever he raises an armpit? If he is so drenched with his favourite cologne that hugging him makes your eyes water and you can taste the fumes on your tongue, you tend to wonder what kind of odour he is trying to cover up!

This test involves hugging your Mark hello on purpose, ensuring that your nose is well positioned into his neck to enable you to inhale a large dose and make an assessment. This is best done at the beginning in case you almost vomit at his stench and need to employ an immediate emergency exit strategy.

When enveloped in his hug, what impact does the smell of your potential Mark make on you?

Do you want to: 1. Nuzzle your nose further into his neck or chest inhaling his scent more deeply, feeling like you want to eat him then and there because you can't get enough of how good his scent is to you?

Or do you want to: 2. Vomit or hold your breath and run from the nostril burning stench of stale sweat, strong spices, garlic or the overpowering stench of cheap cologne?

Smell? What smell? Did you even notice your Mark's scent; if not check again. Ensure that you inhale deep enough each time as this is an important test. Should you still come up with nothing, you may be suffering from a cold or blocked nose and an impaired sense of smell.

If your answer is A … your Mark has aced this test. There is nothing better than inhaling the aroma of a man you find delicious! PASS.

If you answered B … run now Vixens! Put your escape plan into action and leave post haste. You know it won't become any better, so don't waste your time. Employ the sudden migraine or friend in trouble emergency action plan before you even order a drink, leave as fast as possible without being rude. If your answer is C ... you are either sick or not paying enough attention. Shame on you, Vixen! Retest and determine whether this Mark has potential or not.

Adventure Vixen

Time Warp

We walk back inside the lounge room to relax. His thigh is against mine—quite close but not so close that I feel crowded—on the comfortable black leather couch. To break the silence, I turn towards him with a cheeky grin.

"So, do you own any good music, Master Krystian?"

"Oh yeah, of course, Miss Arleia! Let me find something in my collection I think you will like."

He scans the selection of DVDs and CDs on the shelves of the loaded bookcase while muttering to himself about what I might like to listen to. I'm wondering what music this might be, as he slots something into the DVD player. Annie Lennox appears on the big flat screen television.

The popular eighties music floods our ears as we sip on our wine and chat in the flickering candlelight. The Eurhythmics' music brings back memories of my youth. The beat of the familiar tune is travelling through my body, mingling with the wine in a warm pleasant tingly sensation, making me want to sway to it.

Setting down my drink, I slide off the couch and start to move to the rhythm of my youth. I loved to dance to this song in the nightclubs I frequented many years ago. Of course, in my head I am still that age at times! Krystian joins me.

Wrapping his arms around my waist, he begins to sway with me in time to the beat, his hips move perfectly in time with the rhythm of the eighties tune. I smile to myself in approval. I like that. He dances closer so our bodies are brushing against each other, still moving to the music.

Glancing up I see a sparkle in his eye, and a seductive smile on his lips as he draws me hard up against him. Dancing together in perfect unison to the beat and sound of Annie Lennox's voice, we are bound together under her spell. He pulls me closer into his arms, and his lips graze against mine, questioning.

Smiling back at him, I tilt my chin upwards so mine is a breath away from touching his. With a low growl seeming to come from deep inside his chest, he crushes me against his hard chest. His lips swoop down that last millimetre capturing mine. With confidence his tongue darts along my lower lip. I want to open my mouth wider and allow his tongue to dance with mine. His lips move in an expert fashion, drawing me in. Making me want more as my hands slide over his broad shoulders and back exploring new territory.

I'm drowning in the magic of the music, the kiss and the wine. Deja vu hits me and I'm transported back in time twenty years. Dancing against the body of an anonymous male in a darkened club to this same Eurhythmics song, our lips passionately locked together.

I ignore my past vision and go with the feeling and the moment, surrendering myself to Krystian's experienced kisses. Clinging to his broad shoulders, I crush my breasts against his chest, and deepen our kiss. An indeterminable time later I am pulled back to the present by Krystian's inviting voice in my ear.

"Would you like to come into my ... office, Miss Arleia?" A come-hither smile spreads across his face. A shiver of delight flashes down my spine at his words. I'm turned on at the thought of him naked. Hmmm ... What to do? Do I say yes to sex on the first meeting or not? Society's general view is that you should never agree to 'spread your legs' on the first date. Never ever. Ever. Should you choose to flout the rule, you may be forever labelled as a slut, a harlot, a loose woman. The threat of this alone forces many of us to shake in our boots at the possible consequences of having some illicit fun, even if we're dying to do so. Why are society's rules for men the opposite? They are encouraged and congratulated on 'sowing their wild oats'!

If I want to participate in sex on a first date, whose business is it of anyone else's but my own? Oh, and of course the guy who I'm considering having sex with! Why do people judge everything as either good or bad? Who gets to determine which is which? Isn't sex a physical urge I can choose to satisfy when I want to? Is there anything wrong with this? As long as it is consensual of course, in whatever form you and your partner (or partners) are happy to proceed, who does it harm?

The act of touching another person does us a lot of good. Close physical human contact can be fantastic and is also an amazing stress and tension reliever. It makes one experience pleasure and releases the feel-good endorphins which surely can't be a bad thing!

If I am practising safe sex and enjoyment is being had by all parties involved, what's the problem? Once one becomes older and wiser it's easier to view the bigger picture and break free from society's shackles, and the infernal rules enforced by guilt.

Choose to cast these old-fashioned ideas aside, oh Vixens! Start with a fresh mind, wipe clean the whiteboard of your mind and rewrite the rules which suit you now. I don't live according to someone else's idea of how I should conduct my life. Why should I feel guilty when I'm feeling horny and in the happy position of being offered sex with a guy I am attracted to? Why worry about what others think?

Remember, as a Vixen, light-hearted play is the aim! Even if I only go on one playful date with someone and don't want to repeat the experience for whatever reason, there are plenty of other suitable Marks to choose from!

I am letting go of the emotional hang ups and want to enjoy sex for what it is—a lot of pleasure and an adventure, with no expectations of anything but the present moment. If I want to repeat the antics, I can. If once is enough, my curiosity satisfied; I can move on to the next one!

Therefore, for Vixens it's advisable to see several men at once. Should I not hear back from one, I probably won't realise it for a couple of weeks, because I am too busy enticing and playing with the other men on my current list. With my attention divided between a few Marks at a time, it is far more difficult to become attached to any one of them. I am aiming for short-term Marks, excellent for playing, not for long-term relationships. Vixens are here to play, not get hitched! I've cast away the shackles of doubt forced onto me by society - as long as there's mutual respect and honesty between us, that's good enough for me.

Krystian manages to put me in the right mood by being respectful, humorous and playful as well as a damn good kisser with natural rhythm. My mind is made up.

"Lead the way, Master Krystian."

Sensing the mutual internal excitement and anticipation building, he takes me by the hand to lead me down the hallway and into his bedroom. I am surprised and impressed at the scented candles burning on the bedside tables and windowsill. He pushes me back gently on the bed, then eases himself down beside me to continue the delicious kiss we've been sharing.

Now I could go into intimate details about his performance, technique and cock size ... but I won't. There are some things a Vixen likes to keep to herself ... for now! A couple of hours later I have experienced his superior skills; kissing is not the only thing he is good at. I will definitely consider coming back for more!

"How about a dip in the warm spa, Miss Arleia?" He brushes the stray hairs stuck to my sweaty forehead back from my face. Fortunately, I prepared for this eventuality underwear wise as I didn't want to be naked outside in his spa ... well not to start with. Ridiculous, I know, after what just happened—but a darkened room is different to a flashing bright spa!

My tight black camisole and bootylicious silky black knickers with lace edging are a perfect choice. I hope that the knickers will cover some cellulite on my butt, while the fitted cami will be more attractive than my lily-white stomach and keep my rounded belly flatter.

Satisfied that I will be comfortable in my underwear, I slip into the perfect bubbling water while the ever thoughtful Krystian disappears to prepare us some drinks. He joins me in the hot tub with a splash and sighs, 'This is heaven!'

With the warm water pulsing out of the designer jets from my shoulders down to my feet, and the music surrounding us from the spa's internal stereo, I am fast sliding into a comfortable and relaxed mode. Krystian gives me a lazy smile as the water swirls around us inviting us to sink in deeper.

We chat together for a while, sipping our drinks, mingled with the occasional kiss, enjoying each other's company. I did not expect this. Krystian is a happy, positive person with a great sense of humour. He is a 'no bullshit' kind of guy, and even when relaying the basic story of his previous relationship, he doesn't act negative or bitter.

Hallelujah! I think, relieved. The last thing I want to do is to hear about a guy's problems! The present moment is about enjoying it together without all the residual crap that exists in the real world intruding on our time. He does an excellent job of staying present and does not wallow in stories from his past. Another 'Pass' for Krystian, I decide.

Although he has the perfect unsuitability criteria for a Vixen's Mark and is not a long-term relationship possibility, he might become a real friend in the months to come. I'm surprised by this thought since we have only just met.

After hopping out of the spa into the beach towel Krystian holds out for me in a chivalrous manner, I can't stop an uncontrollable shiver as the cold air hits my wet skin. My icy, dripping clothing is not helping so I strip them off while keeping as much towel wrapped around me as possible to stave off the cold night air. I set a speed record for dressing with my bra as the only underwear beneath my jeans and top. My wet knickers are wrapped in the towel, and I call out to Krystian for a plastic bag. Note to self: Always put a spare pair of undies and a plastic bag in your handbag before heading out on a date—you never know when you may need them ... for a variety of reasons!

Krystian and I share a warm embrace and a last, lingering kiss once we reach his front door, before stepping out into the chilly night.

"Be safe on the drive home, Miss Arleia!"

I jump into my car, turning on both the motor and the heater, while lowering the window.

"Oh I shall, thank you Master Krystian!" I smile cheekily. "Thank you for the lovely evening!"

His face glows in the headlights as he grins down at me.

"We should go out together again sometime." I beam up at him.

"Mmm ... I'd like that!"

I'm grinning the smile of a Cheshire cat presented with a massive bowl of cream.

He waves me off as I speed off into the night, giggling like a maniac as I head home through the now quiet streets towards my home and cosy warm bed. I can't wipe the smug grin off my face the entire way home. After a long drive I'm ready to sink straight into my bed. Exhausted but happy, I congratulate myself on my first successful venture. It was superb! The evening's events swirl around in my head. What other adventures and happenings are in store for me? I look forward to my next expedition into dating land, and the life of a Vixen.

A brief flash of white light illuminates my bedroom for a second before being drawn greedily into the book on my bedside table. But I do not notice this, unconscious beneath my eyelids, already asleep.

Correct Vixen Attire

Sexy lingerie ahoy! A vixen is prepared for any occasion with a plethora of cute and sexy lacy lovelies to choose to wear under her regular attire. Her collection may include the following:

- ✓ Chemises and baby dolls (floaty and sexy to entice your lover to bed)
- ✓ Corsets (excellent for flattening a tummy and gaining more curves)

Adventure Vixen

Disaster Date

My week flows around me in its usual busy fashion of seeing clients, taking phone calls and keeping various appointments. Between all this I make the time to answer Krystian's daily texts. He sends them at random times, messages like, "Have an osome day, pretty lady!"

Or, "It's a beautiful day today sexy lady, I hope you are enjoying the sunshine!"

They are pleasant, welcome ones, not too over familiar, not stalker-ish, invasive or rude. Little messages are a cute daily reminder that I am in his thoughts, which is quite satisfying.

All of a sudden, the week has flown by and it's Friday morning. My appointment with Mitch is tonight, and the meeting time is fast looming! Between the flurry of calls and appointments through the week, I do manage to chat on the phone to him one evening.

He has a sense of humour and seems interesting enough that I think he should be OK in person. There is some over-complimenting going on, but I assume it is just nervousness on his part. It can be difficult to gauge a person by a phone conversation, so I give him the benefit of the doubt.

Our tryst is at a cute heritage pub in The Rocks area near Circular Quay at eight o'clock, so there's just enough time to race home after work and try on half a dozen combinations of outfits. Clothes end up strewn all over my once neat bedroom, but at least I am almost ready by seven o'clock!

The choice of my navy skinny leg jeans, low heeled black ankle boots, a black tank top with a teal jacket and necklace for tonight is final. With expert make-up and my long blonde hair parted on the side with a sweeping angled fringe, I'm ready to go and meet my man for the evening.

Walking to the train station, which is a convenient five-minute stroll down the road, warms me up for the short journey into the city. I do prefer to drive my car, but if you are going to be heading to the city, the train beats a car any day. It's not until my train is pulling into the station that I realise I forgot to consult the Book about Mitch. *Shit*.

With one foot on the platform I consider running back home to do so. People push past me, giving me looks of annoyance at me half blocking the train's doorway. I'm jostled into the train as the whistle sounds and the doors close. Too late! Why did I make time for vodka but not for the Book? Internally I berate myself. What sort of Vixen forgets to use the tool that's most helpful in my quest? I didn't even consult my Goddess cards. The success of my date with Krystian must have addled my brain! I sigh in resignation, unsure of what tonight will hold now.

I meander alongside the glistening dark water's edge. The quay's lights are reflected in a mesmerising fashion, making it difficult to concentrate on weaving through the throng of wandering people and buskers as I head to our designated meeting point.

While I stroll along, the nervousness and anxiety dancing in and out of existence take a back seat. I calm myself by directing my thoughts and attention to the sparkling harbour. I appreciate the magnificent view of a living city against the water and the night sky, bobbing ferries and boat lights twinkling into the dark water.

Perhaps the lack of nerves is due to the rather strong vodka I downed in a flash minutes before I walked out my door? On an empty stomach one drink can work wonders in spreading a delicious warmth through my entire system, dispelling all my nerves (well, most of them) and putting me in a quite happy and bemused state. Hm ... Will drinking before a date instead of consulting the Book become a new habit?

I cross the street and arrive at the hotel where we chose to meet. With a sinking feeling I realise it may be harder to find each other than I first thought. I feel the vibrations from the live band within, pumping out of the venue's open doors. The sound mingles with the swelling, inebriated chatter of dozens of people milling outside of the quaint pub which seems to almost be alive.

Luckily, I spy a couple leaving and I swoop in to nab their spot. I take note of the varied types of people out this evening. Businessmen still dressed in suits are engaging in their after Friday night drinks ritual. A gaggle of young, undernourished girls sporting massive manes in short brightly coloured pantsuits teamed with glittery platform shoes, vacant looks and incessant giggles loud enough that they should be reported for disturbing the peace. You can tell who the tourists are too. People looking flushed from too much sun, thirsty after a ferry ride in their crumpled clothes and sensible walking shoes. The last of the old men who have called this old watering hole a home away from home for many years trickle out of the doors heading for their real home. They don't like what their familiar, comfortable pub turns into at night—a seething mass of writhing bodies, spilt drinks and shouted conversation as the band ramps up the volume of the music.

I begin to rethink the wisdom of the choice of venue. With so many people around, how will I ever recognise Mitch? Pulling out my phone, I type out a quick message:

"Sitting at a table outside. Come and find me if you are here!" Send! Not a minute passes before I get a reply.

"I'm inside near the bar, I will come out and find you."

Well thank goodness! I wasn't going to give up this table with several other patrons milling around, hoping to snare it the second it becomes free.

I see a smiling older, balding guy weaving his way towards me.

Holy crap! This must be Mitch!

My mind does a quick flash back to the online picture he used. It must have been taken at least ten or fifteen years ago! What is with that?

Seriously, if you are planning to meet with a girl, you should post a reasonably up-to-date picture of yourself on your profile! How can you put up an old one and hope that the person you are meeting won't see the twenty extra lines marking your face or the hairline that's receded much further now than when the picture was taken? How ridiculous!

To be honest, if Mitch had posted a current image on his profile, I doubt that I would have started talking to him. Mitch at thirty-something was way more handsome than he is at forty-three. Seeing that I'm here now and he is fast approaching, I need to make the best of this situation.

"Hi … Arleia?" His grin is tinged with an edge of uncertainty that comes with meeting a new person on a date for the first time.

"Yes! You're Mitch? Lovely to meet you!"

When presented with an awkward or sticky happening, I go into 'working actress mode'. I can talk in a polite and friendly manner to whoever I am with about anything and not appear ill at ease or nervous. I am going to need to employ this skill for the evening. I pull myself together and with a smile plastered on my face, I gaze across at him.

"Who would have known that the pub would be so busy tonight? I don't think I would have been able to find you inside. Have you been here for long?" Mitch relaxes into the chair across from me. "Can I fetch us a drink?" he continues.

Thank God! A glimmer of hope for the evening—more alcohol!

I ask for a glass of the house bubbly and I watch as he weaves his way through the crowded sidewalk and back into the hotel. A happy sigh escapes me. I'd much rather be comfortable sitting here at the table watching people, than fighting my way through the throngs of Friday night revellers waiting to be served!

A good fifteen-minutes later Mitch appears with two drinks, still full to the brim—a sign that miracles can and do happen! He smiles flirtatiously as he passes me my glass of bubbly.

"Wow! You are gorgeous!"

A little embarrassed at his enthusiasm, I am appreciative of the compliment.

"And your smile! Fantastic! Oh and you smell delicious too."

His face lights up in pleased satisfaction, whereas my smile feels frozen into an icy grimace on my face. One compliment? Yes, lovely! But this is almost too much, and we are only twenty-minutes into the date.

"Well, thank you for the compliments." Awkward! Work mode Arleia, work mode!

"So, Mitch, what is it you do for work?"

I hope to gain time to gather my thoughts and to decide how long I am prepared to stay on this date! He chats on about something business related, as my eyes glaze over. I focus instead on downing my delicious bubbly as fast as possible. Again, I feel grateful for the effects of alcohol.

Sadly, with empty glasses all round someone is going to need to do another bar run. We decide to both brave the crowded hotel, and I feel obliged to buy him a drink this time. Edging closer to the bar, I indicate with a wave of a fifty dollar note what I am doing. Mitch smiles and melts back into the sea of faces.

Squeezing through a convenient gap in the crowd, I almost bang into the guy standing right in front of me, getting a good glance at him. He's in his late twenties, wearing a tight-fitting t-shirt which emphasises his lickable massive biceps. I can't peel my eyes away from them! With dark hair, broad shoulders, a narrow waist and the cutest round butt I have seen in a while ... I almost forget what I'm doing standing at the bar. Delicious! Mmm, exactly the way I like a man.

I am having a hard time not grabbing him with both hands to caress the solid muscle underneath the skin ... perhaps lick them, and him. Oh dear. I'm almost drooling as the lush young hottie turns from the bar, drinks in hand and smiling flirtatiously at me. Grinning back, I step aside.

"Thanks cutie!" He grins back at me as he slides his gorgeous body against mine to move past the line up and away from the crowded area. My night might not be so bad if this is the kind of eye candy available to perve on here!

Drinks in hand after a fifteen-minute wait, I weave my way back to where Mitch is standing. Inside I wish I was dancing with big bicep boy instead! As I hand him his drink, he leans forward and inhales deeply.

"Mmm, you do smell delicious!"

I give him a distant smile in return and lift my glass to my lips. Yeah, you said that at least five times already mate. His over-complimenting is wearing thin, and my ability to hold my tongue is disappearing fast. Thank God for alcohol! I think to myself for the fiftieth time this evening.

Someone in the passing throng jostles Mitch forcing him to step forward and bang into me.

"Oh! I'm sorry! Ooops, I touched your breasts then!"

What a moron. I find it's an effort to muster a wry grin in reply.

"I did notice."

"I'm so sorry Arleia, I was ... "

Before he can even finish his insincere apology, he's knocked again, and he again ends up with his body pressed into my breasts.

"Oh no! It happened again!" It's obvious that he is pleased with the crowded hotel working in his favour tonight.

"Don't worry about it."

I step as far away from him as possible with the milling crowd surrounding us. I wonder if the Book has a sense of humour and is laughing at me right now; its unheeded red warning glow lighting up my empty bedroom. How much longer will I stay on this date? I want to bail right now.

We chat a bit, but we need to yell into each other's ears to be heard. Mitch leans forward, his breath tickling my ear in a rather unpleasant fashion.

"Do you ever get worried being a single female walking around the city by yourself?"

I consider the question.

"No, not really I don't. I learnt karate for a few years, so I can pack a mean punch if I have to!"

"Well, what would you do if someone grabbed you in a dark alley?"

This is a weird question.

"I would incapacitate him for long enough to allow me to high tail it out of the alley unharmed and raise the alarm!" Mitch is amused at my reply and nods in agreement.

"Well, escaping unscathed would be a good thing to do, if you're able to do so for sure."

I ask him what he would do in the same situation.

Grinning in a boyish fashion, he suddenly appears younger than I'd seen him all evening. "I would drop to the ground into the foetal position and emit a bad smell to drive them away!"

I am speechless. Are you kidding me? What sort of dumb, idiotic answer is this? Maybe your mates might think letting out an eye-watering pong from your butt is a cool thing to do ... in PRIMARY school! The hilarity is completely lost on me! My nose scrunches in dismay.

"Really? Like a skunk you mean?"

My top lip morphs from a forced smile into a grimace at an extremely visual image of him curled up in the foetal position in an alley. Butt cheeks vibrating to emit deadly smelling fart bombs to drive his assailants away, choking to death on the fumes as they stumble away, tears streaming down their faces.

Now in one way, that's kind of funny. But right now, the vision in my head is not. Would you choose farting for self-defence as an interesting topic when out on a date with a new woman whom I assume you are trying to impress? I think not!

Apart from him dropping this gem, I am getting sick of the constant over-complimenting. I love a good compliment, but we all possess our limits! Too much flattery quickly becomes creepy and insincere. It's like when you're seeing a new guy and he tells you he loves you in less than two weeks ... Creepy! Dude. *Really?* You don't even know me yet! Premature and exaggerated declarations of love make me want to put my sneakers on and hightail my butt out of the relationship as fast as possible.

By now I have endured almost two hours of this disaster date and it is well past time to end my torture. Why didn't I leave earlier and use my back-up plan which is always at the ready? Well, quite simply because the bulging bicep boy is hanging out close by. I have a perfect view of those incredibly hard and huge biceps over Mitch's left shoulder. Time goes a lot faster when I pay more attention to sexy biceps man than to my date!

I watch as the young hottie walks towards us, staring at me. A sexy smile flashes across his face. My eyes flick back to Mitch, whose attention has been drawn to the football on the big screen for a second. Bicep boy slides his body against mine as he passes, and I feel a tug at my jeans as he slips something into a back pocket. Startled, I looked over my shoulder at him. He winks and blows me a kiss. My cheeks flame and I grin in appreciation of his cheekiness as he's swallowed by the crowd.

I'm dying to check my pocket, but Mitch demands my attention. He's asking me if I'd like to go to a café nearby to continue our date. *Hell no!*

"Oh! Look at the time! I'm so sorry, but I am going to need to get going."

I try to appear sad about leaving, but I'm not sure if I can pull it off.

"Sadly, work starts early in the morning," I arrange my face into an apologetic look. "And I still need to get home from here too!"

The blow of me ending the night in this abrupt way is slightly softened by my regretful appearance. He draws me closer and plants his lips on mine. Whoa! That is unexpected! The alcohol zinging around my system allows the kiss, which, though pleasant enough; does not curl my toes or rock my world. I pull away from him, and draw back even further when I realise he's about to try his luck a second time.

"Uhm, must go or I will miss the train!" My feet are itching to run.

"It was lovely to meet you though, thanks Mitch!" The Vixen is always polite.

He leans in for one more hug and kiss goodbye, but I avert my head at the last second, so that his lips only connect with my cheek. I draw back with a bright smile.

"Well, I've got to go!" Turning towards the door, I take one long last look at the delicious bulging bicep boy and weave my way as fast as I can towards the exit, and freedom. I take a deep breath of fresh air, and start jogging towards the train station, heedless of my heeled boots.

I'm dying to see what message bicep boy left me, but I need the safety of the station first. As soon as I reach the platform, my hand dives into my back pocket. A folded piece of paper emerges, and I unfold it, my hands trembling. The words above his phone number make me burst into laughter, startling other people nearby.

Ditch the old guy, sexy! ☺ Joshua… call me x

The train squeals to a stop in front of me as I scrunch his note up and shove it into my jeans. In the half empty carriage heading home, my mind can't help but replay the events of the evening, my thoughts lingering on Joshua's lick-able biceps. I'm startled out of my daydream by a loud message alert sounding on my phone. Who the heck is messaging me at this time of night? I wonder to myself, as I rummage around in my bag for my ever-elusive phone.

My handbags, even the smaller ones, all seem to resemble the Tardis from *Dr Who*. They appear small, unassuming and awfully pretty from the outside—it doesn't seem as though I could hide anything at all in such a small area. However, the interior is a cavernous black hole which swallows up and hides even the largest items.

At last my hand finds the evasive phone and I can retrieve it from my bag. Mitch! Oh fantastic. What does he want to say, I wonder? It's bound to be more uninteresting nonsense. I open the message to read its contents.

"Thanks for a great evening babe. I'd love to see your gorgeous self again xx."

Ugh! Throwing my phone back into my bag, I ignore his message and sink back into my seat.

I fully realise my mistake tonight. *I should have consulted the Book before I left*. No surprise that this night was a disaster!

With a shrug I sit back again. Nothing I can do about it now. Instead I think about bulging bicep boy, Joshua. I pull out the crumpled phone number he slipped me and a shiver of anticipation runs through me at the thought of a date with him ... I can't wait! My weekend ahead is free, so I will have plenty of time to find more potential dates—and possibly add him to the list.

Meeting Your Date

Always plan to meet your Mark at the destination rather than travelling together. You still don't know him well enough to trust him, and it is better to keep the air of mystery, distance and allure for longer.

Your freedom to leave whenever you like is also important should something unforeseen happen. The ability to leave alone when you want to, is imperative at this early stage.

Adventure Vixen

Dr Jekyll

Saturday morning dawns, and I roll out of bed and into my gym clothes before I am even awake. To be pre-prepared seems to be the best way for me to make my way to the gym consistently. If all my things are out ready the evening before, I don't need to think at all in the morning.

I try to tell myself that if I don't go to the gym in the morning, I will just go in the afternoon instead. This sounds first rate in theory, but do I do it? No. Never. I don't understand why going to the gym is so hard for me to do, but I now must accept the fact that if I don't go first thing in the morning, I don't go at all! After recovering from my morning session and feeling more awake, I decide to ignore all household chores in favour of increasing my contact list online.

To gather the essential items I need for successful fishing is second nature by now. This time I remember the Book too, so I can consult it for each Mark I consider meeting. I take everything outside with me, seeing that is a pleasant, mild winter day. The outdoors is beckoning. The glass panes of the lounge room door lead out to a small, private, leafy patio area which is the perfect place to sit while fishing. The gleaming glass topped table has plenty of room for my laptop and supplies. There are cushioned chairs surrounded by decorative raised beds of lush plants with a huge market umbrella shading the cosy area. I arrange everything within reach, and settle in for a few hours of fun hunting, with my feet resting on one of the chairs and the radio blasting a top forty hits countdown from the lounge room. Now, what I will find online today? Giggling in anticipation, I my account.

What the heck? Stunned, I realise that a total of twenty-seven new contact requests are waiting for me to respond! I can't believe my eyes. Surely there were only a couple on my list the last time I checked this site. Switching to invisible as fast as I can, I give myself enough thinking time to go through the mountain of new potential Marks. OK, here I go! I am going to need to be ruthless!

My criterion for the first round of elimination is height. It's the easiest thing I can think of to start with, and height is a huge deal for me, as you know. I can't stand to go on a date with a guy who is the same height or shorter than me, so fast eradication is the name of the game!

The second removal round will focus on the profile picture. Wow! Half an hour of quick decision making, and I am down to five suitable candidates to become the next Mark. That didn't take too long! I accept the five remaining contact requests, and before long, one of them pops up online.

"Heyyy ... thanks for the add, I'm Roshan!"

Like a pro I click on his profile again to obtain an idea of who this man is.

GREEN TO THIS Male 29 Australia

Have Photos. Will unlock or just ask :-)

Hi, I'm tradie/part-time model looking for someone to hang out with and get to know. I enjoy travelling and can be mature when I have to but also fun most of the time. If you would like to find out more, drop me a line.

Cronulla New South Wales| Australia

Seeking Criteria Members anywhere in Australia.

Casual Dating with a female. Between 18 and 35 years of age.

What I'm Looking For: Someone who is easy going and chilled to get along with.

Details: Relationship Status Single

Drinking Habits: Socially

Height: 5'8" / 176cm

Body Type: Fit

Education: University Student

Occupation: Tradesperson

Sign of the Zodiac: Gemini

Interests: Cars and Motoring, Going Out, Health and Fitness, Movies, Music, Sports

Ohhhh, well hello! There is not much information in the profile, but OMG, there are some wicked looking abs in his picture! Couple these attributes with sparkling eyes, a smouldering smile that would melt chocolate with the smoothest looking delicious mocha coloured skin. He looks yummy enough to eat! Before I become carried away, I need to check my unsuitability criteria. Ohhhh yes, he does meet that—he is too short for my preference!

Only a couple of inches taller than me equals no heels when going out. Perfect. MWAAAHAhahahahaahahaaaa!

As I prepare myself mentally to start chatting to him, another message appears on my screen.

Dr Jekyll: Well, Hello there!

Wooaaahhh... now I need to do a quick check of this potential Mark's profile! How else will I know how I want to answer him? Hmmm, even less information on this one. Guys are hopeless!

DR JEKYLL-I was sucked in by this dating site's ad on TV! Damn you television with your flickering lights and hypnotic promises. I can unlock my pic when we chat.

34 Sydney New South Wales| Australia Seeking Criteria Members anywhere in Australia.

Casual Dating with a female or friendship with a female. Between 18 and 45 years of age.

What I'm looking for: You! Who knows ... if you click you click right?

Relationship Status: Single

Hair Colour: Black

Eye Colour: Blue Height: 6'0" / 182cm

Body Type: Muscular

Sign of the Zodiac: Aquarius

Interests: Cooking, Going Out, Reading

Hmmm. Even though there seems to be a serious lack of information on his profile, he does seem to possess a good sense of humour, and a slight quirky streak too!

ATrixenVixen: Well hello yourself! You're blaming the TV's lights for being here? Original ...

Dr Jekyll: Hahahahaaa yeah well you know how sneaky these suckers can be!

ATrixenVixen: Indeed ... distinctly hypnotic! It's obvious you couldn't avoid them. Totally impossible!

Dr Jekyll: Exactly! How can I resist? Hmm ... a woman who knows the score ... I like it!

ATrixenVixen: Hahaaaa! Oh! A man with a quick wit AND sense of humour? I like it!

Dr Jekyll: Ahaaa: Well I am pleased to meet you! I'm Adam.

ATrixenVixen: Well most interesting to meet you Adam. I'm Arleia.

Dr Jekyll: Ahhhh ... a lovely name to match the beautiful face and smile. I'm almost bewitched already!

ATrixenVixen: Hahaaaa! Watch out, oh evil doctor, I do have the power to bewitch. You should fear for your safety and run, for I am a Vixen.

Dr Jekyll: Oooooh, a Vixen, hey? Not sure I've enjoyed the pleasure of meeting one yet. Intriguing.

ATrixenVixen: You should be running, not intrigued! ... Or else you may find yourself ensnared in my web of delight!

Dr Jekyll: Oh? Web of delight? Are you sure I'd want to escape?

ATrixenVixen: I'm just giving you fair warning, good doctor ... It's the least a Vixen can do, before she dazzles you with her charms.

Dr Jekyll: I do like to be dazzled on occasion! Do you do windows as well? Hahahahaaa.

ATrixenVixen: Oooooh! Cheeky! You can find your own slaves to do that thank you!

Dr Jekyll: I might do that ... The lazy sods are just lounging in their cage at the moment.

ATrixenVixen: Their cage? I'd not think you would be so heartless as to lock your slaves up in a cage!

Dr Jekyll: Ahhhh, but of course I am kind—I did throw in a few of the latest gossip magazines for their entertainment, plus I wheeled the cage closer to the heater ... What more could they want?

ATrixenVixen: Ohhhh Of course! How remiss of me to think you would be unkind in any way oh evil one!

Dr Jekyll: Exactly! I even have hessian sacks in the cage too.

ATrixenVixen: Hessian? Isn't that cloth a little scratchy for them?

Dr Jekyll: Not when it is covered with straw it's not ... and of course there are a few bright coloured throw cushions in their cosy prison too to complete the ambiance!

ATrixenVixen: Baaahahaahahahaahahaa!

Hmmm ... Fast witted, funny, imaginative ... What are his unsuitable criteria here? I'm going to delve further! I need to see a picture ... Bet he's got a face only a mother can love!

ATrixenVixen: Hmm, thoughtful and decorative. I like your style oh evil doctor! Perhaps you should entice me further by flashing me your private picture?

Dr Jekyll: Hahaha! A delightfully worded request oh Vixen, your wish shall be granted!

OK! Result achieved! Let me take a quick glance—I am dying to view what he's like ... Ohh, hmm ... quite attractive, I am highly surprised! Dark blond curls atop of a cheeky, friendly smile with a hint of naughtiness about him. Oh crap. Wait. There needs to be something unsuitable about him.

Heyyy…. His profile says black hair. Hmm, something is afoot here. He does exhibit some classic signs to look for! He has penned little to no information in his profile at all. You can see he is not giving up any real information about himself, other than his sense of humour and playfulness.

Whenever you come across profiles like this one, it is wise to proceed with caution! The Book says there is a reason these men write so little information on their page. Lack of detail is often something big enough to make a difference on how you view them. With this in mind, I continue the conversation.

ATrixenVixen: Mmmm ... you look quite cute for an evil doctor!

Dr Jekyll: Ha-ha! It's when I practise my evil laugh that you need to watch out, Vixen!

ATrixenVixen: Oooooh ... Well, I will do my best to remember oh evil one, but you'd better be warned you cannot win when you tangle with a Vixen ...

Dr Jekyll: Hmm, well with that sexy, naughty smile of yours, as well as your eye-popping cleavage, many men would fall willingly into your web!

ATrixenVixen: Yes, it should be no surprise, I am head Vixen after all! Mwaaahahaahaaahahaaa!

Dr Jekyll: I can see I could be getting myself into trouble here.

ATrixenVixen: Indeed, you may. Right now, I could be lazily languishing upon my lounge, luring you in ...

Dr Jekyll: Oooooh! It's like lustful literary longings.

ATrixenVixen: Don't even try to outdo me, mere mortal. You've got no chance!

Dr Jekyll: Hahahahaaaahaaahaa!

ATrixenVixen: Soo ... what brings you here good doctor? One of your calibre is surprising! Do tell ...

Dr Jekyll: Umm ... well, I may have a slight confession to make, oh sexy vixen.

I knew it, I just knew it! Whatever this is will clinch the unsuitability criteria section for me; I can feel it coming ... thank goodness for that! Someone so witty, funny, and flirtatious must be hiding a downside somewhere or I would need to stop talking to him and RUN!

Holding my breath almost without realising, I wait to read what his response will be.

ATrixenVixen: Well? I'm waiting, oh doctor of secrets!

Dr Jekyll: This is harder to tell you than I thought it would be.

ATrixenVixen: Oh for God's sake, just spit whatever it is out man! LOL

Dr Jekyll: OK ... here goes ... I'm in an open relationship.

Bingo. We have a winner! That does top the unsuitable criteria for a long-term partner! You know, I did wonder once before whether I could ever agree to be in an open relationship. In theory it sounds satisfying. You could both experience some fun on the side, be open and honest about what you're doing, and even set down rules.

Maybe couples research open relationships on the internet first, gathering ideas of what good sound rules would work for them. Where their limits are, what is acceptable and what is not. How to implement the new agreement, what each other's expectations are, and how it would best work for each couple considering the path of an open relationship.

When I contemplate it like this, it seems quite logical. Almost easy to do; after a little preparation. It would certainly be much better than cheating and lying. Once trust is lost between each other, it is difficult and sometimes impossible to regain that trust. But a well thought out plan together as a couple could work, couldn't it? Or would the green-eyed monster rear its ugly head and start niggling at me in the back of my mind?

Would I wonder if the other girl he is having sex with is better than I am at satisfying him? If she knows more stuff in bed than I do? Whether she is more attractive or cuter than I am? Smarter? Or has bigger breasts? Even worse, does she possess the ability to steal my man's heart away? Would I even care? Or would I be safe in our cocoon of love, knowing with an innate certainty he will always come back to me, as I will to him, because we are soul mates?

Do soul mates even exist? Or are they a myth created by the machine of commercialism with Valentine's Day, weddings, anniversaries and the like, to squeeze more money out of us? That question is too hard for me now. Seeing that I've not met my soul mate, I am not an authority.

Back to the open relationship debate. I am sure we are all different. This is a good thing! However, I am pretty sure that, if I ever fell deliriously in love with someone, I'd want to scratch the eyes out of any woman who is too flirtatious with my man, in some crazy fit of jealousy. God knows what I might do if he ever slept with another woman.

Shit. I'm waffling on again. When I should be concentrating on my next move here. Should I go for a guy who is attached, even if he says he is in an open relationship? Even though he is explaining to me at this very second what the rules of their deal are? Does his girlfriend agree to this, or is it only him who is aware that they are in an open relationship? He does seem to present well thought out and quite involved rules ... he may possibly be for real.

Perhaps I will take a chance and see how this unfolds.

ATrixenVixen: *Well, that is interesting! And you say the reason why you came to this agreement is because she is working overseas for months at a time?*

Dr Jekyll: Yes, that's right Vixen. Do you still want to talk to me, knowing this? I don't blame you if you don't!

ATrixenVixen: *It's OK, I do appreciate your honesty. I couldn't be in your situation, but I do understand where you are coming from. You shall be allowed to keep conversing with me. For now!*

Dr Jekyll: Phew! Thank goodness! I would be devastated to miss the chance to talk with a real-life Vixen!

ATrixenVixen: *Well, perhaps you will be lucky enough to do so ... we will see!*

The moral dilemma! I need a break so I can digest all of this. I glance over my screen to see the Book's red glow of disapproval regarding this potential Mark. Of course!

In the meantime, I have been asked out for drinks with the other delicious looking Mark, Roshan, who seems like a sweet but naughty kind of guy. Excellent, just what I like! Mwaaahahaahaahahaaaa!

Hmm, it also helps that he is model-level attractive, a construction worker and part-time model/stripper with an edible body. It sounds like he is a lovely guy too! Unsuitability check? Yes! All good attributes, with a glaring unsuitable fact: he is too short for my long-term criteria!

In a moment of sudden exhaustion, I snap my laptop shut. Blinking a couple of times, I refocus my eyes back to the reality of my surroundings. The leafy plants and garden around me come back into view. Glancing at my watch I am stunned to realise three hours have passed—no wonder I'm having trouble unbending myself from this position!

I glance down and brush the remaining crumbs from my earlier snacks into my empty glass. With a satisfied grin I stand to stretch out some of the soreness in my muscles, thinking about what a productive three hours they were—a definite date with a hot mocha model and an interesting witty and intelligent conversation with another. I may need more time to think about that one!

Still trying to diminish the stiffness in my legs, I realise the day is clear enough to go for a walk. I set off towards the park before I can talk myself out of going. I can't help but entertain thoughts of this morning's successes. I think about all the times in the past that I have been to a club, a bar or to listen to a band. How many hours did I spend at these places, eyeing hot guys, hoping to catch their eye and have them speak to me? I would giggle with friends over a whole group of attractive men in the corner, but rarely pluck up the courage needed to go over and approach one, let alone a whole group of guys, saying, "Hi, my name is ... I think you're cute, want to dance?" On paper appears so simple, yet in reality it seems to be almost impossible.

Of course, if I ever did pick up the courage after a few drinks to approach a cutie I spotted earlier, chances were he already had a girlfriend, or just left for the night, while I was at the bar busy getting sloshed to gain false bravado ... and I missed my chance!

It is so hard to approach guys in person. Is it little wonder the traditional style of going to clubs and pubs for the sole purpose of finding a half decent guy that you fancy snogging, is getting a little tired?

I would rather be comfortable in my own home, browsing the online catalogue of men available and deciding which one or ones I might like to meet. At least I don't need to doll myself up for the night and come home disappointed! I can relax and peruse the many choices at my leisure and choose one I might like to be bothered dressing up and getting out of the house for.

Now it does take a while to become savvier in choosing attractive, unsuitable Marks who will not drive me to clock watching after the first fifteen-minutes of the date, but this is what the Vixen's handbook is for! I'm thankful I noticed its warning about Adam before I wasted any more time with him. I am happy to report my meeting is now organised with the hunky Roshan, so bring on my next adventure!

Red Light Warning—Forbidden Marks:

- *Vixens are not to set their sights upon any man who is married whether they are happy or not*

- *Men in monogamous relationships are not to be pursued*

- *No vixen shall meet with a Mark whom she knows is seeing a sister vixen, unless the vixens previously agree on terms*

- *Do not target Marks in an 'open relationship' that their partners are not aware of*

Failure to adhere to these rules can incur extreme misery and persecution from wronged women.

Vixens are of light and wish to avoid negative drama in their lives. Knowingly entering into vixen play with an attached Mark of any kind is forbidden.

Adventure Vixen

Green to This

Thank God It's Friday!

I'm rushing around trying to finish work for the day. I hurry towards my car surrounded by a chorus of "See you next week!" and "Have an excellent weekend." Tonight is my tryst with Roshan, and I want to make sure that there's enough time to shower, change, decide what to wear, then do a lightning fast tidy up of my house, in case I do entertain an unplanned visitor later in the night!

Now, I know that the Vixen's Handbook includes rules about first time meetings, and a protocol to follow, but on occasion I may bend the rules. If I am meeting the man out in an appropriate public place first, spend time chatting and getting to know the measure of the Mark, I may decide to invite them back to my place for a coffee if I so choose!

This thought spurs me into high speed action around the house, almost magically tidying up and putting things away in a flash. All this amazing cleaning happens in a shorter time than I would ever have thought possible. Yes, it's true, miracles do happen. If only my fairy godmother existed to wave her wand and instantly produce the perfect outfit for me too - or the perfect man! I may be convinced to find a permanent partner again one day, but not until I've had my fill of playful gratification with as many Marks as I like first!

How else will I discover what qualities are essentials to me in a man unless I experiment with many, and take note of all the things I require in a mate? I need to focus on the attributes and personality quirks that are attractive to me. While I am enjoying the variety of men, I could focus on the couple of personality traits and qualities I am drawn to. I will start a list and pick the best quality and the most attractive trait of each gentleman I meet, collate them all together in a super list to describe my imaginary dream man … for if and when I am ready to attract him to me!

That is certainly something to think about. Mwaaahaaahahaaahahaaaaa!

Of course, that time is still far away, and I am currently in full Vixen mode and loving the adventure. Checking my wrist, I see that there are now only forty-minutes left to get ready to meet him ... I'm going to need to make this into a sprint! In the shower I hear my phone going off with a message.

"Oh God, please don't let this text be him saying he is early, and at the pub already waiting for me!" I slide out of the shower, with shampoo suds sliding down my nose. Swearing, I slip on the tiles and bang my knee on the door frame. Ouch! Quickly I check the text on my half-charged phone, still cursing while rubbing my sore knee and dripping water through the hallway and kitchen. The message is indeed from Roshan, and I sigh with relief as I read that he's running late himself and will be an extra half an hour. What a break!

Calmer now, I jump back into the shower. I stand under the cascading water in a more relaxed state and finish getting ready at a more leisurely pace, still mindful of the time. I am down to the last fashion choice to make for my outfit—the shoes, when I remember that Roshan is not very tall, and there is no way I want to be towering over him in heels like Xena, the Warrior Princess! No. That won't do at all.

Rummaging through my shoes, I hunt for suitable choices. Finally, I find a cute low- heeled pair of long black boots with buckles up the sides—perfect! OK. Ready ... but perhaps I will do a final check before leaving. I feel a warm prickling at the back of my neck and the Book beckons me. Its golden glow of approval about tonight reassures me, letting me know that if I like Roshan, it's safe to bring him here afterward.

Maybe I should get a second opinion from my Goddess cards too, since I screwed up with the Mitch date. Taking the cards from their box, I shuffle with my eyes closed while asking for guidance about Roshan. I feel a card flip from the deck and open my eyes.

Isis: Past Life

This situation involves your past-life memories. Your roots upon this planet are strong and deep. Some of these roots have anchored you in past memories, so that you are paralysed when it comes to moving forward. Sometimes you bury those memories to shield yourself from pain or embarrassment, so you won't remember those awkward moments when life tested you to the maximum. Reveal those lessons to yourself now, strong sorceress, and move forward with the confidence that you have sage wisdom behind you.

You've known the person you're enquiring about in a past life.

I'm surprised by this message. It's not what I was expecting. I mull over the card as I slip on a pale pink lacy bra and matching knickers with a silky lace camisole, under a pink floaty low cut layered tank top and a black straight line maxi skirt with side slits. My low-heeled long boots and a fitted black jacket finish the ensemble. After a final twirl in front of the mirror with a last minute swipe of extra lip gloss for a more luscious shine, I am out the door!

Congratulating myself on my cleverness in choosing a bar close to home this time *and* remembering to consult the Book and my cards, I pull into the car park in less than three-minutes! I don't want tonight to be a repeat of the disaster date with Mitch.

I walk through the hallway to the outdoor beer garden, surveying every person. Luckily for me not many people are in the bar or the beer garden, so I'm confident that I've raced him to the hotel ... which is like a miracle for me, the habitually late one!

My lungs fill as I take a deep steadying breath to calm my nerves before stepping towards the bar to order a glass of champagne. Glass in hand, I wander outside to the pleasant outdoor area with landscaped plants and cosy cushioned seats. A small corner table with a leafy background located away from the other patrons is perfect.

This is the best position to be in, because it gives me a clear view of all three entrances Roshan is likely to appear at, and a few precious seconds to check him out before he sees me! Seated on the charcoal wicker chair, I take a large sip of my drink to help gain more Dutch courage before he appears. Preferably the guy should buy me a drink but in this instance, I want the champagne to line my empty stomach and help me to relax while I wait for him. Searching for my phone in my handbag, I realise I have another message from Roshan. He had better be coming ... Or else I will be seriously pissed off!

I read his text and relief runs through me when I read that he is running a few more minutes late, but that he is on his way. I glance around the bar, checking out the mix of people - some there for dinner, others with their eyes glued to the big screen watching the latest rugby match, while others keep their eyes stuck to the Keno screen, hoping to hit the jackpot.

Just as I sigh and wonder how much longer he is going to be, he appears. Weaving his way through the couches and tables towards me, he flashes a grin of greeting. His white teeth sparkle from the growing wide smile which matches the rest of his yumminess as he saunters towards my table. His smiling familiar eyes know the answer even before he asks if I am Arleia.

"Yes, I am! And you of course must be Roshan!"

I stand to greet him as he leans forward and pecks me on the cheek. " Hmmm, this could be an interesting night indeed!" I think to myself as I sit back down, glad of my flat shoes.

"Can I buy you another drink before I join you?" He is exceedingly polite in his enquiry. Manners do impress me, as does the rest of him!

"I'd love another glass of champagne, thank you." Flirtatiously grinning up at him, I find it hard to resist the urge to bat my eyelashes at him and giggle. As he makes his way over to the bar for our drinks, I can't help but admire his broad shoulders, narrow waist and rounded butt, which must have been sculpted in the gym.

Mmm, yum! I think to myself in appreciation, a good score for Roshan so far! Polite, thoughtful, spunky and immensely delicious ... It's hard not to undress him with my eyes! Before my thoughts can dissect him more or wonder why his eyes seem familiar, he is back with our drinks. He slouches in a relaxed pose across from me, after apologising for his tardiness.

There is a momentary second of awkwardness as we stare at each other across the table. His eyes are mesmerising. I break the silence by telling him how great it is to meet him (even though he was late), but that perhaps he was worth waiting for!

This elicits a spontaneous laugh from Roshan, and I can see him relaxing a bit more with me.

"So, Roshan ... What did you do today that kept me waiting for you?" The Book suggests I start the conversation with an open-ended question on any date. This helps me to force a man to express more than a yes or no answer. The question style also allows me a moment to take a sip of my much needed second drink, which is joining the first in a happy zing around my body.

If I can make him talk to me, it gives me the opportunity to find out if he is interesting or not. And time to formulate my next words. Which I'm hoping comes out as witty and amazing as they sound in my head! I'm operating on a full glass-and-a-bit of champagne on an empty stomach! It is pretty nerve wracking to be on a first date with an attractive, sexy twenty-nine-year-old man and come up with something entertaining in the first sentence. He tells me about his day, but instead of me thinking of something intelligent to reply with, I am immersed in his smiling brown eyes, dazzling smile and biceps.

Dammit! Focus Vixen, focus! Trying for another dainty sip of my champagne, I almost slosh it all over my top while trying to set it back down on the table. Oh fantastic. Way to go with making a positive lasting first impression, Arleia! You need to get better at drinking in public! This is not quite going to plan. Roshan glances across at me, mirth dancing in his eyes.

"Are you OK?" he kindly enquires, as I struggle to return to my normal level of awesomeness.

"Yeah, thanks!" My laugh is uneasy with a nervous edge. "Luckily I rescued it and didn't spill a drop of my drink—can't be having good champagne going to waste!" I joke back. Thank God he laughs with me, and both of us relax enough to enable us to slide into a relaxed, witty banter for a couple of fun-filled hours. Our conversation flows so easily it's like we are old friends. I remember the card's words and wonder if we did know each other in another life. I'm drawn from my musings by his next words.

"You live around this way, right?" His smile is suggestive, and a smile of my own threatens to break free. Ah gotcha, my flirtatious Mark! I know why he is asking and think to myself ... Oh hell yes! Do I want to be alone with you? Definitely, you delicious man!

"Yes, I do! Why ... are you angling for an invitation to my place perhaps?" I'm trying to maintain my cool, seductive manner, and don't want to appear too eager! His broad sunny grin makes my body respond with an answering pull of attraction towards him.

"Mmm, thought you'd never ask!" He runs his fingers over mine in a light feathery caress. I shiver in anticipation, licking my dry lips at the thought and peering over at the delicious specimen in front of me.

"Ohh ... Is that an invitation?" Teasing him is quite amusing.

"You know it is, Vixen!" His laugh is flirtatious. "Let's blow this joint!" Giggling, I allow him to pull me along as he heads towards the exit.

We stroll hand in hand in the direction of our cars. Almost wanting to skip in excitement, I control myself. Appear cool, Arleia ... don't get too excited — he hasn't passed the next test yet. The KISS! Which is a terribly important test indeed. Coming to a halt in front of my car, he stops to stare at me. I stare back across levelly at him, which is a weird thing for me to do—I am used to looking up at taller guys than him! Mwaaahaaahaaahahaaahahaaa!

Without warning he leans in, caresses my face with one hand, and softly kisses me on the lips, coaxing them apart so he can greet the tip of my tongue with his. I move closer into him, drawn in by the deliciousness of the kiss, and the hard smoothness of his muscled body. His other hand snakes around my waist, drawing me in closer to deepen the kiss. He is heedless of the fact that we are still in the hotel's car park, oblivious to any observers who may be present.

"Uhmmm ... "I murmur against his lips, wanting to continue, but knowing we would be much more comfortable in my Vixen lair than in this public location.

"Go!" His voice is confident and commanding. "I will follow you."

A grin brightens my face. Giggling with glee in anticipation I make sure his car is behind me as I pull out of the car park. Now I am glad I did an amazing speed clean of my house. Phew! It wouldn't do to see my bedroom looking like the wardrobe sneezed! Running inside, I turn on the heater, put on some music, and light candles and incense before he even walks down the driveway to the front door.

"Come in, come in!" Swinging the door open, I welcome him with a smile. He does not need to be asked twice, and steps inside the hallway, wrapping me in his arms. Pushing me gently up against the wall, his mouth seeks mine, and immediately our tongues are dancing together while locked in a passionate embrace, still in the entrance way, with his hand cupping my breast through my tank top. My nipples harden and ache in response.

I pull back a little after what seems like ages, but in reality is only a few minutes. I ask Roshan if he would like something to drink, while mentally giving him a big tick for passing the kissing test.

He smiles wolfishly back at me and replies, "The only thing I want to drink in at the moment is you!" I blush, pleased at his response. "How about we find somewhere more comfortable to continue this?"

The veiled hint is coupled with a lazy grin so sensual; it makes me go weak at the knees. Or is my inability to walk easily due to the four glasses of champagne I consumed? With my best alluring grin, I grab his hand. Walking backwards down the hallway towards my bedroom, I lead him over to my soft comfortable bed. He pulls me with him, so I end up sprawled across his body on the bed. Gazing down at him, I bat my lashes flirtatiously.

"Well ... hello there! Fancy meeting you here ... in fact I fancy you a lot!" He leans over me, covering my torso with his. A deep growl erupts from his throat. He lowers his lips to my ear, and whispers "Oh I do ... very much fancy meeting you here too, sexy Vixen!"

His hot breath on my ear and neck, his hard chest pressed against mine is too much to bear, and I can't help myself. I turn my head to face him, my mouth swooping towards those delicious lips as he moans in agreement. He slides his free hand over my thigh and hip towards my underwear. He'd better take note of how cute they are!

The longing for his touch is growing as he circles the exact area of where I want his hand and fingers to touch, making me even wetter and hungry for his touch.

I can't help myself and tease him by rubbing my fingers across his hardness, smiling in satisfaction and approval at the sudden increase in length and stiffness in response to my caress. His head dips toward my breasts, he pushes back my bra, and takes a nipple between his teeth with care. His tongue rolls around the tip as he sucks on my breast, coaxing it to harden.

Running my hands over his broad shoulders, and down his back to cup his smooth round muscled butt, I squeeze hard, giggling. He looks up at me with a quizzical expression and makes a tutting sound. "Ohh, you're going to pay for that Miss Vixen. I'm going to lick you until you moan and beg me to stop!" His warning makes me shiver in anticipation.

"Oh dear. How awful!" My protest is loud, but inside I'm thinking like any hot-blooded woman—oh YES please! He slides further down the bed, kissing and caressing my skin as he goes, while I lie back enjoying the attention and thinking, 'Mmmm ... hope he knows what he's doing down south, or I'm going to be super-disappointed!'

He murmurs his approval of my sexy lingerie before sliding them down over my ankles. Roshan nudges my thighs apart as I groan in approval, his wet tongue laps against my skin in exactly the right spot which is aching for his attention. A stifled moan of pleasure escapes as he demonstrates that he is no stranger to this game, and I grin to myself in a Vixenly way. Oh, this night is going my way so far! Even though he fails my height criterion, height does not matter when we are horizontal.

Mwaaahaahaaahahaaahaaaa!

Several damn good orgasms later, rehydrated and happy, I flop down on my couch in sated exhaustion. Roshan gave me another spine-tingling kiss before heading off, assuring me he had an excellent night, and thanking me for my company. With a wicked grin my thoughts retrace the evening. Delicious, is my final verdict. A skilled kisser and experienced lover, who goes down on a woman without being asked or expecting oral sex in return, and a damned pleasurable cock indeed. I'll give a massive 'thumbs up' to this Mark so far—I will be seeing this hottie again!

My bedroom looks like a bomb exploded from under the bed. Everything is in a tangled mess … But I don't care. I fall into bed to enjoy the best sleep in weeks as soon as my head touches the pillow.

Now how about that? Restful sleep is an added benefit of Vixendom—the healthy advantages of a fabulous sleep are endless! Could sex be prescribed for depression or sleep disorders like insomnia? Perhaps I will research whether there are any scientific studies done in this area linking sex and health benefits... I'm sure some must have been some conducted!

The next morning, I replay the night in my head and conclude that I am quite proud of myself for finding such a great Mark! The Book was right again, and the Isis card adds to my curiosity about Roshan. Could I have known him in a past life? Our initial connection was strong, and it does feel like I have known him forever, which is certainly strange.

I wonder what the rest of the weekend will bring?

First Meeting Guidelines

Important safety rules are in place for all Vixens to follow ensuring their wellbeing and control. The following will enlighten you in knowing what both acceptable locations and unacceptable choices of meeting your potential marks are. These rules should be upheld at all times except when extenuating circumstances are present.

- **Unacceptable First Venue Choices: Car Park Meeting—** This reeks of a guy wanting only one thing from you. This choice of location tells you he does not think you are worthy of meeting in a bar or cafe … not even a park! Vixens are much more expecting of appreciation of their assets to even consider this location … FAIL

- **Dark and Isolated Locations—**This does sound like it may be fun and mysterious rather than unacceptable and dangerous for a first meeting choice … However the fun and mystery of a dark, isolated location is only present with a Mark you are familiar with and trust, not someone you are meeting for the first time.

Location examples include: Parks, playgrounds, alleyways.

- **His Place**- An incredible tempting option indeed! What if your Mark is not alone in the house as he first claimed? What if the guy answering the door does not resemble the picture he presented online? What if four of his huge mates are also at his house wanting to join in with you?

  You may:

  ✗ Jeopardise your personal safety

  ✗ Waste time on someone not worthy of your attention

  ✗ Be disappointed he is not the guy in the picture. This creates an awkward situation if you want to leave his place immediately

  ✗ Be detained against your will in a private residence

- **Your Place**- The convenience of your own lair is tempting, but if you don't like him ... he now has your address. This can put you in danger of being stalked by an undesirable Mark in the future. Guard your location until you are sure the Mark is trustworthy and mentally stable. Allow only the worthiest of Marks the address of a Vixen's lair.

Adventure Vixen

Shopping Addiction

Saturday dawns with a bright shining sun to encourage me to go outside.

When I stick one leg out from under the sheets, I realise that my impression was misleading. The frosty bite stinging the air makes me retreat into my warm cocoon of a bed for a bit longer. In my hazy daze, I laze between being awake and asleep for longer than I thought. The alarm clock is not as patient as I would like it to be and shows only a measly hour left to prepare. Damn.

Get out of bed and hurry to the shower, you idiot! I ignore my messy bedroom on purpose and run out the door in record time. Thank goodness I only have a few hours of work to do today. My head is pounding from moving this fast with a hangover.

Pushing myself forward into the car, I crank the heater up, and console myself with the thought that at least I will spend the afternoon shopping online for new Marks, or call bicep boy! A grin spreads across my face as I zoom through the still empty streets to arrive at work on time.

This experience has been so much fun so far, and I have been extremely lucky to find two awesome guys in such a short time. This is only the start of my adventure into Vixendom … I want MORE!

With a loud chime, my phone message jars me out of my daydreaming at work. I smile as I check my inbox, and to my surprise not one but three messages are waiting for me! Gee, how did I miss those? They must have arrived while I was showering or blasting my hair dry, I decide. Two texts are from Krystian, and one from Roshan. I can't help but chortle in glee. Krystian's messages first. Awwww, how cute! He still calls me Miss Arleia, even in texts! He wishes me a good morning, tells me he had an awesome time with me, and suggests another date to catch-up with him if I like? Oh yes, I'd like to alright! I need to check Roshan's message before I can reply to Krystian—my curiosity as to what his message will say is massive!

His message is really similar to Krystian's—he had a fantastic time, I am one gorgeous, sexy and fun lady, and he would love to catch-up with me again ... really soon. Excellent! I'm quite pleased with myself and flattered by the attention I am receiving from these men. I can't wait to find out what happens next! In record time I punch out a reply to both.

Work passes by in a blur of busy-ness, and before long I'm back home. I am tempted to pull my laptop out as soon as I get home, but the enormity of the uncleaned mess and bedroom disaster smacks me in the face as I walk in the door. Dammit, I forgot about that! My heart sinks as I survey the chaos, and I realise I'm back to square one in the cleaning department.

Why, oh why can't every house come equipped with a cleaning fairy? If only such a thing as a regulation house cleaning fairy existed! Sighing to myself, I start to pick things up off the floor, gathering speed as I go. In a little over an hour and a half I can see the fruits of my momentous cleaning effort, and my untidy home for once is sparkling clean and tidy.

At last! I grab my computer and a drink to take outside into the surprisingly mild winter's afternoon. Setting myself up in comfort on the patio, dragging a second chair around to use as a footrest, while I place everything else within arm's reach, and turn on my computer.

"Oh my God, this is unbelievable!" I exclaim aloud. I've logged into my new favourite dating site, and to my amazement a total of thirty-four contact requests are now awaiting my decision! Wow. In a matter of only a couple of days of not being online I have amassed over thirty guys who are waiting to talk to me!

A sudden noise of the site's alert bell sounds loudly in my ears, then again, and yet again! What the heck? Peering at the screen intently, I try to discover what the alert means.

It takes me a while, but eventually I figure out that each time the bell sounds, a potential Mark is looking at my profile. How do they know I am online? I'm puzzled. After searching for the problem, I realise that my profile is set to the online status. No wonder I am getting so many hits right now!

My availability and visibility are far too high for my liking, so I scramble to click on the invisible option, breathing a sigh of relief. How can I cope with the more than the thirty-four possible Marks already awaiting my attention? With a thoughtful sip of my drink I contemplate who I should check out first.

After doing a quick scan of the list of possibilities I conclude that this may take me hours if I'm not careful! I'm going to whittle down my choices by being ruthless again before I start viewing individual profiles. I start with the easiest and most obvious choice—to remove the Marks that are out of my age range. Anyone forty-five and over gets deleted immediately! A mere five-minutes later my daunting list of men is reduced to a more manageable twenty-seven.

Oh yes, that's a little better now, but I have one more fast eradication run to make. I couldn't help but see a few profile pictures in my list which would earn the immediate deletion, so I scroll down the list once again. I do not like the look of a shaved white shiny head on a guy—a bald snow-white scalp makes me wonder if they went through treatment for illness. The bald head factor alone makes me delete another six profiles. I delete another only because he appears so stern and unhappy in his profile picture, I feel depressed just looking at him! Yet more get dropped off the list for their ages, not for being too old this time, instead for being too young!

Now how young is too young for me? Where do I draw the line in the sand on the age issue? I am clear on what is too old for me ... but what age is too young? I never considered the fact that I might receive contact requests from cute guys as young as nineteen!

Admittedly, I am flattered being admired by young hot boys, but I wonder what these boys are looking for? Do they contact older chicks purely for entertainment and sex, with their focus on learning things from an older woman? Are they expecting us to be their private teachers and guide them through the do's and don'ts of oral sex? Or is it possible that they are searching for a mother figure to love in an alternative kind of way? Are they looking for a long-term relationship with someone twice their age so they can say that their girlfriend is a cougar?

Perhaps bagging an older woman is for the thrill of sharing a sexual experience with their mates about their own personal Mrs Robinson? I wonder if they've simply always admired and been attracted to older women—more so than they are to the girls in their own age group. I can't help but check out the profiles of two of the twenty-one-year-old guys on my list. Both are real cuties, and if I'd been closer to their age, I might have considered adding both to my contact list. They are so baby-faced though. I want to pinch their cheeks more than their butts!

Now I'm not one to judge, and if you like them half your age; fantastic, why not? But to me, these guys' appearances are too much on the boyish side of the spectrum. My interest lies in the Marks who are men not boys! After much thought, I decide that twenty-six will be the absolute youngest age I will accept on my contact list for the moment. Mwaaaahaahahaaahaaaahaaa!

I send declines to another six on my list. Finally, I am ready to inspect the remaining potential profiles. Some of them do not show a visible profile picture, so I decide to start with them. The two Marks I choose first to check out, because their snippets of information seem interesting, end up both being duds in the photo department.

One bloke appears as if he is overdue to give birth by at least a month with a huge beer baby, and the other guy must be at least fifteen years older than his listed profile age of forty-two. Delete and delete again I say! In less than half an hour my bountiful list of thirty-four potentials is whittled down to a mere handful of Marks to consider. Oh man, does even one guy exist in this group that I would want to talk to, let alone meet?

Scrolling down the page again, I finally come across a profile which snares my attention. He is slightly younger than me at thirty-nine, into music, and seems alternative in his thinking. I start to read his profile in depth, while admiring his private picture. The image shows a cool looking dude with dark shoulder length dreadlocks, holding the prized possession of a guitar.

Profile name first. "Unique Opportunity". After reading his words, I must agree! The further I read, the more intrigued I become. This guy is into dominant and submissive stuff, and I'm painfully aware that I possess NO knowledge in this area yet. Part of me is curious, while the other part of me is fearful and apprehensive of the unknown. What exactly does he mean? This is unfamiliar territory to me, so I re-read his whole profile.

UNIQUE OPPORTUNITY Male 39 Australia

D = Dom, s = sub, I am either/both, but I do prefer the second if given the option. I want someone nice, open-minded, experienced, or not, it doesn't matter, I am experienced and more than happy to share what I know. Safe words, respect, limits. FUN and Laughter, with a little bit of ouch!

Sydney New South Wales| Australia

Seeking Criteria Relationship with a female or casual dating with a female. Between 30 and 50 years of age.

What I'm Looking For: Someone who knows what I'm talking about and rocks their world as much as it does mine, or this play type at least enters their thoughts. I know it sounds like with all this I am looking to play, and while yes play is fun, I do want to find someone for something a little more serious than a session on occasion. I'm also happy to talk to like-minded people of either gender.

One other thing, yes this profile is incredibly specific, and possibly a little different, but I am way more than this interest. I also love kisses and cuddles, and spooning, and hanging out with my girl, I love music and motorbikes. I'm well-travelled and intelligent ... just have a few kinky desires, are they yours too?

Details: Ethnicity White (Caucasian)

Relationship Status: Single

Drinking Habits: Socially

Hair Colour: Light Brown

Height: 5'11" / 180cm

Body Type: Muscular

Interests: D/S, Whips, walks on the beach ;) Rope, Collars, Motorbikes, Music

I notice the whips, rope and collars strategically placed between the innocent walks on the beach and music interests and wonder what that collection of words means in a practical sense. I am certain I don't want anyone to whip me, that's for sure! What would I do if a guy wanted me to whip him? Could I? Would whipping hurt them? Do they like the pain?

The only previous experience I've had with a whip was as a child, watching an uncle on a farm kill a snake by cutting it in two with a crack of his whip. I'm pretty sure this guy's reference to whips means something a bit different!

I'm more than a little intrigued at the idea of learning about something new. I've never considered this line of thought before. Do I tie him up, or does he tie me up? I'm not sure I would like to be restrained—it's not an appealing concept to me! Hmm ... Or is it? How would I know the answer, if I've never really tried any fetish stuff?

Years ago, an ex-boyfriend asked me if I was 'in the mood' for trying restraints, and even went to the trouble of making them himself! I thought what the heck I'll give it a go! He tied both my wrists and ankles, securing them to each of the four bedposts, but in a comfortable way. I found the experience quite sexy while he was tying me up, kissing and caressing my body as he went ... even erotic.

I was enjoying the attention and about to voice that thought when he said he was leaving the room. Um ...

Excuse me? I was confused. I thought 'OK I guess ... Perhaps he is going to the fridge for some ice cubes or some whipped cream to continue the game with?'

Spread starfish on the bed for a while, I was thinking this is going to be fun for about the first five minutes. After that I got annoyed. 'What the hell was he doing?' Left alone I frowned and sulked. Another ten-minutes went by, with no sign of him coming back to the room. I was getting pissed off and muttering under my breath.

'What is the bloody point in this? I have no interest in being tied up and left here; it's utterly boring to be honest!'

The start of an itch tickled the side of my nose, which of course I couldn't reach. I thought ...That's it. I've had enough of this bullshit! If he's not going to come back, well there's no way I'm going to yell out for him to come back. Instead I'm going to break these stupid bloody restraints he made and he can get fucked with his idiotic idea of fun! I started pulling on the wrist ones first, determined I'd break free. Using all my power I gave them a hard yank to weaken the bonds. Luckily for me my boyfriend wasn't a talented seamstress and had done a shoddy job of securely sewing the heavy-duty Velcro on to the bands. After a mighty effort and some serious cursing, I managed to pull one of my hands free, and give my nose a well needed scratch!

I then set about untying my other wrist and ankles. Freedom at last! My wrists needed fierce rubbing to encourage the circulation back into them. Down the hall I stomped into the lounge where I found my boyfriend sprawled across the couch with a beer and chips, munching loudly while engrossed in a program on the television. He was surprised at my thunderous expression as I stood in front of the TV and threw the remains of his restraints on the floor in front of him.

"Don't you ever do that again you idiot! I'm happy to play along with your idea, but what is the point in leaving me alone on the bed for so long, you moron!"

Bewildered, he looked at me, not quite believing I was as angry with him as I appeared. His eyes focussed on his now destroyed handiwork on the floor.

"Babe, what did you break them for?"

A stupid question asked in a puzzled manner. He frowned while examining his wrecked workmanship and ignored me. How could he not realise what the problem was? Stamping my foot, I yelled louder.

"Well if you are going to leave me alone, tied to your bed for over half an hour, what do you expect me to do? How is that pleasurable for me in any way? I bet you forgot about me, didn't you?"

His sheepish look at the TV behind me and the game being played on the screen told me all I needed to know. That was it. I was done with him. My scowl and pissed off manner told him he'd better not even speak to me at that moment lest I threaten him with physical violence.

With my things gathered I stormed out of his apartment, slamming the door as I went. After that failed debacle, I needed to stop off on the way home—for a well-deserved bottle of wine and huge block of my favourite chocolate to lessen the disaster of the evening.

You can see from that story how well my foray into something different within the bedroom ended, so I've never been tempted to try it again!

Mood Quiz by Mark Test

You have a Mark in mind that has progressed thus far through the Vixen testing process, but be vigilant, oh Vixen, as the real test is here. Some Marks start well, masking their true intent. Passing the first tests and conversing well enough to keep your attention so far. You may be lulled into thinking he is a suitable Mark to meet until he asks the fatal question:

"Are you in the mood?"

Seriously? I mean, come on guys. You need to do something first before we are close to being in the mood to even meet you, let alone agree to having sex with you! Dazzle us with your wit, humour, clever innuendos and fast thinking. Compliment us in the appropriate way, play with us and make us laugh. Then you may be worthy of meeting a Vixen.

Should a potential Mark want to test your mood with this stupid question expecting you to reply that yes you are in the mood for sex with an unworthy stranger...**FAIL.**

Adventure Vixen

Dom or Sub?

Now that I think about the question, maybe I am not a submissive a kind of person. I am impatient and like getting my own way, but dominant? I stare at Unique Opportunity's profile for another minute. Yes, I am going to add this dude as a contact, I decide. His profile is intriguing enough that I want to learn a bit more about him. For a millisecond I pause, then press the 'Add to Contact List' button. There. Another addition to my list is done!

I wonder what he ... oh! He is online NOW. Holy crap, he is writing a message to me right now! Oh shit. Am I ready for this yet? Too late, I realise as his greeting flashes up on the screen.

Uniqueopportunity: Hi there

ATrixenVixen: Hi yourself

Uniqueopportunity: Thanks for accepting.

ATrixenVixen: Curiosity got the better of me lol.

Uniqueopportunity: Fair enough. Not gonna argue with that! I'm Sean.

ATrixenVixen: Hi Sean, I'm Arleia.

Uniqueopportunity: Nice to meet you ... Sooo. Curious huh?

Arleia: Well I do possess a curious mind.

Uniqueopportunity: That's an asset.

ATrixenVixen: Yes indeed ... but not sure I like much pain. But hey what do I know, haven't tried it.

Uniqueopportunity: It's not all about pain. It's about sensations. About the psychology. Respect of limits, fun.

ATrixenVixen: I know. I'm teasing you.

Uniqueopportunity: Hmm naughty girl.

ATrixenVixen: I also have a teasing nature to go along with the curious mind.

Uniqueopportunity: I like your teasing.

ATrixenVixen: Lucky, I guess.

Uniqueopportunity: So, are you more sub or dom? Or both.

ATrixenVixen: To be honest I have no idea ... I know in theory what it is about but not in practice. So who knows?

Uniqueopportunity: Cool. Hey, sorry I must head back to work. I'll be on in an hour or so if you'd like to chat more?

ATrixenVixen: Cool, catch u later!

I can feel my heart pumping and nervous energy still affecting me as I sit and contemplate our conversation so far, glad of the temporary reprieve so that I can gather my thoughts. He does seem like an interesting but mysterious Mark and I can't help but want to find out more about him, as well as his fetishes. I think about his question.

Am I a more dominant person, or a submissive one? Can one be both? Some quick research online is required so that I can gain a better understanding of what each one means, instead of saying something I may regret later! An hour and a half later my eyes are popping out of my head from my efforts. Fetish stuff is much more complicated than I'd imagined! I think I've come up with some sort of answer though. I seem to possess elements of both a submissive and a dominant type within me, as far as I can tell.

Who would have thought! I suppose I am ready to respond to his difficult question and find out how far my response takes me. In this game of unfamiliar language, I realize I am swimming way out of my depth. But I do like to take a risk sometimes, and I'm a strong swimmer, so I take the plunge and punch out a reply to him. Hang on … I need to do something to increase my confidence before I send my answer to him. Deep breath ... Mwaaahaaahaaaahaaaaaa!

OK. Now that's better. I'm ready.

ATrixenVixen: OK I thought about your question ... I'm both.

Uniqueopportunity: Lol. Sounds good to me.

Oh man, I didn't expect him to be online under the same 'invisible' setting as me.

ATrixenVixen: Haha oh hi there

Uniqueopportunity: How have you been? Lol. I'm still at work so may take time to chat back.

ATrixenVixen: Hahaaaa. I'm excellent thanks. I am also busy so delayed replies here too.

Uniqueopportunity: That's cool. We all need to get stuff done. Any big plans for next weekend?

ATrixenVixen: No big plans as such. I'm working all day Saturday, so it wipes out half the weekend lol. What about you?

Uniqueopportunity: My sister is moving tomorrow-should be fun. Have my daughter tonight and tomorrow as well, so enough to keep me busy. So what did you think about that made you decide you like both Dom and sub?

ATrixenVixen: Hmm. Good question. I visualised in my head to see what I'd rather ... and the answer I came up with ... both. (I am not going to admit it took me almost two hours of online research, as well as a lot of inner searching to come up with this answer!)

Uniqueopportunity: Cool. So how do you feel about meeting?

ATrixenVixen: I'd be happy to catch-up for a drink and chat ...

Uniqueopportunity: Perfect. When are you free?

OMG, OMG! My heart is pounding in both excitement and trepidation at the thought of meeting up with him, but I need to sound cool and chilled out online, not like a scared or excited loony! I take a couple of deep breaths to calm myself and continue.

ATrixenVixen: Good question. Weekend or weeknight?

Uniqueopportunity: I'm thinking Sunday afternoon?

ATrixenVixen: OK, I could do late morning but I have something on from early afternoon onwards. What do you think?

Uniqueopportunity: I could make 11am or something. Though I'm unsure of my Sat night plans ... May be hungover.

ATrixenVixen: LOL quite fair enough I'd imagine ... 11am sounds like a reasonable time.

Uniqueopportunity: Cool, so Sunday it is. Do you have a preferred location? It has to serve quality coffee.

ATrixenVixen: Yes a cafe for a coffee sounds perfect ... Manly beach front cafe?

Uniqueopportunity: Yes x

ATrixenVixen: Great, I will see you then!

Oh. My. God. I made a date. With a guy so far out of my dating comfort zone I can't believe it. What am I thinking? Breathe now, just breathe! Both apprehensive and curious at the same time, I contemplate the upcoming event, while slurping on the dregs of my drink.

At least I agreed only to a daytime meeting, and in a heavily populated area, so I'm not worried at all. OK, possibly slightly. After all, what could he do in a crowded Manly cafe? Tie me to a chair and whip me in the popular cafe?

My imagination runs away with me at the thought. I imagine him deciding he likes me a lot, so reaches into his duffle bag (that he conveniently carries in circumstances such as these), for some rope. While I'm frozen on the cafe's chair like a stunned mullet with my mouth open in surprise holding my coffee cup in the air, he fashions the rope into a cowboy's lasso.

Brandishing the rope like he's in a paddock catching a cow, he twirling the noose over his head in an expert fashion, and flips it neatly over my shoulders, pulling the noose tighter so that I am drawn closer towards him.

The other patrons' mouths drop open in shock as he flips the rope around me and exclaims, "Gotcha, my pretty!" in a triumphant manner, like he won a prize.

Then he drags both me and the chair to the open glass bi-fold doors onto the sidewalk outside.

Equally improbable would be the production of a whip, collar or anything else he may hide in his bag of tricks while on a first date in public. Thank goodness! So I think I am feeling safe enough in meeting him next week. I guess I am a curious Vixen who is interested in learning new things and expanding my thinking, which I'm sure Sean has the capacity to do. Our meeting may be extremely interesting ... or shit-my-pants scary!

I'm going to have to read up in the Book again to prepare for a date so far out of my comfort zone, before I freak out and cancel it. Why didn't I think to check what the Book's coloured glow was while I was talking to him?

Adventure Vixen

Delicious Darz

After all this contemplation I am exhausted!

Snapping my laptop closed, I belatedly remember that another thirteen contact requests are waiting online for my attention. I was too busy being side-tracked by curiosity and making another date. Mwaaahahaahaaahahaaa!

I waver. Should I reopen the computer and perhaps chance a quick glance? Hmm ... *So tempting.* If I stay invisible this time, I will have a better chance of not being interrupted by more requests or messages while I do a quick sort through and cull any unwanted Marks who don't meet my criteria.

I should be hanging out my washing, doing the dishes or cleaning my car, but all these mundane tasks pale dramatically, compared to the exciting things that are awaiting me in the online supermarket of lust.

Screw it! I'll call bicep boy Joshua instead. At least I know what he looks like in person. I cast my mind back to where I left his note, and my recent cleaning effort. My eyes widen as I realise that I may have thrown it out in the trash. Oh my God, don't tell me I did. Please no!

I race inside and check my jeans, the bin, under the bed and in my drawers. The note has vanished. My shoulders slump in disappointment. The vision of me squeezing Joshua's biceps while I'm suspended mid-air kissing him vanishes along with the note.

Dammit, I think to myself as I sit back down after my fruitless search and log in online again. I'm so annoyed at myself now. Why didn't I punch his number straight into my phone when I had the chance?

The chores can wait. I want to determine whether any more of these men are worthy of my attention. I need to add more Marks to my contact list to distract myself from the disappointment of losing bicep boy's number! If we are meant to meet again one day, the universe will make it happen.

Feeling more positive and confident on this website now, I scroll through the first three profiles, dismissing them immediately. One is too busy berating other guys for contacting him and sounds too negative for my liking. Another bores me to tears with his over-the-top love for his dog, who is in every single picture of him. The third provides almost no information about himself and it's such a poor quality picture that I can't even tell if he's male, let alone make out any of his features.

There, that was easy! Three down, and twelve to go. Wait. Twelve? Oh crap! More men have added themselves to my now growing rather than shrinking list of potential Marks. Who would guess that keeping up with requests could be this hard? To simply read through all the requests and keep up with this side of things takes a lot of time, let alone time to chat to any Marks!

I decide I am going to be even stricter on my criteria and read on with determination. With speed I delete a few more. A football lover, one guy who seems to state watching DVD's and movies as his only interest, and two who are way too sleazy for me to contemplate. It's another easy obliteration for the man parading his wealth, education and self-assessed fabulousness right from the first sentence. That's a delete for the sap who's 'looking for his soul mate', and for another wanting to 'just be friends', and berating anyone who dares ask for a picture, as image requesting is the epitome of shallowness, according to him.

Maybe ... No ... Nope. Definitely not ... bye-bye!' I make super quick decisions as I speed through the list of contestants.

Oh. Hey now, wait a minute. Helloooo! This dude sounds pretty good. Don't tell me I found another potential Mark to add to my list? After another thorough read of his profile, I get a positive vibe about this guy. He sounds normal and interesting. Conveniently also the owner of a cute picture showing a killer body I could drool over.

Well hello Darz! I'm thinking you might be my next mark if you pass the Vixen's first test.

Mwaaahaaahaaahahaaaahaaa!

DARZ007

Age: 28

What to write ... ... you'll have to find out. Sorry for lame pics. Hard to write on the internet. Hardworking, very loyal, easy going, caring, sweet, no baggage, no dramas, positive, driven, stable, career focused, fit & healthy! LOVE LIFE :)

Surry Hills New South Wales| Australia

Seeking Criteria Members anywhere in Australia.

Relationship or casual dating with a female. Between 18 and 45 years of age.

What I'm Looking For: Cute, smart and nice smile is always good. I'd like to meet someone to go to beach with, wine and dine or like my dance/trance. Would love to travel more and experience life.

Ethnicity: White (Caucasian)

Relationship Status: Single

Drinking Habits: Socially

Hair Colour: Dark Brown

Eye Colour: Brown

Height: 5'10" / 177cm

Body Type: Fit

Interests: comedy, conversation, dinners, friends, music dance, rock ... anything, sports again, technology, my trade, beach and summer, going out, health and fitness, movies, music, sports travel, photos.

Mmm, yes definite potential with this guy! As I tap on the 'add to contacts' icon, a grin of satisfaction crosses my face.

Wow, I'm quite pleased with myself! I am starting to grow a satisfying little list of Marks here, and think I've picked reasonably well so far. There was the exception of Mitch (yuck, I shudder at the memory!) but surely finding the right men is nothing more than a numbers game. When you choose with care and ensure that you always consider your strict criteria, you will quickly gain a stupendous list of potential Marks to work on and entice. Oh! Darz007 is online now! Hmm, I'm curious ...

darz007: Howdy ... I'm Darz

ATrixenVixen: Hey Darz. I'm Arleia!

darz007: How u been?

ATrixenVixen: Really good thanks. And u?

darz007: Not too bad, don't like winter at all hey ahha! How was ya day?

ATrixenVixen: It was a good day ... worked and caught up with family. Why don't you like winter?

darz007: It is messing with my fragile body.

ATrixenVixen: Ahhhh yea I get what you mean ... why can't it stay warm dammit! Ha-ha

darz007: Yeah that's it.

ATrixenVixen: Aww ... your poor fragile body.

darz007: Ha-ha that's it! My body is fragile ... I'm waiting for you to break it.

ATrixenVixen: Hahaha! I don't like to break body parts ... if I can help it! LOL

darz007: Well thank God for that! I'm sighing in relief now. I was worried! Ha-ha

ATrixenVixen: I almost heard that sigh of relief. Lol! I like fun things not breaking things ;)

darz007: I could turkey slap ya for better hearing?

ATrixenVixen: Oh, u will huh, what a kind offer.

darz007: Umm ... hey is it?

ATrixenVixen: Hmm ... Aren't you drenched by the sarcasm dripping off my words? LOL

darz007: I can see something else dripping from your mouth ... in my head that is though! Hahaaaa

ATrixenVixen: Heehee Oh, I do believe that was a tad rude

darz007: lol

I do a quick re-read of our conversation so far ... No inappropriate endearments, correct usage of emoticons. This guy is passing a few tests here! He also demonstrates a good sense of humour and fast thinking. Cheeky, but he's still respectful enough. I think I quite like him so far!

ATrixenVixen: Uhmm, I think it's safer for me not to comment at this point! Hahaaaa ... so are you off out partying tonight?

darz007: Partying? I'm too old for that shit! Ha-ha

ATrixenVixen: OMG yes. You're right ... sooo very old.

darz007: I'm thinking about telling you the truth.

ATrixenVixen: ...?

darz007: I'm thinking about joining my pisshead mates.

ATrixenVixen: Oh ... and what's wrong with that?

darz007: Well nothing, except I'm fragile.

ATrixenVixen: Hmm ... why is it you're fragile, pray tell...? Just the weather? Emotionally? Physically? Mentally? Or all the above? LOL darz007: I think it's the weather ... honestly last two months killed me! LOL sounds like a princess. I'd rather cuddle and drink coffee ... fookn weirdo ME! Ha-ha

ATrixenVixen: LOL nothing wrong with being weird either.

darz007: Just put a movie on, touch, talk, touch, talk.

ATrixenVixen: Hmm ... I can't see anything wrong with that either. Nice to mix weekend activities up.

darz007: Yes indeed

ATrixenVixen: Almost forgotten about things like that lol

darz007: Oh ... you have?

ATrixenVixen: Yes ... the thought occurs to me I can't even remember the last time I had an evening like that.

darz007: Mmm should have one tonight.

ATrixenVixen: Ha-ha u think so hey.

darz007: ha-ha Why not?

ATrixenVixen: Well as tempting as your offer is ... I'm going to a dinner planned with a group of friends tonight. Another time might be an excellent idea though.

darz007: Great it could be a lot of fun! Hehe I might go join my piss head friends then for one warming drink LOL.

ATrixenVixen: Oh I think you should! OMG I have just seen the time ... must run. Sorry! It was delightful to chat with you though. I'm sure we shall again!

darz007: How can we not? I need a movie night! Ha-ha ... Enjoy your night Arleia ... talk to you soon.

ATrixenVixen: You too... Byyeeeee!

Logging off I stand and do the biggest stretch towards the sky my cramped muscles can manage. "Ohhhh I feel so stiff now! Ouch!" Then my attention turns to my butt, which seems to be sore and flattened from being sat on for so long.

Enough! I declare to myself. That's it for today, and what an excellent day it was for fishing. A solid date set with the mysterious Sean, and promising potential for another with the delicious Darz. The only problem with watching a movie with him on the first date, is that the Handbook advises to limit all first dates to only an hour or two — which cuts out the movie idea. I shrug, not wanting to be reminded of the rules right now and carry on with my celebration.

'Life couldn't get any sweeter!' With a little victory dance of happiness, I twirl around grinning like a cat who ate all the cream. A glance at the clock tells me there's only an hour to get ready now, to be on time for dinner with my girlfriends. I hot foot it inside to change and prepare myself for a fun evening with three of my amazing friends.

While dressing I wonder what they will think of my dating adventures so far? I've only managed to fill one of them in, and I can imagine the others will be clamouring for some juicy details of my exploits, which, of course, I am happy to share with them!

The Top Forty Music Hits program comes on, so I turn it up and dance towards the bathroom to finish getting ready for the enjoyable evening ahead. I'm hoping to make our meeting at the restaurant on time for a change, but I'm sure my friends don't expect this kind of promptness from me by now!

Mwaaahaaahaaahahaaaahaaa!

First Meeting Duration

Length of First Meeting: One to Two Hours.

This gives you plenty of time with him if you click, and a perfect excuse should you be champing at the bit to flee the date. If you hint that you have nothing else planned for the entire day it could be detrimental later in implementing your escape strategy.

Once you have clicked and the sparks and compliments are flying, you can choose to extend the time for as long as you wish. This is the ideal outcome of meeting a potential Mark.

Adventure Vixen

Girls Gossip

"Wow! I can't believe I'm here! You witnessed a miracle tonight, girls—I am on time with even a whole minute to spare!" My three close friends appreciate my joke, knowing I am more often late than on time. We are seated around the cosy table in our favourite local Thai restaurant. The friendly, helpful waiter led us over to our preferred table upon arrival, smiling in welcome at our familiar faces.

Lulu, a dark haired, curvy, alluring Italian Vixen herself, sits to the left of me. She grins and leans over closer to my ear and whispers, "Sooo ... how's the new expert in dating doing so far?" Her eyebrows wiggle in an exaggerated, suggestive manner. Then she nudges me so hard that I almost fall off the chair. I grin back at her.

"Oh my experience has been excellent so far. I have so many stories to tell and I'm only just starting!" Purposefully I flick my hair over my shoulder trying for a casual 'damn but I'm good and got my sexy going on!' type of gesture, winking at her in mischief.

Lulu is so excited she can't contain herself, clapping her hands together and turning towards the other girls. "Franni! Billie-Rae! Hurry up and decide what you want to order girls!"

They look up from their menus, startled. "Why? Are we being timed and limited on our food decisions here? Is making a food choice now a race?" Francesca drops her reading glasses further down her nose and blows a few of her unruly foiled blonde strands of hair out of her line of vision, pretending to be offended, but nods. As she peers over the top of her glasses with a smirk, her hazel eyes dance with suppressed laughter.

"Luckily I completed a super speed-reading course earlier this year … I'm sure to win!" She gathers up her menu with confident lightning speed, her shoulder length hair swishing across her face as she pretends to speed read the whole menu in less than ten seconds. Billie-Rae rolls her eyes in response and shakes her head, elbowing Francesca so hard that it is now her turn to almost end up on the floor.

"Stop being stupid, you nutcase!" The admonishment from Lulu is stern as she snatches the menu out of Francesca's hands. "You are reading the wrong one! You should be starting on the wine list, not the food. I'm parched and dying for a wine!" Making thirsty gasping noises to prove her point she waves the waiter over, acting more like she is drowning than thirsty. She orders a bottle of bubbly for us to all share.

"Why do we need to hurry up, Lulu? Is there a fire? A shortage of food perhaps? Or did you book a hot booty call after we finish here?" Francesca is always teasing Lulu.

"Oh no, it's not me for a change!" Lulu pokes her tongue out, while beckoning Francesca and Billie-Rae closer. My eyes can't help but roll at the dramatic way she is behaving.

Adopting a serious expression, she exaggerates a glance left and right as if to check whether anyone else is listening to what she's about to divulge. "We need to order our meals as fast as possible, because Arleia has new dating gossip for us! I'm dying to hear it, and I know you girls will be too. I don't think I can wait much longer, and if we don't order now it could be eleven o'clock before we start eating our meals, and I'm starving now!" Lulu sits back in her seat to watch their reactions.

"What?" They both stare at her, shocked. I was watching the dramatized exchange in quiet amusement, but now I have something to add. Leaning in to talk, I accidently knock over my water glass.

"Oh shit!" A couple of fellow restaurant patrons glance over to see what I did, but my quick reflexes steady the glass after only a few spilt drops. The girls snigger as I mop them up with a serviette, muttering as I do, "Nothing to see here! Move along, no raunchy talk here!"

"C'mon!" Francesca beseeches me. "I must hear at least a small titbit of information—you can't make me wait for the damn waiter. Look how busy he is now!" Feeling sorry for her only because I know how I would feel if she did the same to me, I relent.

"Well so far girls, I've gone on three dates. Two were excellent, which I shall of course share in detail, but the third one I wanted to use my best exit strategy as fast as I could!" We all giggle at the thought, for it's not an unusual occurrence for any of us. As I am about to launch into further explanation, our waiter appears at the table. Of course, we'd all forgotten to choose our food, but also don't want him to disappear again.

"Are you ready to order yet, ladies?" He smiles while looking from one face to another. Sheepish grins meet his smile as we admit that we are not quite ready yet, but if he stayed and waited a moment we would be! We have dined here many times before and are all familiar with the menu.

The crowded Thai restaurant on the North Shore is popular with locals, and we don't want to lose this opportunity to order. We ask him to recite the specials of the evening to give us a moment longer to decide.

Billie-Rae comes up with the brilliant suggestion of ordering more wine first, so by the time he returns with the fresh bottle, we are ready. We order our meals in record time, then again are left alone at our table to continue our conversation. To be honest, I can't wait to share my news of dates with Krystian, Mitch and Roshan;

as much as the girls are eager to hear all about them! They devour the juicy details in delight, as I regale them with the funniest date stories first, and even manage to get the basics of all three dates conveyed to the girls before our main meals appear.

As I eat my delicious meal, I contemplate telling them about the possible new Dom/Sub mystery man Sean, but I decide against it. I am not sure how they would all take any fetish talk yet, as the fetish world is outside the realm of our usual type of guy. Hell, for that matter it's quite out of my comfort zone too! Billie-Rae would freak out, and Francesca would want to give me a strict safety lecture, in case I'm going to somehow end up chained up in a dungeon of some type in a seedy part of town! No, I decide she is better off hearing about him after the event happens, rather than before. She's the type who would hide in the cafe where my date and I planned to meet and watch over us like a hawk. Not an ideal thing to happen on a first date.

Lulu's eyes are boring a hole into me, so I turn to her with an innocent expression.

"Yeeesssss?" Drawling in an enquiring manner, I bat my lashes at her, smiling.

"I know there's more, missy!" She hisses at me, trying not to alert the other two girls busy chatting to each other to our conversation.

In response I laugh my triumphant Vixen laugh softly. "Mwaaahaaahaaahahaaaahaaa!

"Indeed you are right, but at the moment, extra dating information is for your ears only, Lulu." She understands what I want to convey by the slight nod of her head and twitch of her mouth.

I can tell she is dying to ask me but will wait until we can be by ourselves to devour the extra details that I don't want to share with the others. Our other friends are observers, whereas Lulu is also a Vixen type.

After much discussion and delicious food, we step out of the restaurant with a flurry of coats and jackets being donned against the fresh cold air outside. Shivering at the change in temperature from the warmth of the restaurant, now eager to go our separate ways. After hugs are exchanged and amidst a chorus of goodbyes, we rush off to the relative warmth of our waiting cars.

Lulu and I parked close to each other, so we head along the brightly lit busy street in the same direction together. We arrive at her car first and both jump in to escape the bone chilling wind picking up in strength outside. Lulu starts the car and turns the heater on high, which make us both shiver more as a cold blast of air assaults our feet. Barely able to contain herself a second longer, Lulu turns to me. "Spill the dating info, sister! I bet there's a lot you haven't told me yet, you dirty stop-out!"

Laughing at her expression of mock anger, I update her first about the possible Mark in the apparent open relationship, Adam. Then I fill her in on Darz, the latest cutie I am considering. I get to Dreads, and I can't help but laugh as her eyes widen more with each story. To finish, I regale her with the nose wrinkling rimming tale. Lulu shakes her head and emits a low whistle of admiration at my impressive achievements so far. She almost acts proud of me as she fires a couple of questions at me about Dreads.

There's not much more I can tell her, seeing I've not had much contact with him yet. I bring up his online dating profile on my phone and pass it over. Within two seconds she is scrolling down the page, reading Sean's profile with a grin on her face. A couple of unladylike snorts later as she finishes reading the whole thing, she is now squinting at the only picture there is of him on his profile.

"Hmmm ... *Very nice!*" She examines the image in appreciation, almost licking the picture. "I can see the appeal there, although I personally don't like dreadlocks at all!"

I grin back at her. "He is hot enough that I'm curious to see him ... What can I say?!" Like schoolgirls we giggle together, enlarging Sean's image to examine it better, and re-reading his profile.

"Have you ever dated a guy who is into this kind of thing, Lulu?" She shakes her head. "No, not yet. But do you remember the dude who lived near the northern beach area that I used to see a few months ago? Knicker-sniffer?" She reminded me of her nickname for him with a laugh.

"Oh yeah, I do remember you talking about him!" I couldn't help but snigger. "He's the one with the fabulously large cock which stayed hard for hours, right?"

She sniggered along with me exclaiming "Yeah, and that's not all!" The suggestive wiggle of her brow brings the memory back clearer.

"God, yes! That's right, now I remember! He was up for almost anything, hey! Extremely naughty; just how we like them in Vixen mode. Hey, did you ever get your favourite two pairs of G-strings back from Knicker-sniffer?" I couldn't help but laugh at the thought. Maybe he has collected a whole drawerful of different women's underwear and sniffs each one to remember who the owner is. Ewww!

Whenever us girls talk about men we are dating, it's unusual for us to use their real names, unless they are long-term keepers. This maintains the guy's anonymity, helps us to remember certain quirks or traits of the guy, also whether we would want to see them again, and makes us laugh!

We say our goodbyes, and I head to my car only a few paces away, waving as Lulu toots her horn at me while she speeds away.

Adventure Vixen

Home Delivery

Once I arrive home I realise the evening isn't quite over yet. It seems so much later because of how much darker the sky is in the early winter's evenings now. I'm surprised to find eleven o'clock is still ages away—my head feels more like it is well past midnight! I'm not sure I am ready to sleep yet.

"Hmm, what shall I do with my time?"

Still as a statue in the lounge room, I am undecided, weighing my options. In all honesty I could do with an early night, but the thought of lying in bed trying to sleep is not appealing to me. One option is a movie, or perhaps a programme I've recorded, and have been meaning to watch. My eyes flicker over the TV, but then are drawn across to my laptop, innocently sitting on my kitchen table.

No. I shouldn't, I think, ignoring the fissure of excitement at the shopping wonders the internet may hold. God knows how long the computer might hold me in front of the screen mesmerised, once I logon the dating website! Immobile and undecided, I stare at my closed laptop for a few more moments.

"Oh, fuck it!" Yanking the laptop from the table, I flop down on the couch with it on my knees, already open and humming to life. 'I will take a quick look—for an hour, tops! Then I am going to bed,' I tell myself sternly, as my fingers fly over the keys punching out my now familiar login details, before sensible thoughts have the chance to enter my head. Straight into invisible mode so I can peruse the site with less interruptions, in secret I discover which delectable dishes are on offer tonight.

Ohh. Well, hello Darz! My latest addition and possible Mark pops up as being online. I have not had the chance to talk much with him yet. When I have chatted to him though, he seemed like an attractive guy who might be worth meeting. Perhaps I will decide on him tonight!

I flash a 'Hello, sexy!' message across the screen to him, and in an instant get an enthusiastic reply. With the pillow adjusted behind my back, I'm ready to settle in for a chat. I'm feeling a bit horny—must be all the talk of my adventures earlier this evening with the girls!

Whatever the reason, I am in a naughtier than usual mood, and can't help but let cheekiness filter into our conversation, plunging me into saucy Vixen mode. After a short banter and discussion of our earlier exploits of the day, Darz suggests coming to my place for a coffee.

My place? Hmmm, better than his place I guess ... but for our first meeting? Now THAT is against the rules! Damn. Could I consider breaking the rules, just this once? I'm not sure yet. I need to check the Book for guidance first. If there is any trace of a red warning glow, then there's no way he's coming over here!

ATrixenVixen: Not my style to invite people I've not met before to my house ... or to watch movies, touch and talk.

I stall for time so I can retrieve both the Book and my Goddess cards. I decide I'll need a double confirmation from my guides before I will agree to before I hand over my address!

darz007: Cool, stranger danger hey?

ATrixenVixen: Lol well yea ... I think I'm more conscious of it as a friend of mine was stalked by some chick - it's been so bad he needed to get the police involved.

darz007: Lol cool, I understand.

ATrixenVixen: Not that I think you are weird or anything. Ha-ha-ha! I prefer to meet at a pub or somewhere close even before giving my address.

darz007: Good way to be.

ATrixenVixen: Plus, there are a couple of cosy pubs close to me

darz007: Don't worry, I'm not a weirdo! Hahaaaa

Well, that's important to know, I guess ... among other things! I think with a smile, wavering slightly in the face of such normality and understanding. If he tries to push the issue of coming over straight away, I'll tell him in no uncertain terms that he can piss off! I excuse myself from the conversation for five-minutes to gain some guidance with this situation. I start with the Handbook. A faint glow of gold surrounds it, and I sigh in relief. But wait. There's something else happening. Between the pages I can see a growing purple light. I drop the Book in surprise as a flash of light is sucked into the pages. What the hell? I search my memory for the words of the stranger who gave it to me.

When the Book's owner needs new guidance or learns a new lesson, the information is drawn from the universe appearing within its pages. A white flash heralds the change - a purple glow leads you to the answer.

That's it! I flick through the Book, searching for the answer I need. My mouth drops open in surprise as I read the shimmering words.

- Guard your location until you are sure the Mark is trustworthy and mentally stable. Allow only the worthiest of Marks the address of a Vixen's lair*.

Wow. I'm still puzzled at how these words appeared here. I didn't truly believe all of the mysterious woman's words about the Book until now. But here they are, in glowing purple to be exact. My confidence in inviting Darz over grows. Shit! I must get back! He'll think I've lost interest in him.

A TrixenVixen: I do believe you ... and for the record neither am I. Lol ... nor a stalker, I mean, who's got the time? Ha-ha

darz007: Lol oh wait, I have a mouthful of nuts ... wouldn't you like some young firm nuts ... fresh as these?

ATrixenVixen: Heeheeheeee... oh. Uh ... fresh nuts hey?

darz007: Is that a yum?

ATrixenVixen: LOL, there is no mention of nut tasting in the coffee or movie idea is there?

darz007: I can bring the nuts ... Mmm, yummy vixen and yummy nuts.

ATrixenVixen: Hahahaaaa

darz007: These are small, so easy to fit in my mouth and eat Ha-ha.

ATrixenVixen: Oh ... Ermmm well my favourite are cashews and almonds.

darz007: So what r you up to tonight?

Tonight? Is he kidding? It is fast heading towards midnight, and the time where I am in bed, not considering inviting someone over for a coffee or a movie. Can't have me sounding like an uncool stick in the mud, though. I'm going to need to make something more exciting up than just changing into my nightie and hitting the sack!

ATrixenVixen: Well... I've been invited by friends to go to a pub, but I can't be bothered—went out earlier already this evening, so it would be better to be somewhere less loud and crowded.

darz007: SAME. Hmm ... movie/coffee?

ATrixenVixen: Mmm ... sounds much easier and still as much fun.

darz007: Even though it's the weekend, a hot coffee would do me. Sometimes I'll be in mood to party, other times I want to relax.

ATrixenVixen: LOL to be honest I don't drink coffee this late ... but yes same here.

darz007: So, u got any movies?

ATrixenVixen: I do ... only a few yes.

darz007: Would be some on TV... porn? LOL

ATrixenVixen: LOL Noooo! Just back from a Bali holiday and got a couple while there.

darz007: Ha-ha! Oh did you?

ATrixenVixen: Yea ... had a blast there too!

darz007: Omg you're horrible smuggling XXX rated movies from Bali.

ATrixenVixen: Haha! Oh funny boy ... yikes imagine that. Who knows what sort of porn it would be!

darz007: Lol true, what movies did you get?

ATrixenVixen: I don't own any porn at all I'm afraid lol ... but let me go check. I can't even remember!

darz007: Ha-ha! OK then.

ATrixenVixen: I own a huge selection of eight new movies.

darz007: U seen any yet?

ATrixenVixen: Nope, none of them! I don't think to put a movie on to watch by myself for some reason.

darz007: Why not? Need some else to press play?

ATrixenVixen: LOL oh sooooo funny! No ... to massage my shoulders ha-ha.

darz007: I can do that lol

Now he's talking! A shoulder massage would be heaven ... Yippee, he has said the magic words! Let me do a quick appraisal—no ridiculous use of emoticons, not over-familiar endearments, good sense of humour, no pushiness, a little naughty and suggestive, but respectfully so ... He is looking pretty good so far! I wonder if he would come out at this time of night to my place ... and whether a shoulder massage would be the only thing happening, apart from coffee and a movie. I glance over at the Book. Its' soft golden glow settles my nerves about inviting Darz over.

ATrixenVixen: Hahahaaaa, well if you give me a relaxing shoulder massage, I might return the favour. If you're lucky and considering your current fragile state!

darz007: Invite me ... I'm not a weirdo.

ATrixenVixen: Hmm ... should I bend my rule? Ahhhh the dilemma lol.

darz007: Yes you should, omg, relax girl!

ATrixenVixen: LOL! I'm relaxed. And yes OK.

darz007: YAY Hmm ... did we swap numbers?

ATrixenVixen: I think so yes.

darz007: Let me send u SMS... or u send me one.

I grab my handbag and check my phone. Oh yes, I do have his number! I send off a quick message with my address for him and finish the text with a smiley face before I can think too much about what I'm doing. Excitement and trepidation skitter through my body. I did it! Now I think I need an immensely strong drink to settle my sudden nerves.

darz007: Oh wow, that was quick.

ATrixenVixen: Lol no mucking around here ha-ha.

darz007: I can come around and view a movie of your choice Miss Vixen, and give you a shoulder massage ... do I need to dress up?

ATrixenVixen: Lol what do u mean by that? Not a suit or tie no.

darz007: I'm in shorts, just put jumper on, shall I put thongs on ha-ha... is that bad? Goshhhhh

ATrixenVixen: Haha ... may as well be comfortable. What's the point in having a comfortable night if you can't be comfy with cold legs and feet?

darz007: Cheeky! ... but true.

ATrixenVixen: So whatever you want I guess. Perhaps not naked lol.

darz007: You'd like naked though.

ATrixenVixen: Hmm ... not for a first meeting hard to concentrate on the movie lol! Plus, this is a posh suburb you know! Heeheheee

darz007: HA-HA! I will see you soon, Miss Vixen x.

ATrixenVixen: great ... hurry up—it's late! Ha-ha

I glance at the clock to gauge how long before Darz will be knocking on my door. Holy shit! Twelve thirty-five am ... lucky this extra adrenalin is coursing through my veins or I could be asleep before he gets here! I snap my computer shut and spring off the couch, intent on the alcohol cupboard housing and the unopened litre bottle of vodka. With the strong thumbs up from the Book, I won't need to consult my Goddess cards tonight! I slide them both safely into the cupboard as I pull out the vodka.

With a good measure sloshed into a glass, I hunt in my fridge for something palatable to mix the spirit with. A fresh bottle of Coke lazes on the bottom shelf—perfect!

Like a whirlwind I speed around the house, drink in hand, making sure candles are lit, incense sticks burning, appropriate music playing and that all of my mess is gathered up and dumped into the spare room. Sculling down the last of my drink, I feel the strong rush of alcohol invade my limbs, making them feel heavier.

Shit! What am I wearing? Did I check if I'm wearing slinky knickers? Where's my 'suck-me-in' lace chemise?

Do I have a cute enough bra on? No! OMG! This getting ready for Mark's business, and looking Vixen-like, is not an easy thing to slap together in twenty-minutes under normal circumstances, let alone with this vodka coursing through my veins and at this time of the night ... or morning!

Hmmm, will these sexy things even be on display? I wonder for a second, wavering. We did agree on only a shoulder massage, coffee and a movie ... Oh crap. A Vixen's motto is to be prepared for anything! I'm going to execute a quick lingerie change, just in case.

On one foot while I try to replace my shoes after replacing my knickers with sexier ones, I hop around, checking the time again. In a panic I realise that twenty-two minutes have already passed since we spoke. This convinces me that now is the time for a quick second stiff vodka before he arrives. Which could be any minute now!

Pitfalls of Marks in your Lair:

× You have less control over when he leaves, and the date is over

× Extra time in preparation needed for cleaning of lair

× Higher monetary cost due to pre-purchase of drinks and nibbles

× Extreme organisation of schedule to allow for shopping, cleaning and preparation

× It is your bed which has the wet spot to avoid sleeping in, should the date progress that far (which equals another load of washing to do later)

Adventure Vixen

Breaking the Rules

My heart leaps as I hear a sharp knock at the door, so I take a couple of deep breaths to calm myself before opening it. Oh man, I hope I didn't make a mistake in inviting Darz here ... and that he will leave when I ask him to! The door swings wide open. A nervous grin crosses my face when I see him for the first time. Oh yes, well hello there! In an instant we are aware of a mutual attraction to each other. His friendly grin that reaches all the way to his eyes, makes me feel comfortable and relaxed, as well as excited and turned on. He steps into the entrance way and envelops me in a huge warm hug.

Kissing me on the cheek, he grins and winks at me as he says, 'Well, hello Miss Vixen. It is a pleasure to be allowed the privilege of being invited to your lair!' I laugh, relieved at his words that assure me he is worthy of my invite.

"Well, don't thank me too soon. I may kick you out again quick smart if you're not an awesome shoulder masseur!"

He laughs as he follows my lead into the lounge room and sits down on the couch with me. My nerves have been calmed by the vodka, I run my eyes down his body in appraisal, and what I see, I like very much! He has short stylish brown hair and an open, friendly face which is cute—in fact even more handsome than in his picture. Phew, what a relief!

His biceps bulge from years of gym visits, and his jumper stretches across his broad shoulders, moulded to the shape of a delicious body. I wonder if he owns a six pack ... or an impressive package in those jeans! That thought makes me grin in wickedness, right as he catches my eye.

"What is the mischievous grin for? I swear you are looking at me like you want to devour me!"

The heated flare of embarrassment flashes across my cheeks. "Ooops! Guilty!"

We both laugh as he slides closer to me on the lounge, his warm thigh now pressed hard up against mine. He eyeballs me up and down, his eyes lingering for a second longer on my breasts, and he lifts his hand to my cleavage, tracing a finger down between them until his finger is trapped in the warm cocoon between them.

Watching his finger trace my skin, my nipples start to harden in excitement. I want him to be bold, and take my breasts into his hands, knead my nipples, bare them and suck on each one until they became rock hard.

In the back of my mind floats the vague realization that perhaps only one strong drink of vodka was enough for me. The second one has tipped me towards a dangerous carefree edge heading to beyond caring, and into wanting to get intimate with this guy much faster than normal.

Our laughter fades, as the sexual tension almost sizzles in the air between us, and our faces become more serious. He leans in towards me, cupping me around the neck to draw me closer to his parted lips.

Without protest I let him. Knowing I too want to taste those lips, to touch my tongue against his and sample his kisses. I press my breasts against his hard chest, causing him to groan and deepen the kiss, while running his fingers through my hair. Sighing softly against his lips, I grin as I draw back from him.

"Well! There doesn't seem to be many coffees, movies or shoulder massages going on here!" I imply in a cheeky manner, trying to come to my senses and not rip his clothes off within the first ten-minutes of meeting him in person. My fingers are itching to trace over the rather large looking bulge in his jeans but I'm trying to hold myself back for at least another few minutes!

"Mmm, so there isn't!" He flashes a naughty grin. "But I will say that this is so much better than watching a movie, Miss Vixen. I love the way you kiss; I'm thinking I need another sample."

"Ohh, now that is smooth!" I'm impressed. Of course, I also do my own assessment of his kiss. If the dude is a terrible kisser, no way would I bother going any further with him! Of course, this is one of the reasons why you are better off going anywhere but to your place. What if he's an awful slobbery kisser, or moves his mouth faster than a speeding rally car? Or if he thinks shoving his entire tongue down your throat is a turn-on? You don't want to be stuck with any of those scenarios!

My relief at him being a good kisser makes me much happier about my decision to invite him over, so I agree to his proposal of another test, rather than offer him a coffee!

Darz gathers me closer, coaxing my lips apart gently with his tongue, while sliding his hand from my jawline, down my throat, and flicking open the top button of my shirt, sliding his hand inside of my lacy bra to cup my whole breast, squeezing and teasing my nipple to attention with his fingers. I can feel his grin of satisfaction against my lips.

"Well two can play at this you know!" I slide my hand from his knee up along his muscled thigh to the zippered junction that is my aim. Bolder now, I press my hand against his ever-tightening jeans, feeling the thrill of sexual power as he groans and pinches my nipple even harder.

I'm sliding down along the familiar slippery path of desire. Part of me wants to rip open his pants and encircle his hardness with my fingers, which is so clearly straining against the zip. The other part of me really wants that promised massage, the reason for the invite in the first place.

Darz recaptures my lips with his, so I wiggle closer to him, hooking my thigh over his while our tongues dance together. He murmurs something against my lips, his free hand slips under my skirt to caress my bare thigh, sliding upwards towards my new lingerie. I stop his hand by slapping my free hand onto his.

"Hey, where's my promised massage, mister? There are no more shenanigans until the knots in my shoulders have been relaxed to mush!" He sweeps the couch cushions off with a grin, gesturing for me to lie face down, so he can deliver on his promise.

"Oh wait! You have too many layers on for this to be beneficial enough, woman!"

Shrugging out of my top layers but leaving on my lingerie, I allow him to straddle me and start kneading my shoulders. His strong hands have an immediate impact, and I groan aloud in pleasure, letting him know he is massaging the exact spot. I can feel my whole body relax as he slowly makes his way from my shoulders down to my lower back, melting me into the couch. His hands venture lower, rhythmically kneading my cheeks until my hips lift involuntarily.

Groaning softly, I part my thighs another inch to allow his wandering fingers access to where I want them. His fingers slide inside my wetness then massage my butt cheeks. I can't help myself—after another few minutes of torture, I unzip his pants. Almost feverish, my fingers pull his underwear down to allow his hardness to spring free of its clothes prison.

He hauls me upright, moaning against my throat while biting my neck, and pushes harder against my fingers as my thumb slowly circle the tip of his head, which is already wet and slippery. The blood pulses fiercely along his length, so I squeeze a little more as I stroke my hand along his smooth skin in a slow rhythmic way.

In response, he slides his fingers further inside, pressing them forward while his thumb circles my clit, bringing me closer to the edge in a matter of seconds. The familiar energy of desire ripples through my body, getting stronger, my body silently urging him on, wanting to go where he is taking me.

My hand slides over his hot throbbing skin faster, my palm covered with his natural lubrication, my fingers flicking over the wet head teasing him to the edge, as he does to me. Our breaths mingle as we kiss again, our tongues twirling faster in their dance, as our bodies get nearer to exploding in ecstasy. Almost whimpering with need, I want him to take me to completion. I'm so close I can taste it.

My hips rising to meet his fingers as my own work his rigidness into a frenzy of need. Both of us panting now, kissing each other, bodies pressed together, beads of sweat glistening in the flickering candlelight. With one last amazing stroke of his thumb against me in the perfect place, I am transported, crying out against his lips in pleasure, causing him to groan a low deep growl as he tips over the edge with me, his dick convulsing in my hand as he comes. We both fall back against the couch in happy exhaustion, sated.

Long minutes later I rouse myself enough to open my eyes.

"Holy crap, that was good!'" My sigh is one of pleasure, a huge grin on my face. He opens one eye, peers at me and laughs.

"Phew woman ... what did you do to me?" He shakes his head as if in awe. "Amazing, Miss Vixen! You must have hidden magic in those fingers of yours!"

I giggle drowsily in response. "Well, I could say the same for you. That was an awesome massage! Oh my God, I think you broke me. I can't move a muscle now. I'm too relaxed!"

I make a half-hearted attempt to stand but settle for sitting, as my legs are not quite steady enough to hold me yet. Darz is trying to pull his clothes back on, but still having difficulty with limb coordination. "Well, I couldn't ask for a better evening ... even with no coffee or movies to be seen!"

I flash my Vixenly grin and laugh. "Mwaaahaaahaaahahaaaahaaa! Now there is no escape for you ... you are entwined in my deadly web, mere mortal!" We giggle together like naughty kids, both able to now stand without falling over and walk to the front door.

"Hmm, I think I quite like the sound of that, oh Vixen!"

He plays along and gives me a light kiss on the neck, while slapping my butt cheek. I laugh, but unconsciousness is approaching at an alarming rate, so I decide that his time is up.

"Well, we will make another time to catch-up. Perhaps we can even meet at a pub this time for a drink first?"

I open the door and virtually shove him out with a grin. Good naturedly, he smiles back squeezing me in affection.

"For sure! What about Wednesday night? I will text you the location and time once my brain is working again!" I nod in agreement as his lips captures one last kiss before he leaves. Now close to three in the morning, I throw myself on the bed, peeling off clothes as I go, heedless of the mess on the floor. Exhausted but smiling and satisfied, I fall straight into a deep slumber.

When in vixen mode, we are looking for the right type of hot playful guys we click with immediately.

Not 'Mr. Sweet and might be nice when I get to know him eventually' guy.

Adventure Vixen

Sunday Date

The next morning, I awake with that annoying feeling like I've forgotten something.

Shit! What is it? Wracking my brain, I wipe the sleep out of my eyes, trying to remember what is swimming around in the back of my mind. Blearily I glance over at the alarm clock, to discover that the time is 7.13 am. Geez, what am I doing awake at this time? Disgusted, I sink back down into my comfortable cocoon.

This is way too early to be awake! Last night's fun adventure with Darz flashes across my mind, and I smile a naughty smile of happiness, and stretch in satisfaction at the thought. Even though we met so late in the evening, he's a hot Mark, and interesting enough to keep me awake—even re-energise me!

The thought of seeing him again next week sends a shiver of anticipation down my spine. I lie snuggled up in my warm bed, drifting in and out of consciousness for over an hour, until a startling thought pops into my head. It is Sunday. *Sunday morning to be precise.*

Oh crap. Dreads! The thought of him springs my eyes open immediately, and I'm blinded by the sudden influx of light flooding my room. Well, at least the weather gods are smiling. Outside my window, the sun shines brightly through a few fluffy stray clouds. A tiny spark of excitement shivers through my body at the thought of meeting this guy, the most mysterious of all so far!

I wonder what Sean is like. Will I like him, or feel intimidated by him? I am swimming out of my depth here, but I'm too curious to turn back to safety. No matter! I am a strong swimmer and float like a buoy, so I'm not nervous ... am I?

My fanciful musings make me waste another hour in bed. Giving myself a stern lecture on hurrying up and not being late, I swing my legs out of the warmth of my bed, and into the fresh morning air. Diving into the shower with a shiver, I wash my hair and body in record time.

Once wrapped in my warm dressing gown, I retrieve the Book and my Goddess cards from the cupboard that I shoved them in last night. If there's ever a time I need guidance, this is it! The Book has a faint golden glow as I flick through its pages, re-reading the wisdom within. Its words reassure me, but I'm still a bit worried. I feel the need to double check with my cards.

Shuffling the gold edged cards, I concentrate on projecting my question out to the universe. After my fourth shuffle, a card flips face up in the deck with my answer.

Lakshmi: Bright Future

This is a kind universe, and everyone within it is working in your favour. There are no obstacles in your way except your own projections of fear into your future. Take a moment and hush your mind, quietening it from worries and fears. Why would you wish darkness upon yourself when light shines all around you? Step into this brightness by lightening your thoughts and feelings. Clear your heart of fear. Stop worrying. Everything is going to be fine.

A huge sigh of relief escapes me. I feel so much better about going on this date now. Until I catch sight of the clock hands racing towards ten o'clock. Damn! I agreed to go to a cafe at Manly beach, which is quite a drive from my place, even assuming the traffic on a Sunday morning would be relatively sparse.

A bit frantic now, I search through my clothes for something suitable to wear for a Sunday morning date. Hmmm. What the hell would that be, I wonder? It is daytime, but I want to appear tempting, so a basic t-shirt and jeans combo is out. To some this would be a sexy outfit, but with my breasts being on the larger side, a lower neckline suits me better. Plus, my boobs can draw the attention away from the other bits I would rather he not notice.

Hmmm, possibly a black miniskirt, low cut top and edgy studded high heeled black boots for this occasion? How about a studded collar to match? Now I'm being silly! Besides, fetish wear is a night-time attire thing, isn't it? I can't help but imagine me turning up for coffee in a casual beach cafe wearing a latex dress, thigh-high boots and fishnet stockings—or a collar! The thought makes me giggle.

Focus Arleia, focus! I scold myself and switch into high gear, throwing on the clothes I finally choose for the day. An Aztec patterned flowing skirt with thigh high splits, low-heeled long black boots, a black scoop necked tank top and an emerald green jacket, and I am done! Sliding the straightening iron through my hair set at 'warp speed', I grab my make-up and handbag and I'm ready to go. I take one last glance at the ensemble I've chosen, making sure that my outfit is comfortable as well as impressive enough for a first date, without looking like I put in too much effort!

I race out the door, cursing at the time flying by. In the car I slam the gears into reverse and zoom backwards down the driveway. I am going to need to pray to the traffic gods for all green lights if I'm to make the journey in the twenty-measly minutes left before meeting my Mark.

For God's sake! It's not like I was doing anything this morning to allow for a reasonable excuse for my lateness! I'm frustrated with myself at the careless dawdling.

I need to study quantum physics, to learn how to make myself appear in two places simultaneously. Maybe then I will be able to fit more things into my life. It's unfortunate that scientists haven't made this a reality yet! Physicists can make a single dot of light appear in two different locations at once, but the same dot being in two places is still a *long* way from a single human living in two locations. For all we know of the universe, we could be living in a parallel universe right now!

I glance at my clock on the dash. I'm making good time, but I am still going to be late. I need time to bend or be elastic! I punch out a quick, "Sorry! Running late, be there in 5!" message to Dreads as I pull into the closest car park I can find.

With a quick glance in the mirror, I realize my face is still bare of make-up, which I planned to apply as I drove here to save time. Instead I got caught up in a daydream and completely forgot my plan! I swipe my make-up across my face in haste and do a final mirror check to ensure all is where it's supposed to be. There's no lipstick on my teeth, so I am good to go.

Jumping out of the car, I trot at high speed towards the cafe. Now the nerves rush back at me causing butterflies in my stomach. Breathe, just breathe and be calm! I instruct myself as I trot down the busy road towards my destination.

Once inside the packed entrance, I spot him immediately. That is the good thing about him having such a unique hairstyle, I guess—much easier to find! At least I can head straight over to him with confidence. Sean, aka Dreads, stands up to greet me as I approach.

"Well hello!" he exclaims with a big smile on his face. "You must be Arleia!"

"Indeed I am!" Grinning back at him, I notice his cute dimples flash as he smiles. "So sorry I am a few minutes late!" He nonchalantly brushes my apology aside. "No matter! You're here now. What can I order for you to drink?"

"I'd love a hot chocolate in a mug, thank you!" I'm a little shy now.

He nods with a cheeky grin, and gestures for me to sit down while he goes to the counter to order for us.

I check out the decor of the café from the quirky orange two-seater couch. Furnished in a charming retro style with mismatched chairs, tables and couches scattered haphazardly around in groups, the café's interior sends out a cosy feel. The smell of freshly ground coffee wafts through the café.

Fifties style billboards cover a couple of walls, advertising products no longer in existence. A few of the classic fifties style pin-up girl posters adorn another wall. They fit in well with the surrounding furnishings, adding extra warmth to the eclectic mix.

I stare across at Dreads while his back is towards me at the counter. Mmm, cute butt! This thought has me grinning in appreciation, but I glance away quickly, not wanting to be caught staring as he turns back to walk towards me, drinks in hand. Placing them on the table, he slides across the couch next to me.

"I hope you don't mind me sitting next to you, instead of across from you?" His thigh brushes against mine.

"Uhm, no that's fine!"

Inside I am a little wary. Plus, what am I going to say? *No you can't! You're too close for comfort and I am way out of my comfort zone!* I shift my position on the couch so I can face him more, and only our knees are touching rather than our entire thighs, so I feel more comfortable. I recall the message from my cards and take a deep breath to relax. That's better!

"Sooo," he drawls, while looking me up and down in appreciation. He almost makes me want to do a slow turn like a prime piece of meat being chosen by the butcher. I gulp nervously, and take a quick sip of my drink, unsure what is to come next.

"What did you think of my profile, Arleia? It's a little different to most!" He stares at me with a lazy grin spreading across his face, his eyes twinkling in amusement. I'm flustered at his first question, like a schoolgirl who wants to give the right response but is unsure of what the correct answer is. I buy some more time with another sip of my hot chocolate before I answer him.

"Well, you are right!" I agree with a nervous laugh. "I can't say I've met anyone quite like you as yet in my dating adventures!" He chuckles at my response.

"Well, I am a regular guy, who likes a bit of kink in his relationships. Nothing too scary!"

Huh. That's easy for him to say. *Nothing scary indeed.* I'm almost shaking in my boots from fear of the unknown! However, as we chat my curiosity overcomes my fear and I start to ask him questions.

"What do you mean by kink? I'm new to this concept, so you might need to explain the concepts and what fetishes imply in a practical sense!" Not used to talking about this, my cheeks flame and I want to squirm in my chair. He grins at my obvious discomfort.

"Well Arleia, sometimes I like to be the dominant partner, and other times I like the woman to be the dominant partner, and I am happy to be the submissive one. Sex can be thrilling when I have a strong woman dominating me, telling me what she wants me to do. I will obey her. I mean I will do *anything* she wants. If I don't, she can punish me in any way she sees fit. The punishment may be a simple spanking over the knees, or some lashes of her whip. I can even act as a footstool and table for her feet and drinks—it varies, depending on the mistress."

I try not to appear too shocked at what he's divulged, so I rearrange my face on purpose into a neutral 'Mmm, that's so interesting' worldly facial expression ... I hope!

He continues, "The mistress may want her feet massaged, or to be serenaded by a guitar, or she may want her house cleaned or garden tended to."

My ears prick up. Woah! *Now* you're talking my language! Foot massage? House cleaned? Served food and beverages? Serenaded? Yes please to all those, thank you! I'm not so sure about the whipping and spanking business, but this bit I can handle.

"So are you more dominant or submissive, Arleia?" Dreads grins into his coffee cup.

Oh man! I'm now thinking we should have met in the pub where alcohol can help me answer these awkward questions without blushing like an innocent virgin!

"Uhmm ... Ermmm ... well ... " I stutter and feel the first hot flush of red travelling up my neck to burst forth onto my cheeks. I want to fan my face, but he would think I am even more of weirdo if I did. Wait, what am I saying? Isn't it HIM who is the more unusual one here? He is waiting for an answer that I don't possess yet. I've never contemplated this before, or seen myself in those terms, so I am not prepared with an easy answer.

"Umm, guess I'd be more dominant, but also a bit submissive perhaps?" I respond in question form, feeling silly and out of my depth. "I think I could whip or spank someone easier than allowing someone else to either whip or spank me!" I am desperate to change the subject to something a little safer for now.

"So, have you met many women from the dating site yet Sean?"

"Yes, I have met a few. But so far there are none I would want to see again. Perhaps my thoughts will change after our date!" His lip curls in a suggestive manner. "After all, I don't bite, unless you want me to?"

I find myself laughing with him, which eases the tension the difficult questions were causing.

"Mmm well yes, you never know what may happen!"

Thankfully the conversation turns to topics I'm more comfortable with, and we chat easily for quite a while about our lives, work, hobbies and music. I relax, happier with these mainstream topics. Engrossed in our conversation, we consume two hot drinks each, and a lazy pleasant two hours pass with ease. Dreads eventually peers across at me with a quizzical expression.

"Hey, how about we blow this joint and head to the pub for a drink or two and keep chatting?"

For a millisecond I hesitate. Oh what the fuck, I still have time.

"Fantastic! Let's do it!"

I decide that I do like him as a person, as we saunter along the street adjacent to the almost deserted beach, towards the closest place which sells alcohol. Conveniently the nearest pub is located a mere block away and sports an amazing view of the ocean.

Though still chilly, I appreciate the beautiful sunshine filled day in contrast to the dismal dull days we have been getting. This puts me in a happier mood, and I am looking forward to getting alcohol zinging into my system, so I can be braver in my questioning. I am so curious about the whole slave/master thing, but still unsure how much I can ask or cope with!

We enter the trendy up-market pub with a fresh, alive feel; the opposite to the run-down old pubs where the stench of stale beer lingering in the atmosphere is complimented by sticky psychedelic patterned carpets. The bar is busy, but not so crowded that it is impossible to snare a barstool and table. We pick one overlooking the beach front. The bi-fold windows are pushed back to welcome the fresh sea breeze, giving the impression that you are almost sitting right on the sand. I grin, thinking aloud that this is the perfect spot to be enjoying the day.

He agrees, and enquires as to what alcoholic drink I might like. I smile back and ask for a glass of bubbly, while inside I'm thinking, OMG I need alcohol *now*! Hurry up ... and make my order a whole bottle to start with!

Of course, all I say aloud is that a house bubbly would be amazing, thanks! I smile a small Vixenly smile and take a couple of deep, calming breaths as he turns towards the bar.

This is the perfect opportunity to check my phone for messages. Seeing this date is a little off the beaten track, I earlier told two of my best friends — Lulu and Billie-Rae - where I am going and with whom, to be safe. They will be wondering how we are doing so far.

Lulu has sent me a cheeky message asking if I am too tied up to answer her. This makes me laugh but I realise she is concerned, so I flash her a quick message back saying that all is fine, no ropes and still on date, before he returns from the bar with our drinks.

A couple of sips later, my empty stomach causes a fast reaction to the alcohol spreading through my system. The spread of the warmth makes it harder to censor my words and thoughts.

Peeping up from my glass I see Sean staring with intensity at me, and I'm captured by his eyes. For a long moment time stands still, and I can't seem to force myself to tear my eyes away from him. A sudden loud burst of laughter nearby breaks the spell, and I down the rest of my drink nervously, wondering what he's thinking about right now.

"You know, you would be so hot and luscious in latex."

The statement catches me by surprise, and I stammer an unintelligible reply of "Ohh. Ermmm ... what?"

"A latex dress. Have you ever worn latex before, Arleia?" He tosses the question at me in a casual way, as if it is a normal and natural topic of conversation. This throws me off balance.

"Latex? No. No, I've never worn anything made of that." I reply to him with a smile, but inside I'm thinking to myself ... Latex? Where did this come from? What do these dresses or outfits even look like? I start to imagine short shoestring-strapped dresses you pour yourself into, with cut out butt cheek holes or nipple circles. My mind races through the only latex images I can summon, and the only other thing popping to mind is a pair of gloves!

"Oh yeah, latex clothing is amazing!" enthuses Sean with a grin and an unsettling, knowing wink. "Any size body at all is attractive in latex. Even the smell, touch and taste of the material is such a turn on!"

"Hmm ... Uhm I'm not sure I can picture exactly what type of dress you mean!" I laugh as I can't help but admit I don't have the foggiest idea what the hell he is talking about. *The taste?*

"Oh, here, I will show you!" Five seconds after my admission, he pulls up a latex clothing website on his phone so I could see what he means.

"Here! Check out this page, Arleia! Here is an excellent site with awesome sexy latex designs of all types. They are pricey, but good latex outfits are worth spending the money on!"

Absurdly I want to agree and say, *oh yes! Latex is usually expensive!* But I possess so little knowledge about this fabric that I'm feeling too out of my depth to banter back in my usual fashion.

He pushes his phone over to me so I can view the website, so I scroll down the page. Admittedly they do look amazing, and super shapely too. They are less sleazy looking than I thought they would be ... well, most of them! There are even a couple listed I thought I wouldn't mind trying on myself, if only to find out what it looked and felt like to wear a latex dress.

I soon come to my senses when I check out the price of my favourite dress. A mere two hundred and fifty British pounds! I almost choke on my drink as I convert this figure into Australian dollars in my head. Perhaps I will need to wait for a rich handsome man to buy me one as a gift one day rather than invest this much cash into something I'd be able to wear on limited occasions. It is easy chatting to Sean and after the second drink I can ask him a few of the things I'm curious about. I'd no idea so many people are into all sorts of fetishes, and my curiosity only grows from our conversation. I'm amazed to find we've spent over four hours together on this first date—much longer than I would usually allow or expect!

Sean definitely is cute, and extremely intriguing. I'm not sure this is my kind of thing, but then again how could I know with no experience of this world yet? How can I form an informed opinion about the dominant/submissive world if I have not tried it? Silently I ponder over some of the things Sean revealed while I gather my things and wait for him to join me. We meander over towards where I am parked, still chatting. I stop at my car, and gaze at him with a grin.

"Oh, this is my ride right here!" Ready to say goodbye and dive in, Sean surprises me by grabbing hold of my hand. He steps closer towards me with an odd grin on his face which I find hard to read.

"Well, it's been incredibly interesting to meet you today, Arleia!" He drawls in a flirtatious, suggestive tone.

Is his tone really suggestive? Or is it the alcohol making my head fuzzy and giving me mixed messages?

"Oh! Yes, it was also really cool to meet you too Sean!" I almost bat my lashes at him, the alcohol making me more flirtatious than usual, and lowering my inhibitions.

Without warning he steps towards me, sliding one arm around my waist and drawing me hard up against him, while his other hand captures my chin, lifting my head to the perfect position for his lips to swoop down and imprison mine. Melting into him he deepens the kiss, his thumb caressing my jaw as he wraps his fingers around the back of my neck and draws me even closer still.

I can't help but reciprocate, my arms sliding around his waist, my tongue dancing with his in the moist warmth of our connected mouths. A low groan rumbles deep within his throat as he holds me even tighter against him for a few moments. When he finally releases my mouth, it takes a second or two for the bright sunny day and public surroundings to become visible again.

We grin sheepishly at each other, like kids caught by their parents for doing something naughty that they shouldn't be doing. I need to break the silence and speed the hell away from here!

"Well, it was interesting, Sean. Much more so than I originally anticipated!" My laughter has an edge of surprise.

"Same here, Arleia! It was a real pleasure meeting you!" An innocent, boyish grin flashes across his face. "Drive safely, won't you?"

He sweeps me up into a hug so tight I can hardly draw a breath before he suddenly lets me go. Swaying, I regain my balance and grin back at him in the not so innocent fashion of a Vixen — but toned down a little in caution. I am still way out of my depth, but my enjoyment of his company is genuine.

Our farewell over; I jump into my car as he strides off to where his car is parked. Motionless for a couple of minutes, I take a few deep breaths. Wow, I was so out of my comfort zone on this one, but I did it! The date was quite interesting and only a little scary. I'm proud of myself for stepping out of my comfort zone!

As I drive towards my brother's house for a family get-together, I mull over the time spent with Sean. I will not be discussing my morning activities with my brother or family!

Stopping for a moment to buy the drinks I promised to bring along, I fire off a quick report of my morning's experience to both Billie-Rae and Lulu to ease their concerns about me meeting Sean, even in broad daylight! Relieved replies spring back to me, making me laugh at the alternative scenarios my friends suggest—me being tied up in a dungeon or suspended by ropes in a fetish club. Their fears are laughable ... that's not a daytime activity! *Is it?*

I can't help chuckling aloud at my morning's dating experience. Of course, I don't want my brother finding out anything like that—he would freak out at the very thought, even though nothing happened! I guess older brothers can be protective like that, so best they don't know ... for their own good, of course!

My dating life is something to be held close to my chest and examined in the privacy of my own home, not to be discussed at family gatherings, so I push all thoughts of my morning aside, grab the drinks for the barbecue and head inside to greet everyone already amassed under the peaked pergola.

At least, with enough going on with the fifteen other family members to distract me, I can give them enough of my attention and enjoy the day together. But part of me still wants to go back home and reflect on my date in solitude, as well as check the computer for any other messages from my Marks waiting for me online. Uhm ... Perhaps I am getting too addicted to this new pastime of mine. Lots of handsome men are falling all over me and I love the attention. Can you blame me? My brother and his wife only seem to talk about their renovations, between complaining about their gorgeous kids and bore me with a discussion of which dishes they ordered from the menu at the Greek restaurant last night.

Little do they know there is a Vixen in their midst actively nourishing her inner light and going on adventures, but in the dark is how I am going to keep them! I'm pleased that I remembered to change my phone to silent mode before I arrived, so that they wouldn't question me on the many messages I received this afternoon from my Marks wanting to organise a meeting or three with me ... Mwaaahahaahaaahahaaa!

After a few hours I escape the family fold and once home I collapse into bed, exhausted but happy. Before I fall into the depths of dreamland, I reply to my messages from Darz, Krystian and Roshan, as well as from Sean thanking me for the excellent company that morning.

I think I might need to go shopping soon! Visions of sexy corsets mingled with latex dresses and lights shining through bodies float across my mind as I drift into a deep unconsciousness. But while I'm fast asleep, I miss the new glow of the Book, flashing a soft red warning light in contrast to the warm golden light it usually emits when all is well.

Acceptable Venue Choices

Many excellent options are available for a first date venue with your potential Marks, and public places are always the safest. All you know about the Mark you are arranging an initial meeting with, is the information he wrote on his profile, and the conversations you engaged in.

This alone is not enough to determine if he is a trustworthy person or not—he may not be the person depicted in the online pictures, so it is wise to practice caution. Flirting in public can be a turn on for both you and the Mark, and should you be lucky enough to find one you like and the feeling is mutual; all sorts of fun can be had even on a date in public.

Venue Suggestions:

- ✓ **Bars:** Find out which bars near you possess either leafy beer gardens, quiet intimate lounge areas or have been transformed into up-market bars with no 'front bar' in sight.

- ✓ **Cafes:** An easy non-alcoholic choice or morning meeting place. Acceptable for 'coffee only' dates—choose the meeting time wisely so you are not coerced into a meal while you are there! They often have cosy indoor and outdoor spaces and are weather friendly.

Adventure Vixen

Brazilian Banter

It is so bizarre to wake up to several text messages per day, and all from different men. Admittedly, it's quite flattering and a huge confidence boost to be given this much attention. The fact that the attention is coming from several men at once gives me such a sense of naughtiness and makes me smile nonstop!

How many guys can you see at once without forgetting a name or date? Or even worse, what if you accidently double-booked yourself and had two Marks simultaneously turn up on your doorstep? Awkward! I am learning that it is very important to record everyone you meet. My mind can be a bit selective at times, and I may forget the reason why I decided not to bother wasting even another hour of my precious time on a bloke I went out with a few months ago. Mitch will not make my 'Must see again!' list. I have not chosen too badly so far and have been getting an above average strike rate with funny, witty and desirable Marks thus far, so the handbook's rules must be working well!

Visions of my latest date with Sean pop into my head. Damn, he is cute! I don't know if I am into dreadlocks or the fetish scene though ... am I? I decide to put him on the back burner. Perhaps at a later time I will pursue this avenue, just for fun and to find out what the fetish life is like, but I am not quite ready to travel that path yet! The idea piques my curiosity, nevertheless. I am having such an enjoyable time with the other guys now that I can think about Sean later.

Any others I might like to meet in the near future, will need to be checked out in detail too. As I have learnt so far, many Marks are lined up ready for the discerning shopper, displayed on the dating supermarket shelf, where they reside daily jostling for your attention.

I do realize that I need to spend more time developing my inner light, and work on being true to myself. I didn't do this at all during the time before I unceremoniously become an *ex*-girlfriend. Even that relatively short time spent pandering to another's needs dimmed the brightness of my soul and made me forget who I am.

No wonder I am not ready to embark on the scary task of opening my heart to any other man yet! How can I do that until I am complete within myself? Of course I have physical needs, but what better way than the Vixen way to inject some excitement into daily life? Until I am ready for my Prince of Weird to come along and sweep me off on an adventure with him instead, perhaps ...

My fingers itch in eagerness to reach my keyboard throughout the entire week, but a series of late-night meetings, birthday celebrations and appointments thwart my efforts. Not to mention the time I spend answering text messages from my current Marks daily!

It's not until Thursday evening that I am able to snatch a few hours to check out the shopping in my newest favourite shopping mall of delights. In a comfortable position, I logon to discover what I've missed in the entire four days that I didn't inspect my profile.

There are a couple of messages from Darz—what a sweet and totally hot guy he is! Reading them makes me smile. He is still incredibly keen to go out on a proper date and suggests several ideas for our next meeting together. I punch out a quick reply to him, agreeing with his second suggestion of a cosy bar located close to my place.

Of course, I am going to choose the closest pub to me now— I've learnt that much! I don't want to waste any more time travelling for hours to meet anyone. A Mark could end up being a complete idiot or grope you inappropriately. Or have a bad case of halitosis, or grown a bushy handlebar moustache since posting his pictures online! Wasting an entire evening on a guy not worthy of a Vixen's time or attention is to be avoided whenever possible.

I'm interrupted mid-thought by an answer from Darz popping up on my screen. "Tomorrow night. At the place of your choice, sexy lady. At 7pm?" The message surprises me as he shows as offline on my list. I grin and recognise a fellow invisible observer, in stark opposition to many other men who seem to be showing up as online for at least twelve hours each day! I can't blame him for wanting to be incognito—my first choice now is to always go on my favourite dating website under the invisible banner, so that I can peruse the potential Marks who want to meet me. I can also hide from those on my list that I do not need to speak to, or who I'm not inclined to chat with at that moment in time.

I've made the mistake of having my status set as 'online' by accident before. This resulted in me being bombarded by five guys all wanting to converse with me at once! Although this sounds ideal on occasion, the practicality of carrying on multiple separate conversations is incredibly complex and challenging, resulting in missed messages as well as some going to the wrong recipients.

Way too stressful, I can tell you! Having to explain yourself when the message you sent in no way relates to the conversation you are having with someone does shake your credibility with the potential Mark. He may become sulky or annoyed that he is not the only one commanding your attention.

Speaking of which, mine is drawn back to Darz and our flirty chat just became more interesting. Another half an hour of chatting and I am looking forward to our next meeting even more than I did before. This Mark owns a hot body and brain with a witty sense of humour, and floors me with some attractive depth in his character. I am intrigued to learn more.

Once we finish our conversation and confirm our rendezvous for the next night, I move onto the pile of potential Mark requests to slice and dice the obvious rejects out from the potential Marks.

One guy catches my eye immediately. He is Brazilian, which sparks my interest. I've never met anyone from Brazil before, and Brazilians possess a reputation for being skilled lovers. Perhaps that is the thought in the back of my mind when I add him and decide to give him a chance. He shows up online as soon as he is on my list, and I can see that he is fast in tapping out a message back to me. Wow. Talk about instant response!

I re-read his profile, as his polite but admiring greeting flashes onto my screen. I grin and launch into the conversation with ease. His name is Pedro. He's a thirty-two-year-old Brazilian born guy who has lived in Melbourne for the past seven years and works in the banking industry. We banter back and forth for a while before he christens me with Kit-e-cat. The endearment is a reasonable name for me seeing that I can be soft, cuddly and purr like a kitten, but also hide sharp claws sheathed nearby for use if they are ever needed. Again, I study his profile.

His picture is snapped from too far away to make out his features clearly. That is always a valid concern. I do not want to waste my time on a man that I don't find attractive, so I do need him to send me a better one before I decide—especially since he is flirting hard with me. I am not sure that I want to be drawn in yet.

Teasingly I admonish him for such an unclear picture on his profile, stating that he needs to give me a better one before I can decide whether I will meet him or not. He agrees and a moment later a private photo is posted on his profile. I check the picture out straight way—it's a Vixen rule!

Pedro's image fills my screen. In his chosen image he shows a buff, bare chest but his head is thrown back, so not all of his face is visible. I can make out a strong jawline and nose, glossy black ringlets down to his shoulders slicked back with product, and rounded biceps hinting at frequent gym visits.

"How do you like my picture, Kit-e-cat?"

"Hmm, not too bad, but it is a shame that I can't see your face or eyes in the photo!" My reply is cheeky.

"Well, you can stare into my eyes when they are looking at you from between your beautiful thighs!"

He makes me laugh out loud, and I give him points in appreciation of an impressive line thrown out in a flash. What can I say to that? No retort comes to mind that can beat his reply right now, so I wonder why he is reticent to show me his full face.

I decide to give him the benefit of the doubt for now and keep conversing—at least he is making me laugh with his foreignness peeping through in his sentence structures and phrasing of things. What a shame that he is in a different city though. I will not travel to Melbourne for him. If anything, he would need to come here to meet me—and all I can promise would be a coffee, the rest being unknown until we meet, as always with each dude. I lament the fact that he is in another city and that makes meeting more difficult, but he is unfazed and tells me that he travels to Sydney on a regular basis for work, so seeing me here is no problem at all.

"So you see Kit-e-cat, you may run, but you cannot hide. I will come after you like a cheetah hunts a gazelle.
"

"What makes you think I will be hiding at all? Kit-e-cat owns sharp claws under her soft alluring fur, it may be you who runs and hides!" Giggling to myself I await his response.

"Ahhh, I can see I'm going to have to up my game, sexy woman, lest the hunter becomes the hunted!" he quips back seamlessly.

I laugh, delighted to find he can play along with me so easily. Perhaps he would be worthy of a meeting and surprise me. Maybe I should ask how often he comes to Sydney for business and arrange a meeting. At least if he does come for work purposes I won't feel as guilty if I only give him an hour of my time before I decide he is not for me. Finally, glancing at the clock, I realize its past time for me to be in bed already—especially considering the hot date I have lined up with Darz for tomorrow night!

I snap back to reality and quickly end my conversation with the Brazilian boy so that I can obtain enough beauty sleep before my impending date. My head touches the pillow and I lose consciousness immediately, missing the purple flash of light being sucked into the Vixen's Handbook.

Successful Mark Juggling

Once you have gathered several successful Marks to date simultaneously, keeping names and faces clear, separate and remembering each guy can become more difficult. It is the ultimate sin to call out the wrong name in intimacy, so Vixens need to ensure a mistake like this does not occur.

It would be totally offensive to you if he called you Vanessa when your name was Emily, wouldn't it? So as Vixens we can afford to give our marks the same courtesy.

The following is not a mere suggestion. It is a serious rule for a Vixen to follow which ensures that each Mark feels special. Even though he knows you're seeing other men, he doesn't want to be reminded of it by you calling him by one of your other Marks' names accidently instead of his own!

The information you are required to gather for each Mark is simple, but crucial for a Vixen's success, therefore must be recorded for each Mark met.

First name, Nickname and Profile name: These are often different from each other; record correct names to minimise Mark confusion later.

Which website you met on: There are several renowned sites available to shop on and this can become confusing so worth recording this detail.

Age of the Mark: It is the easiest thing to record, but also easy to forget! This is vital, as it is a shocking fact guys lie about their age sometimes. You might think is only something a woman would do (always younger than their real age, of course!) but there are many men who also lie about their age. The strange creatures often increase their age as well as decrease it, depending on their perceptions, making it even more baffling. If you find a Mark has lied about his age you are wise to wonder what else he has not been honest with you about.

Something memorable about the Mark: This can be either a positive or negative. You may make a note of his cheeky smile, bulging biceps, his race, where he works or amazing dress sense—whatever strikes you first as being most memorable about the Mark. This includes negative impressions.

It could be that you don't plan to see him again, but three months later you have forgotten the reason why. This will ensure you don't waste precious time on a dud Mark again. Comments like 'boring and cheap', 'has an annoying laugh' or 'small cock—don't bother!' bring back immediate recollections if why you are better to ignore a random text from him months after your date.

A picture of the Mark: The old saying, 'a picture speaks a thousand words,' is correct. What more do you need as an accurate reminder of who the Mark is? Often the dating websites protect their clients' privacy by not allowing pictures to be copied, so you need to get creative. If the Mark is not willing to send you one you can save, then there is always the option of asking them to send you a picture or press 'print page' to gain the reminder you need.

Record of intimacy: This seems an odd one to add, but our memories fade, and if you have played before with them, chances are they will ask you to play again, and you need to remember whether he is worth a repeat visit or not. If you forget to record the rough, unskilled groper, the two-minute man or the saliva bucket kisser, you may end up agreeing to a date you would rather avoid at all costs.

Star sign: You never know when it is helpful to know a man's star sign. If you know you have never gotten on well with Sagittarians, then you may choose to avoid that star sign. You may also know of good qualities attached to star signs—it is helpful to list these to, and see if they match your Mark!

Adventure Vixen

Dating Darz

At the unwelcome blare of my alarm, my eyes fly open in surprise. I groan and blindly hit out at the offending noise, stabbing the screaming monster to silence.

Since it was me who set it early to have time for meditation this morning, I can't complain. For years I have wanted to make meditation a part of my daily life. I read about it, researched and eventually understood the concept. It seems that prayer is asking God for something, whereas meditation is listening for the answer. It silences my mind and soothes my soul, attracting what I desire into my life.

Our minds are bombarded by advertising material demanding our attention, making us think we lack something. They are right, but what we lack is nothing we can buy. We are missing mind space. We are missing out on remembering dreams and our connection to our soul and the universe.

I sit cross legged on a soft cushion in the lounge, focussing on my long slow breaths, clearing my mind. I know *all* dreams can come true if I have the courage to pursue them. The Book has been helpful in attaining one of my dreams, but it can't help with them all. With a few final slow deep breaths, I finish my morning meditation feeling joyful and energised.

During my meditation I was reminded that I haven't properly checked the Book's advice *or* my cards on Darz as a choice yet! Shit! I race back into my bedroom and pull it from the drawer. I'm relieved to see a golden light of approval. I wonder if I need my cards as well. I've already met him, so I'm quite confident in this date. It's on for tonight!

"I've got a date with Darz tonight, I've got a date with hot, sexy Darz!" I sing under my breath at my desk and try without success to do some work for the day. The added distraction of messages and raunchy pictures from both Krystian and Roshan, as well as two cute messages from Darz, help the day to pass faster. Darz seems silly, cheeky but respectful and hot, so I'm expecting a great night!

Once home, I freshen up and repair my make-up. Shimmying into a patterned maxi skirt with modest side slits, a crimson tank top, casual jacket and low-heeled shoes, I keep in mind that my date is only a few inches taller than I am. A quick brush of my hair, a spritz of perfume and last check in the mirror and I am done. Perfect! Oh, except for the cherry lipstick smudged all over my front teeth. Phew, thank God I checked myself over before I left—lipstick stained teeth are almost as bad as a broccoli-filled smile in public!

Running out the door with one minute to spare before my estimated departure time, I congratulate myself on leaving on time for once. I'm amazed at being so organised! The smug expression on my face soon falters as I enter the busy traffic, giving me a moment of doubt as to whether I'd make it to the bar on time, even though it *is* close by. Perhaps my congratulatory pat on the back to myself was given too hastily.

While ducking and weaving, the traffic gods smile down on me by helping me to arrive at my destination with little more than thirty seconds to spare. Well, that's still a win in my book!

Pushing against the heavy glass door, I enter the warm bar, glancing around as fast as possible to spot him, so that I don't appear like a total idiot loitering at the door for too long. I'm pleased that he is easy to find. Now to transform into Vixen mode. Mwaaahahaahaaahahaaa!

Darz turns from his seat at the bar as I walk towards him. His face lights up in welcome recognition, and he wraps me in an extended warm hug of greeting. Oh, yum! I laugh, my nervousness dissipates, and I agree to him buying me a drink.

Weaving away from the bar, he chooses a perfect table for us. The spot is private should there be any suggestive behaviour at our table later in the night! After a few drinks I find us sitting closer with our thighs touching, staring at each other in a quiet moment. He leans forward, his hand rising to cup my face, his thumb caressing across my lip. He dips his head down to capture my lips with his. An involuntary sigh escapes me, so he takes the opportunity to deepen the kiss, teasing my lips open even more with his tongue, a silent enquiry to advance the kiss, and explore my mouth further.

Swaying closer toward him, I snake my arm up around his neck, pressing our lips harder together. Lips moving in unison, our tongues dance a slow tango. We finally break the kiss, albeit reluctantly, and grin at each other.

"Well verryyyy tasty, Arleia!" His eyes still twinkle with desire. "I could do this all night, given the chance."

"Mmm ..." I manage to stutter with the eloquence of a rabbit stunned by headlights. I shake my brain to force my mind to come up with something better than this. Anything.

"That might just be fun!"

Sliding back closer to him, my hand caresses the top of his thigh. He leans forward, putting his lips to my ear and whispers that perhaps we could organise going to a venue later, that is more private and comfortable. I agree. He is a perfect gentleman, can carry an intelligent conversation and shows a quirky sense of humour ... Holy crap, what was Darz's deal breaking flaw again? He draws me back into the conversation before I can follow that thought.

A few drinks into the date we even discuss a couple of mystical and spiritual topics. I am quite surprised and impressed at the depth of Darz so far. Perhaps I shall consider him as a regular Mark if he keeps performing well in all my evaluations!

"I don't suppose you happen to be free tomorrow night as well, Miss Vixen? I'd love to continue our discussions, as well as several other things, really soon!" With a wink he wiggles his eyebrow, so I can't help but laugh with him. I decide that he is worthy enough to invite to my place again for our next date. He has a flatmate, so we cannot go to his place. We set the time for the following night. By now it is past midnight and I find myself discreetly yawning a couple of times.

Another delicious kiss with Darz in the car park helps dissolve the cold night from my consciousness, but as soon as I get in my car a massive shiver runs through me. I turn the heater on full blast to thaw out again before I arrive home. Despite the bone-chilling wind strong enough to blow me off the road, I can't help but smile all the way home.

The next day flies by and soon after the sun sets, I hear a knock on my door. I give one last glance around checking that the candles are lit and everything is in its place, before I open the door with a smile. Darz stands in front of me, looking delicious in faded jeans and a sweatshirt with a wide grin on his handsome face and a bottle of wine in his hand.

"Well, fancy meeting you here!" I swing the door wider and invite him inside. He gives me a look as though he wants to devour me. I ignore his lecherous gaze as I gesture him into the lounge room and ask if he would like a drink. In answer he grabs me, spinning me around to plant a full kiss on my lips and leaving me breathless in surprise. He grins wickedly at my expression.

"I'd love a drink thanks, sexy woman, but I want another kiss from you first!"

I am a little nervous as he follows me into the kitchen, where a couple of chilled glasses are ready. He takes the bubbly from my hands without asking and dislodges the cork with a loud pop before handing the bottle back.

"Oh, so you're the expert cork popper too I see?" I'm impressed that he is confident enough to do that without asking.

"I'm an expert at many things, Miss Vixen. Perhaps you should find out!" We laugh together and raise our glasses in a toast to our evening ahead.

A couple of glasses later, I find myself wanting the heat of his lips pressed on mine. The alcohol coursing through my veins warms me from the inside and is making me think about kissing him mid-sentence, when he stops talking and gives me an intense stare. Our eyes connect, and we forget what we were discussing as he pulls me to my feet, crushes me against his hard chest and swoops down on my lips, his tongue forcing them apart, finding no resistance. I want this as much as he does.

He pushes me up against the nearby wall, caressing my arm for a moment before grinding his hips against mine, wanting me to feel his body's response from only one kiss, which makes the tendrils of desire curling up within me dance happily. He captures my mouth again and his tongue plays with mine. I reach down to caress the hardness pressing against his jeans. This is going to be a lot of fun! I slide my back away from the wall and we start to walk backwards blindly, still kissing and touching each other as I guide him through the doorway of my bedroom.

He strips off his shirt to reveal the most beautifully carved abs I have seen in a long time. Trying not to drool at his physique, I rake my fingernails down his chest, admiring the contour of his muscles as I go all the way to the top of his jeans. "Oh my God, you've got amazing nails!" He closes his eyes in pleasure, enjoying every moment.

He groans as I undo the button and lower his zip to slide his jeans down to his ankles, kneeling in front of him as I do so. This puts me at eye level with what I wanted to see, and, holy shit, he looks amazing! Now I just hope he knows what to do with that appendage as well ... Mwaaahahaahaaahahaaa!

He pulls me back up and in a smooth motion pushes me back onto the bed while stepping out of the rest of his clothes, stretching his body out beside me. We take our time exploring each other's bodies. A sigh of pleasure escapes me as he bites the back of my neck, managing to hit the exact spot to turn me on.

"I'm going to enjoy every minute of this, sexy woman!" he whispers, tickling my ear with his hot breath, making me agree with his statement wholeheartedly!

A couple of hours later, we both need rehydration considering the amount of sweat we worked up. Once dressed and decent again, we collapse on the lounge with our drinks in hand, both gulping the refreshing water down. After a refill and an easy chat for a while, Darz finishes his drink and turns to me.

"Well, that was damn amazing Arleia! I could get used to much more of this kind of fun with you in the future!"

"I agree with you Darz, you are pretty damn hot and sexy! Hmm, you may even qualify for another invitation to my lair." I can't help but tease him.

"I hope so!" he retorts in mock anger, grabbing me in a huge bear hug and spinning me around before capturing my lips in a delicious goodbye kiss.

As we walk towards the front door, I stifle a groan at the stiffness in my legs. I'm not used to bending in those directions for such a length of time! Darz beams at me as he steps out the door with a promise to talk soon. As I lock the door behind him, I do a little victory dance before almost skipping down the hallway in satisfied glee.

I am so excited that I chose such a perfect Mark, resulting in a fantastic night of frivolity, flirting and of course, fulfilment! Ohhhh yes. I'm liking this lifestyle ... possibly even a little too much? To be a Vixen is intoxicating and empowering, as has been a damn enjoyable experience so far! I wonder where the practice of Vixendom will take me next?

I chuckle when I realize that I have the answer already. It is only a few days away from Krystian's' birthday, and something special is going to be in order for his birthday celebration—distinctively Vixenish of course!

Adventure Vixen

Birthday Surprise

Finally, I awake to a leisurely Sunday morning without a screeching alarm to startle me out of sleep. I smile and turn over, snuggling deeper into my quilt. Perhaps I could stay here all day? Pondering the thought behind closed eyelids, I decide it is a pretty good idea. The rain pelting down outside and the gloominess of the day help me to plan my day's activities. It would be silly not to eat breakfast in bed today, because the sheets need washing anyway.

My breakfast made, I transport the feast to the bedroom, along with my laptop and phone, just in case! I make it back to my cosy cocoon while my bed is still warm. Krystian pops into my mind, and I start to ponder what would be an appropriate birthday surprise. A card?

Perhaps flowers or chocolates? A bottle of alcohol? Boy, this may be harder than I thought!

We've seen each other a few times now and I enjoy his company. A gift seems too much, whereas nothing at all is plain rude. An alternative plan seeps into my mind, and as the idea takes the shape of a lingerie and overcoat visit, I can't help but clap my hands and do my wicked Vixen chortle with glee. He would love it! I pat myself on the back for coming up with such a brilliant plan that will be both unique and challenging.

A couple of weeks ago I browsed online for some new luscious lingerie, and next thing I knew, I had chosen ten different items from the website! They all arrived this week, perfect timing for what I have in mind.

Krystian is going to love me turning up in one of these outfits—concealed only by a long red overcoat. Teamed with gartered stockings and long black high heeled boots, he will think all his birthdays have come at once!

A momentary pang of uncertainty makes me wonder if I can pull this off. Do I possess the confidence to wear this stuff and leave the house in such an outfit? Holy crap, what if I was pulled over by the police? What the hell, I draw on my growing internal bravery. I've got this. You only live once, right? A thrill of excitement at the thought courses through me. I *can* do this, and I will do it with all the sexiness a Vixen possesses!

I examine my lacy purchases, trying to pick which style would work best. I choose the most flattering outfit of a sheer black lace baby doll with a tummy flattening area of satin, trimmed with red ribbon with garters attached to the laced bottom edge. The simpler the better; or I may take all day to contort myself into a complicated lingerie ensemble.

I am pretty sure of my choice, but I will need to try the items on with the stockings, jacket and boots first to find out whether I can really transform myself into a sexy playful siren for the entire night. I feel as if I am preparing to act in a play I designed in my head.

To pull this off with confidence will take quite a lot of effort and organisation, but the thought of fulfilling this fantasy I'm sure Krystian would have is too appealing and exciting to give up. What guy doesn't fantasise about being surprised by a sexy woman dressed in only lingerie and a trench coat?

"Krystian has no idea what he's in for!" I laugh when I realize that I am now both talking and laughing to myself, which would look insane to any casual observer.

After a few lazy hours of scrolling through the supermarket of lust, I decide that I should strip the sheets, and then start my preparations for the surprise birthday present by trying on each outfit. I try the chemise with the boots, stockings and long coat, teamed with cheeky crotchless knickers to complete the ensemble. After a considerable effort, I get my stockings straight and my breasts to sit in the right position without falling out. I am ready to peruse myself in the mirror.

Holy shit! Is that me? I stare back in surprise and wonder if that sexy woman looking back in the reflection is really me. Maybe I *can* pull this off! I should have bought more of this stuff years ago.

The longer I stare at the image in front of me, the sexier I feel. Turning to check myself out from all different angles, I conclude that I don't look half bad at all ... damn good in fact. Well, if everything stays where it's supposed to be, this plan of mine might work!

I practise a couple of smouldering come hither glances in the mirror before dissolving into fits of laughter at my silliness. I must remember not to stare into any mirror when I am giving that expression to any guy, or the sexiness I'm aiming for will be smashed to smithereens! A quick practise session walking in the outfit and boots around the house, convinces me that everything should stay in place as I intended, and I'm satisfied.

Time flies by and I am surprised at how long trying on my lingerie selections takes! Note to self: for future lingerie wearing occasions leave copious amounts of time for leisurely dressing. After losing my balance and falling on the ground in a twisted mess twice, I realise that contorting myself into these crisscrossed, shoe stringy, confusing straps of lace magically sewn together is not all that easy.

Amazingly, these scraps of material are transformed into sexy clothing that can be for a dual purpose. They can look so attractive on a woman's body to enhance her best features, *and* they can be used to disguise the less than perfect bits we all hate.

After all, what normal red-blooded guy is not turned on more by legs clad in fishnets or thigh-high sheer black stockings, than pale naked wobbly thighs? For me it is a confidence booster and wearing this type of camouflage over my rounded belly makes me feel sexier even before I finish getting dressed. A woman with beautiful lingerie is a real novelty or even a hot fantasy for a man. For a small cash investment, the benefits can be huge—a win/win situation for all.

However, I am glad I shopped around first before making a purchase—I found a massive difference in both quality and price on the different sites. I didn't want to spend a fortune, but I also hope to get at least a few wears out of each outfit before they disintegrate!

When shopping in the online lingerie world, you don't want to buy pricey garments until you know what you like. Once you do collect a few items, you can surprise your Marks with seductive lingerie that will blow their minds. A man who catches a glimpse of lace under a woman's clothes can't help but wonder what else we might hiding beneath.

The days fly by and soon it is the evening of Krystian's' birthday. I hurriedly strip and jump through the shower, mindful of the task ahead. With a deep breath I start the contortionist act of trying to stuff myself back into the super-hot get-up I chose for this night. This time I'm prepared for the length of time it takes to get dressed. No wonder this kind of outfit is a special occasion type of thing!

After spending so much time getting the lacy scraps untwisted and the sheer hosiery on straight without putting a run in them, then twisting around blindly trying to do the garter belt up at the back of the stockings, and adjusting all my bits into the right place, I am exhausted.

Men do not realize how much of a process this all is for us women—and I still need my hair and make-up transformed into a matching sexy style too. I admit to myself as I finish my ensemble with a spritz of perfume, that this was a lot of fun. I feel like an inexperienced actress preparing for an unfamiliar role. I am dressed for the part, but with no idea how the play will turn out yet. I glance over at the Book on my bed. Its golden glow reassures me, giving me the confidence boost I need to embark on this new adventure.

As I step out the door an icy cold blast of wind hits me, and I shiver in surprise. Hmmm, I forgot the strength of the winter chill and decide to grab a scarf for warmth. I wrap the woolly scarf tightly around my neck as I run to the car and quickly set the heater to full blast.

Glad of an uneventful drive to a Krystian's, I can't help but smile at what I am about to do. I don my sultry smouldering smile, or so I hope, and step out into the cold. A bit nervous, I check that every strap and lacy ruffle is in the right place before knocking.

The door swings open a moment later and his welcoming greeting reverberates around the hallway as he sweeps me into his arms, twirling me around in a bear hug with a smile.

"Well hello, Master Krystian, and a very happy birthday to you!"

He smiles in thanks, then further comprehension dawns as he does a comical double take. Holding me back at arm's length, his eyes travel down my body, taking in everything I am wearing for the first time.

"Oh my God Arleia, you are one sexy woman!" He captures one end of my scarf, sliding the warmth away from my neck. His eyes are fixed on my cleavage as he traces a finger down my jawline and down to the top button of my coat.

"Just what are you are wearing underneath your long jacket, Missy?"

He unbuttons the first, then second button, pushing the coat aside to catch a glimpse of what I'm hiding beneath. I see the desire in his eyes as he smiles, impressed with what he is unwrapping.

"Woman, you are going to give me a heart attack!" I giggle as he gets closer and try not to show that all the attention is making me nervous and shy.

"Well, I wanted to give you something unique and different for your birthday, and what better gift to give than myself wrapped in provocative lingerie to surprise you?" His eyes light up in appreciation and anticipation as I complete the task of unbuttoning the rest of my coat. His smile looks as if he has been presented with his favourite meal.

"Turn around, sexy lady!" he commands in a low voice.

I drop the jacket and step forward to spin around, like a delectable dessert on a rotating plate, being admired from all angles before being devoured. A growl springs from his throat behind me as he roughly draws me back against his chest, reaching around to cup my breast in his hand, while his other hand slides over my butt, squeezing and caressing my cheek.

"Mmm, I hope this means you do like your birthday surprise then, Krystian?" I venture to ask breathily as I arch back against him. His fingers find my hard nipple and gives it a playful twist.

"Oh man, Arleia ... Yes! This is the best birthday present I have ever gotten!"

I smile in satisfaction—his answer is what I'd been hoping for.

"Mmm, delicious." He murmurs against my cheek, his breath on my ear giving me goose bumps.

"I think you need to be taken into my office and unwrapped in entirety, Miss Arleia!"

He tightens his hold on me, snaking his arm around my waist and propelling me forward down the hallway and into his bedroom. A couple of candles with flames twinkling are placed along the windowsill, and I am pleased to note his thoughtfulness.

"You know, the best thing about this kind of wrapping is that you don't even need to take it off to enjoy your present." I smile seductively at him; powerful and strong, enjoying every minute of this impromptu play so far. He pushes me back to his bed and follows in an instant. For a moment I can smell the vanilla scent of the candles burning before his lips swoop down to capture mine.

I slide my hands down his now bare chest and across his jeans, stopping at his hardness pressed against the denim. He strokes his hand along my thigh heading upwards, to exactly where I want his fingers.

When he realizes the underwear I am wearing is crotchless, he lets out a groan of desire, and grows even harder, almost peeking out from the top of his jeans. My body responds instantly. When he slides a finger to the exact position where I want it to be and pinches my nipple hard, I groan in satisfaction.

Impatient now, my fingers fumble with his zip to remove the clothing barrier between them and his flesh. I yank his jeans down as far as I can reach and squeeze his butt cheeks as he expertly flicks his thumb over me making me want more of him. His shaft grasped firmly, I circle my fingers over the damp head, spreading the moisture over the whole head and around the rim. He moans in pleasure.

I become aware of my hips lifting towards him like they'd grown a mind of their own, and I want more than just his touch. I want him buried deep inside of me. He growls in agreement and takes care of protection before plunging himself into my centre. We both groan in pleasure at the act. Oh God ... Yessss! That is what I was waiting for.

"Damn, you feel so good Krystian!" The words can barely form between the mind-drugging kisses and thrusts.

"God, you are such a sexy woman Arleia ... Fuuuccckkk!"

I grin, feeling even sexier with his words, as he changes positions and flips me over on my knees to drive hard and deep into me from behind until we both come together amid cries of satisfied release.

The pounding of my heart slowly subsides as we lie snuggled into each other's warm bodies, returning to earth and reality. Krystian offers to go and fetch me a drink. I can't lift even a finger after our workout! He grins as he passes me a large glass of water which I gulp down in one breath.

Holy crap, that was great! I lie back on the bed still exhausted from our efforts. An errant bead of sweat trickles down my forehead and I giggle to myself, thinking that this must have used up a good few hundred calories—how many have I burnt off now for the week? With every other type of exercise I tried before, I find myself counting the seconds until the slow form of torture is over, but with this type of workout the minutes fly by—by far the most enjoyable exercise I've ever found. When the session ends, I want to repeat the experience again as soon as possible.

"Now that was awesome, Master Krystian!"

"Miss Arleia, you continue to delight and amaze me. I do mean it when I say you have given me the best birthday present I have ever received in my life!"

He slaps my arse with gentle affection. I'm elated that my plan worked out so well. An unexpected wave of tiredness sweeps over me, making me realize how late the evening had gotten, and that I should leave now. Krystian starts work early in the mornings, so I know he will be fine with me leaving soon. In fact, I never stay the entire night at a guy's place.

I prefer waking up in my own comfortable bed alone to avoid the awkwardness and expectations of the morning after. If I start the habit of staying overnight, I am in danger of slipping into the relationship zone by mistake. This is something a Vixen must avoid at all costs! Until I make the decision that I do want to sail back into relationship land, I don't want to find myself blown into that outcrop of dangerous rocks by accident.

I won't allow myself to become caught in the trap of expectations, rules and emotional vulnerability unless I choose to: when and IF I am ever ready. According to the Book, a Vixen is free to date any and as many Marks as she chooses, but overstaying welcomes can be the first step on a slide down to the dark side. It is easy to fall almost by accident into a relationship without realizing what is happening sometimes! A sleepover night on occasion becomes more frequent-after a few too many drinks, not wanting to drive home as a responsible adult. The next thing you know, every Sunday morning you're awakening to see the same face.

Of course, this scenario is fine if I consciously recognise that this is what I want. In the past I have fallen into relationships with men I think I can change. They have a few things I don't like about them, but on the whole they are nice guys. I tell myself that I 'can't have everything', that I am lucky to find such a reasonable catch or that, at least, being with him is far better than being alone.

I love my own company, to be honest. I can be alone but not feel lonely. Many women I know who are in committed relationships are lonelier than me! If I find a little loneliness creeping in, I always have a friend I can call, meet or message. Or I can call my plethora of

Marks—a few of whom are fast becoming friends as well as fun in bed.

"OK! I must be going, Master Krystian!" I regret having to move as soon as I swing my legs to the side of the bed and stand up, wavering slightly. Oh! Stiffness in my thighs; it was a good workout! He springs off the bed and accompanies me down the hallway, retrieving my scarf and coat for me. He wraps me into my coat, even buttoning a few buttons for me to my amusement while I'm donning my scarf in preparation for the cold again.

"Again, the best surprise ever, Miss Arleia, thank you!"

"Oh, the pleasure is all mine!"

I flick my tongue out at him and step towards the door as he caresses, then slaps my butt. He leans in to give me a final, hot, lingering kiss and a last bone crushing bear hug before he releases me to the warmth of my car.

"Drive carefully!" He calls as I speed off, eager to get home.

Damn. I realize I am still super thirsty. I sure as hell am not getting out of the car, so stopping at a shop is right out of the question. I can, however, go through the drive through section of a fast food restaurant and grab a drink. I glance down to ensure that I appear respectable enough to not engage a pimply teenage boy's attention at the counter as I wait for my Coke in the warmth of my car.

Oops! Half a breast is showing and some black lace—that won't do! Adjusting my scarf to protect my modesty, I'm able to cruise through the drive-through without raising any suspicion. Phew ... I got away with the lingerie fast food adventure too! I giggle to myself as I drive home, with thoughts of the evening filling my mind.

This was the most enjoyable night ever! It is going to be a long time until the smile of satisfaction is wiped from my face, as well as the heady, powerful feeling of being sexy and in control.

Oh, how I love the Vixen life!

Correct Vixen Attire

Sexy lingerie ahoy! A Vixen is prepared for any occasion with a plethora of cute and sexy, lacy lovelies to choose to wear under her regular attire. Her collection may include the following:

✓ Chemises and baby dolls (floaty and sexy to entice your lover to bed)

✓ Corsets (excellent for flattening a tummy and gaining more curves)

✓ Crotchless underwear (perfect for naughty outings or a sneaky surprise for your Mark)

✓ Cheeky lace boy shorts (to show off the curve of your butt and keep the tummy in)

✓ Garter belt (hot fishnets or for smooth sexy and silky feeling legs)

✓ Crotchless stockings to slip over the matching lacy knickers men love this tease and access surprise)

✓ A long trench coat style jacket (for the lingerie under jacket treat)

✓   Maid or Schoolgirl outfit (costumes for fantasy play fun)

✓   Short ruffled tulle skirts to team with corsets and stockings (more exciting with an entire outfit)

✓   Anything that makes you feel like a sexy woman!

It is wise to shop around and look for bargains, especially if you have the power to drive men wild—there may be some tearing of lacy bits in the passion of the moment, and you don't want to present them with a massive lingerie replacement bill! Look online and measure yourself carefully. Be cautious in buying from new sites until you know if their sizing is true. This can save you a lot of time and money in the long run.

Adventure Vixen

Mark Overdose

Another week flies by faster than usual. I'm getting so many messages every day that I find keeping up difficult. Not that I am complaining, mind you, its bloody fantastic! The excellent thing about seeing several guys at once is that you don't even notice or care if you don't hear from one of them in a couple of days.

If I am only dating one guy, forty-eight hours without contact can seem like an eternity. Without warning, crazy obsessive thoughts sneak into my mind and swirl around until I can't help it and I send three text messages to his one, and then beat myself up for being so needy and not waiting for him to answer first. The balance is upset, and I become the chaser rather than the hunted. Note I did not say that I become the hunter. A hunter is a methodical stalker of his prey, whereas a chaser is forever trying to catch someone who is often out of reach.

Oh yes, more thrill in being the hunter than the chaser, I say. I flick through my messages to ensure I respond to each of them. The only potential problem with seeing several Marks at a time is getting them confused with each other. This is something I want to avoid at all costs! Nothing more ego deflating when a guy realizes I called him by the wrong name. A slip of the tongue can be embarrassing when I mix up their occupations or double book an evening and can't remember what I said to which Mark. Although my Marks all know about each other's existence, I prefer to avoid confusing them! Thank god the Book has a solution.

I come to the decision that I need to update and refine my spreadsheet. The essential information compiled about each Mark, including a picture creates the perfect record of current Marks. In fact, every man I meet gets a mention on the spreadsheet—even if it was a disaster date!

Imagine receiving a message from a dude you've not seen or heard from in months. With only a vague recollection of him, but not much more than you might chance another meeting. Ten-minutes into the date you then remember why you didn't pursue him and forgot to text him back months ago. This can result in a wasted evening, or even worse, him thinking you harbour a revived interest in him. Stilted conversation and awkward silences may result, with you wishing you had remembered what a loser he was before making another date with him.

The well-maintained Vixen's 'Mark summary spreadsheet' cures the problem forever! Quick as a flash I can check my summary to refresh my memory on any man I've previously met, and instantly access correct data to help me decide whether I will say yes or no to the request. A time saver, and excellent comparison chart, the Book says an up to date spreadsheet is my best friend.

Vixens who don't follow this rule must again endure the forgotten 'octopus hands man' with an amazing ability to pass his hands through several layers of clothing to your bare skin with no problems, or the work obsessed, boring man with nothing better to talk about than work or his massive movie collection, comprised almost entirely of porn.

Perhaps it is the Mark who is entertaining, but the worst kisser in the world you again end up on a date with. A river of saliva flowing into your mouth as he thrusts his entire tongue in and begins cleaning your teeth with enthusiasm while you try to escape, finishing with a swipe of his dirty hand across his mouth and down his jeans.

A well maintained spreadsheet would have saved me from wasting my precious time with several undesirable Marks in the past. This time, I have been quite lucky. I consider my impressive collection on my list. With one bad experience thus far, and another avoided with the tongue-rimming lover I didn't bother meeting, I can't complain. There are no names I would be unhappy to see pop up on my phone (except Mitch's). Not a bad effort. Three regulars established in a few short months! I can't believe they are all awesome guys who meet the criteria and passed the initial tests, which can be hard to do.

I wonder how many Marks I can date at a time? Don't think I am being greedy—I am still following the Vixen code of telling each Mark that he is not the only guy I see, and its fine with me if he is doing the same, but he needs to be honest about dating other women with me. Knowing that they are dating others reassures me that we are on the same wavelength. I don't want them to fall head over heels for me and declare their undying love!

More disappointing would be them thinking that they need to lie to me about seeing other women, to keep me ignorant and happy because of society's beliefs, traditions or fear of reprisal. I don't want intimate details of their sex life—in fact, if they did share too much information about another woman, I would wonder what they are telling others about me! Also, I do not give out in depth information of my adventures to my other Marks.

I might, however, share an amusing story with them using total anonymity just because we all appreciate a little humorous voyeurism at times. Mwaaahaaahaaahaha!

The single 'NO' out of my list is a testament to how well the assessments work—a damn good average. To be fair to myself, I was only at the beginning of my adventures when I was fooled by a picture taken over fifteen years ago ... I've learnt a lot since then!

At this point I should have realized that pride comes before a fall. My time would be better spent reading the glowing Vixen Handbook over and over until the lessons are seared in my brain like a tattoo. I am too busy congratulating myself on my success to realise that one potential Mark has still not shown me his entire face. This could become a costly mistake. Why do my ears ignore my internal warning signal, but I can always hear the trill of my phone announcing a new message? I've no trouble listening to a friend, or paying attention in a movie, but when it comes to listening to internal guidance from my soul, I become inattentive at times. I always ask for guidance from the universe; so why do I forget to listen for the answer?

My phone's message melody pierces my bubble of thought with three new message alerts. I hate not knowing, so I snatch up the device to discover who they are from. Ahhhh, two from the delightful Krystian, and one from the mysterious Sean saying that he loved meeting me and wishing me an awesome day.

Staring at the texts, I'm conflicted. What should I do about him? Do I even want to travel down a scary, unknown path? I had an enjoyable date with Sean, and there's something about him I like. The conversation was fascinating at times, piquing my Vixen curiosity almost against my will. I'm fascinated with the idea of bondage but am experiencing trepidation about getting more involved.

Knowing that the question is not answerable yet, I put the subject in the 'too hard' basket and turn my attention to easier things—like the two messages waiting for me from Krystian.

A giggle erupts as I read them, noticing his particularly terrible spelling. He's proposing another date to the movies this week, and sends me a link for session times at the cinema near his house. So thoughtful of him! Just as I am replying to him, another message flashes across my phone from Darz. I abandon my reply to Krystian in favour of reading Darz's text, when yet another tone sounds, and Roshan's name replaces Darz's message!

What would the chances of that happening be? I can't believe four different guys all decided to communicate with me in the space of only a few minutes! What a coincidence. Especially as the radio then helpfully informs me that today is Coincidence Wednesday. How bizarre. What do these synchronicities mean? Many say that, if many coincidences or synchronicities are happening in your life, then they are signs you're on the right path. I laugh at my internal musings.

My mind wanders back to the matter of whether I will see Sean again or not. I do already possess a good stash of sexy Marks who are easy and do not require research. Perhaps for now I will concentrate on the light-hearted adventures I am enjoying with these regular guys, rather than delving into an unknown specialty area. I would rather add a couple more to my spreadsheet who are fun, instead of pursuing a research project!

I drag my mind back to my surroundings, almost surprised to find myself at my work desk. Half the office is away from work sick with the flu, so no-one has realised I was daydreaming for a good part of the last two hours! Feeling guilty for being so slack still does not stop me from replying to the text messages first. I then put my phone on silent and slide the distraction into a drawer and out of sight.

By concentrating my focus on work instead of men, the week passes a lot faster than I expected. By the end of the day on Friday I have caught up on everything and even gotten a little ahead with my work. I decide that I can afford a little indulgent shopping in the supermarket of lust.

I stop at a real grocery shop on the way home for a few staples. As I leave the store, I wonder what or *who* I will find online that might capture my attention tonight.

Adventure Vixen

Brazilian Bombardment

My bottom does not even hit the seat in front of my computer before several new messages flash across the screen from my addictive sexy smorgasbord site demanding my attention. I don't know which one to read first, but this time Pedro, the sultry sounding Brazilian, is the winner.

He tells me that he is coming to Sydney for business in a couple of weeks and that he wants to take me out for lunch or dinner. I skim over our previous conversations to remind myself what we talked about and bring up his profile for further scrutiny.

He describes himself as athletic, classy and well-travelled. He's only written a short blurb, but it's descriptive and appealing. His ideal partner must be 'honest, beautiful and self-aware.'

This sentence describes me, so there's a possibility at least! I scroll down the rest of Pedro's profile to remind myself of his attributes before I reply.

He is twenty-seven, single, rarely drinks, doesn't smoke and has a star sign of Aries. My attention is drawn back to his profile. I note that he does not want children, holds a master's degree and works in the banking and finance sector. Interestingly he says that appearance is important, and rates himself as being quite attractive. I wonder why he's got such a pathetic picture on this site. I'd love the reason to be that he is so attractive that, should he show a good photo of himself, he would be inundated with women throwing themselves at him. However, previous experience tells me this is not often the case!

If men show only blurred pictures, or ones where the flash of their phone in the mirror almost entirely obscures their faces, I tend to wonder what they are hiding. Honestly, how hard can it be these days to take a reasonable selfie with the amazing technology available?

Women will take another one hundred and fifty-three if the first selfie is not good enough. Why do men think women will be happy to accept an unfocused image from afar after we invest hours of posing to obtain the perfect picture to post? I skim over the last of Pedro's profile. His description of brown eyes, black hair and a muscular build gets my seal of approval—he also meets my minimum height requirement at 5ft 11". Perhaps I will meet with him when he comes over here. I do a quick glance at the other messages waiting for me before I reply to him.

Woahh! What the heck? What sort of message is this? All thoughts of the Brazilian flee from my mind as I read the message from someone I've not yet conversed with.

Luke03: Hello gorgeous, how are you? My name is Luke, I own a property development company. In July I'm attending a meeting on Hamilton Island to do a presentation on a proposed development of 6 high-end units and a penthouse. Would you come as my pretend gf for $10, 000 cash paid 2 weeks before the trip in person, plus spoiling?

Is he serious? A ten-thousand dollar offer from an unknown person *must* be bullshit! No-one would believe anyone would write this as a serious first message to a stranger. I need to check his profile and discover who sent this. To my surprise there is almost no information on his page, apart from the fact that he is thirty-one with blue eyes and brown hair, is 5ft 10" and resides on the Gold Coast in Queensland. How the hell did he make it onto my contact list? He doesn't even have a picture visible— only a private one. Perhaps I accidently added him in a daze of tired inattentiveness or something? I am curious and reply.

ATrixenVixen: Hi Luke ... very weird first message. Are you serious? And why? How many chicks did you sent this message to? Lol

I wonder if he is online now, and what sort of guy needs to pay for a pretend girlfriend. It's got to be a joke. I'm pretty sure things like this only happen in movies! With no immediate reply, I pull a dissatisfied face.

Instead of wasting my time on questions with no answers, I turn my attention back to Pedro, and my reply to him, telling him I may be interested in meeting him when he is here for business. His "Helloooo my sexy Kit-e-cat!" is almost instant, bringing a smile to my face.

After a few minutes of small talk, I steer the conversation to regular topics to find out what kind of person he is underneath the smooth lines. For every serious question I can come up with, he replies with something bizarre and unexpected. When I ask where he lives, his reply stumps me.

"I live in a dungeon where I entice sexy women who innocently walk by into my den."

Ermmm ... What? That isn't quite what I expected as an answer. I change tack and enquire as to what made him choose to move to Australia from Brazil.

"I heard that an amazingly stunning blonde woman is living in Sydney, so I was compelled to come here for you."

His answers are funny but unbalancing. Why is he being amusing and evasive, rather than straightforward and honest? He works in the banking and finance sector, so for a safe easy answer I ask about his work at the bank.

"Well I am an extremely clever bank robber, baby. They never suspect it is me under the balaclava. But now that I told you this, I will have to kill you."

Yikes! Hopefully this is just his sense of humour and nothing else. I'm used to having an instant response form in my mind—but nothing is coming so I instead laugh off his reply and ask another question. I know he reads a lot, so I enquire as to what he was reading earlier. By now I'm expecting a ridiculous and funny or weird answer, so this doesn't surprise me.

"Reading? Oh no, baby. I am writing my book on methods to kill sexy blonde Sydney girls who know too much!"

Laughingly, I suggest he send me a signed copy and an invite to the book's launch, but I notice that again he doesn't tell me anything about himself. I try to extract a straight answer with my next attempt, to find out what kind of movies he likes.

"All types of movies, Kit-e-cat ... but not gory ones, no. That does not matter though, baby girl. I will not be paying the slightest bit of attention to the movie as I trace my fingers along the soft pale skin of your inner thigh."

I give up my questioning with a laugh, noticing he seems to spout the famed smooth flirty reputation of Brazilians. Perhaps he is interesting enough to meet.

Pedro again messages me, asking for my number as he can no longer stand not knowing what my voice sounds like. Admittedly, I am curious as to what his would sound like too, so I agree, and before I can even refill my drink my phone starts ringing, showing an unfamiliar caller.

I answer and listen to the voice on the other end of the phone. A deep richness seems to ooze from the hand piece like delicious melted chocolate on your lips which makes you want to lick them. Holy crap, this guy has the sexiest voice and accent I've ever heard! He may bring me to orgasm by reading even an innocuous recipe, let alone if he described what he would love to do to a woman. I'm mesmerised , but unsure if this is from the wine I have consumed, or from the voice pouring into my ear.

Abort, abort! Danger Will Robinson! Danger! My weird internal system shouts louder than his smooth hypnotic voice and I shut down the conversation, extracting myself from his irresistible chocolaty tendrils drawing me in to him. My interest in going back online is gone now, so I head to bed. The deep voice with its seductive accent reverberates around my head as I fall asleep.

The next few days a barrage of calls and messages from the Brazilian ensue, and I find hardly any time to keep up with my other Marks in between, though I am looking out for an answer from the mysterious Luke and his crazy offer. I awake to an early reply from Luke that leaves me even more puzzled.

Luke03: Good morning ... yes I am serious. For company ... I asked 2 girls ... you and another.

Aha! How many other girls has he truly sent this to? Probably two hundred! I wonder how far he will take this, and how many girls would consider this if his is a serious offer. What would this entail? Would he be expecting sex? Wouldn't it be like prostitution if you took him up on his offer? I am going to need to view a picture of this guy, so I can obtain more clues as to why he needs a pretend girlfriend.

I reply with a request for a photo and asking where the other girl is from, because I am curious to find out why he did not choose girls who at least lived in the same state as he did. Wouldn't he want to avoid the cost of the flight as well as the ten-thousand dollars he is offering as payment?

I can't help but wonder if he is genuine and what sort of person puts out this kind of offer. I'm eager to talk to the Brazilian too to find out what else I can learn about him. My curiosity about Pedro is distracting me from my other Marks, and we've not even met yet. *A warning sign that I perhaps should be paying more attention to.*

Right on cue a message pops up on my phone from Pedro, and I can't help but smile at his compliments and foreign turns of phrase. With no time to send my reply, he calls me. His warm voice washes over me in his typical over the top greeting.

"At last baby girl, I have you all to myself!" My hello is a little more reserved, but he soon coaxes a grin from me, and the mesmerising pull of his voice is drawing me into his world. Aloud I wonder if he is really only twenty-seven.

"But of course I am twenty-seven baby, there is no need to lie to you."

Normally I wouldn't let a potential Mark get away with calling me 'baby' and certainly not 'baby girl', but the endearment sounds so good in his accent that I can't help but let it slide in his case. Oh dear. Another mistake is brewing. How can this voice possess the power to make me forget the Vixen rules? I fight for clarity within as the delicious chocolatey voice again speaks:

"You make my teeth ache to nibble you all over ... there is no need to worry baby, I am coming for you!" Yikes! That jolts me out of my dreamy dessert delusion and makes me pay attention.

"What? I mean, uhmm ... when are you coming to Sydney?" Almost incoherently stammering in reply, I manage to bang my knee on the dining room chair. Yeowch!

"I have business in Sydney in two weeks' time, Kit-e-cat. Ahhhh ... those eyes of yours baby, a man can drown in them. You are so delicious I want to eat you all up! You may run, but you cannot hide. I will come after you like a cheetah hunts a gazelle ... I shall make you purr all night, and you will scream my name."

Holy crap! What man says things like this? For the first time in my life I can think of no reply and just giggle like an idiot. What the hell is going on here? I'm going to need to end this conversation to regain my equilibrium.

I hastily make an excuse to extract me from his addictive words and compliments and end the phone call. Hot, flustered and in need of a fan, I sink down into a nearby chair to review the conversation. The weekend he is talking about is not far away! I waver between being excited to meet him ... and hearing that protective voice in the back of my head yelling at me to beware.

Finally good sense wins—I am going to demand another photo. This is the Vixen way. No matter how delicious a Mark's voice sounds, you still never know until you are face to face. At least I will have the opportunity to find out sooner rather than later, which is an excellent thing—and he is coming here, which is perfect. I'm glad he is coming for business and not to specifically meet me. That would be too much pressure for a first meeting!

I don't want to drown in the Brazilian's mesmerising voice and accent! I resolve to be more conscious and re-read my Vixen's handbook to regain my mental calm. He can't be as good as he sounds. There's got to be a catch, I just don't know what the catch is yet.

I sigh loudly, wishing the days away until he is due to arrive, so that I can discover once and for all if he is a keeper ... or a stinky blow fish to throw straight back into the sea. Only time will tell.

Immediate Endearment Test

When a Mark addresses you in an overly familiar way before meeting him there is cause for concern. This shows a lack of respect and appreciation of you being a strong powerful woman. When the Mark cannot be corrected in his endearment use, he will immediately fail this test. He is not worthy of a Vixens' attention.

Unacceptable Terms of Endearment:

- ✕ Honey/Hun
- ✕ Darling/Darl
- ✕ Baby/Babe
- ✕ Baby-cakes or doll
- ✕ Dear
- ✕ Hot chick
- ✕ Sexy tits
- ✕ Sweetie
- ✕ Cup-cake
- ✕ Honeybun
- ✕ Hottie
- ✕ Pookie
- ✕ Sugar
- ✕ Sweetie-pie

Acceptable Terms of Endearment:

- ✓ Beautiful or gorgeous
- ✓ Sexy woman
- ✓ Temptress or mistress
- ✓ Vixen

Adventure Vixen

More Money Honey

Time flies toward the impending meeting with Pedro, and I have taken to not answering all his calls, simply because he can talk for hours, and I am busy with my other established Marks. I don't want to neglect them for a guy I've not met, especially one who is resistant to my requests for pictures of his face. He did send me a couple of shots, but again his face was obscured, or he was wearing sunglasses. I still don't really know what he looks like.

If someone misrepresents himself in a picture to hide something, what could he be hiding? Should we girls be more wary and cautious in believing anything a man says on the lie of a single blurry photograph? My answer is yes.

An email notification informs me Luke has replied to me, interrupting my train of thought. Did he attach a picture for me to view? Grabbing my phone, I log in to discover what he's got to say, but more to check out the important attachment I am hoping is there.

Luke03: Closer to me. Why do u ask?

My eyes light up when I see access is granted to his hidden picture, and I brace myself for the unknown as I click the attachment open. Holy crap, he's not what I'd ever go for! My eyes water in protection to shield me from the vision, but I gather my strength, blinking the moisture away to inspect the photo a little closer. I study his image for a long time. Then I look deeper and take in the person behind the outer shell of a man who is desperate enough to approach a stranger with an outlandish proposal.

Luke is a rosy-cheeked, chubby nerd with little sense of style or fashion. He is wearing an ill-fitting blue and white striped business shirt and baggy pants. I feel quite a bit of compassion for him, poor guy. I can see a skerrick of sadness behind the bespectacled eyes. Now I can understand why he would need to hire a pretend girlfriend. His expression doesn't look like he possesses the confidence to even approach an average looking girl in person to say hello, let alone convince her to go out with him. I punch out a reply.

ATrixenVixen: I don't know ... Your request is unusual. Do not know why I thought it would be easier to ask someone closer to you ... It's my naturally suspicious nature! Lol! What do you expect of the person who agrees to your proposal? Also, how many days are you talking about?

Wanting to delve into his mind, I can't help my curiosity at the odd conversation and offer.

Luke03: For 2 nights ... public gf for 10k. Will go up if ur open to more.

What? I re-read his message again. He does seem serious about ten-thousand dollars for an actress girlfriend with *no* funny business at all. How bizarre! Open to more? More cash for sex with him makes me shudder in distaste. I can't help but wonder how much he is willing to pay someone for the full girlfriend experience. For sure I can't do it; no matter how much money is changing hands, or how much alcohol I consume! There is no need to be mean to the unfortunate Luke, though. I feel sorry for him. If he is stuck with no other option available, I would consider granting him the favour of being his pretend girlfriend for a weekend away in the tropics.

Wait, what? Am I considering doing this for real? Perhaps I need more wine. Or less? Surely it's not going to hurt to agree to the hands-off option, but I instinctively know he would want the full girlfriend option taken, what red-blooded guy wouldn't?

ATrixenVixen: Hmm. Sounds reasonable. And no, I am not open to more, sorry. But I am a very nice, genuine person who is happy to help someone out and am an excellent conversationalist also. So if you need a pretend girlfriend to carry an intelligent conversation with investors, I can talk to anyone and put them at ease.

Luke03: So, is that a yes?

Oh Shit. No. Didn't think that far ahead yet, did I? I'd need a hell of a lot more detail before I can decide on something that big. Now I feel nervous and unprepared!

ATrixenVixen: Uhmm. It's a maybe. What are the sleeping arrangements? Also are the days you require in the week or on a weekend?

Phew, I managed to come up with two reasonable questions from my buzzing brain. What would be a fair answer for ten thousand dollars' worth of work?

Luke03: Weekend. For 10k separate beds. 30k to share

THIRTY-THOUSAND DOLLARS?! My jaw drops open. Is he kidding? The shock of his reply makes my initial annoyance evaporate when I read the end of his message. I didn't expect him to come up with such a large figure for only two nights. Wouldn't he be better off hiring a prostitute instead? Hmm, I'm not aware of what the going rate for a top quality one for a weekend is, but surely not more than thirty-thousand dollars?

For someone who I first thought was only joking, he seems to be ready with his answers. Perhaps he is deadly serious about this idea of his and *does* have some investors he needs to impress. He is probably expecting someone to take him up on his offer of ten thousand but hoping he will find a woman who is willing to engage in sex with him for thirty-grand.

I can't help but shudder a little at the thought. What did he mean regarding separate beds? Did he mean a twin-share room and not separate rooms? I would then want to sleep with one eye open in case he jumps on me in the dead of night while I am sleeping. Yikes!

ATrixenVixen: I'm just thinking of work etc. ... I'd not share rooms though ... doesn't matter how much you paid me ... it's not my style.

Luke03: that's OK :-) Hey, can I get access to your private albums?

I laugh, forgetting he hasn't even seen a second picture of me yet, and surprised that he still wants to bother after I have been so blunt with him. I grant him access to the pictures I keep on private and wait for his response.

Luke03: r u positive we can't share at all?

His flattering response makes me smile, but all requests like this will be firmly denied!

ATrixenVixen: I'm not positive because I haven't met you, but I don't think so ... reeks of prostitution or something.

Luke03: :-(

ATrixenVixen: You can see my point though right?

Luke03: Yes I do.

ATrixenVixen: I don't think I will be comfortable if I agreed to that ... you are offering a lot of money—I know this. But money is not everything ;)

Luke03: I realize that

Awwww, poor guy! Hopefully the other girl is more open to his suggestions of full girlfriend. It sounds like he's in serious need of some female company in the bedroom. He needs to realise no matter how much he offers me, I would still say no.

What would I think if a man I am attracted made the same offer? Would I be tempted to say yes? But would a cute guy even make that kind of offer to a woman? I'm pretty sure he would only need to offer to pay for the flights and accommodation for any female and they would jump at the chance of a free weekend away on a tropical island in a resort.

ATrixenVixen: I'm sure you do ... would you be happy taking someone who does not agree to more than separate beds?

Luke03: Yeh maybe.

ATrixenVixen: Lol ... I understand your point of view too ... if I was you, I'd want to find someone who would agree to the $30K option LOL.

Luke03: r u considering 30 at all?

There's no way in hell I am even considering his offer ... no doubt at all! I can't be so mean as to say this straight out in a raw, honest fashion to him of course, but I am curious as to what activities he is envisioning for the weekend's sex-capades that is worth the hefty reward of thirty-thousand dollars.

ATrixenVixen: I don't know. What exactly do you want for this?

Luke03: Full girlfriend

ATrixenVixen: Obviously. But are you expecting sex once on the weekend? Or once a night — or once an hour?

Bleeeyuuuck! I almost stop breathing imagining his response and shudder in revulsion at the thought of sex every hour for two days with this guy. No amount of money or empathy in the world would find me agreeing to anything like that!

Luke03: Lol. Once or twice depending on what u want. That's over the weekend.

He surprises me by his answer. I thought for sure he would want more than that—I mean for a cool thirty-grand for a full girlfriend experience, I thought he'd say closer to four or five times over the weekend at least. Now I feel even more compassion for the guy. I'm going to let him down with kindness and care.

ATrixenVixen: hmmm. Give me time to think about your offer. It is a serious request to consider. When do you need an answer? Did the other girl you asked agree? You may not even need me! lol

Luke03: Within a few days

ATrixenVixen: OK I will consider and message you back

Luke03: Thanks

I heave a huge sigh of relief now that this bizarre conversation is over. I know the answer I will give, but it seems kinder to make him wait a day and let him think I am taking my time considering his offer. What or how did the other girl's conversation go with him, compared to mine? He is not a thrilling conversationalist, and I wonder how hard the weekend would be in his company if he is a hopeless communicator.

Even though I might be surrounded by beautiful resort gardens, and eating delicious food, if the company is not interesting, the two days may drag on forever! I will wait until the morning before I decline his offer. Maybe I will say yes to the possible ten thousand to make up for the two days of incredible boredom. I couldn't help but tell the girls at work of the bizarre offer during the week, and they are all of differing opinions as to whether I should say yes or not.

I am reminded of the Brazilian by my phone. What is his deal? He is still an enigma to me, and I am nervous about meeting him in person after such a build-up.

It is only days away from Pedro coming over to Sydney now, and he is messaging me several times a day, as well as calling me almost every night. I requested a single photo of his eyes, since the eyes are the window to the soul, but he would not comply with my demand. This makes me even more wary of meeting him. His response to my wish is less than satisfactory, and for the life of me I cannot think of a reply to this: "You can stare deeply into my eyes when they are looking at you from between your thighs, sexy woman! I'm going to make you moan and scream, baby."

Right. What do you say to something like this? Tell him he's dreaming? That seems to work alright with Australian men, but with this Brazilian? His way of speaking sometimes floors me, and his one-liners are endless. He has me in embarrassed fits of laughter with things like this: "I'm going to go all jungle style on you, throw you over my shoulder and spank your bottom while I haul you to my car from the café, Kit-e-cat!"

Or this: "Sexy woman! You have been teasing me all day and your tab is overflowing! Give daddy some sugar, baby girl."

Umm ... I have no idea how he comes up with these things. At first I thought that he is quoting from some sort of 'suave lines' book, but seeing that he's always coming out with so many of them, he could write the book! It is going to be interesting to meet him ... one way or another. I hope he will not be disappointing after sounding so well versed in the art of love ... perhaps I will find out this weekend.

Or maybe not, warns a soft voice in the back of my head. I'm half asleep when the bright red warning glow lights up my entire room. Buried under the covers, I miss it. Instead I spend the night dreaming of a Brazilian man with no face and a chubby, bespectacled geek pawing me with one hand while shoving money at me with the other.

Morning comes to my relief, and I can't wait to send my last message to Luke regarding his offer. I sit in front of the computer for a few moments, deciding on the best way to dash his hopes of any possibility of anything physical between us, paid or otherwise.

ATrixenVixen: Hi Luke. I thought your offer through, and girlfriend would be happy to agree with your first offer of pretend girlfriend for $10,000 but not the offer of full gf for $30,000. Your offer is extremely fair, but I cannot and will not prostitute myself for money. I am happy to help you out by coming along and being the classy type of pretend partner you may need for this presentation, but it's all I can agree to.

Phew, I am glad that's over. I doubt that I will hear from him again, as he wanted more than I can agree to, but I do wish him luck, and hope that he finds some gorgeous woman who is happy to do this for him. I glance at the alarm clock and groan in distaste at the time on the display screen, before springing out of bed in a hurry. In too much of a hurry, I again miss the red warning glow emanating from my bedside drawer.

The next thing I realise is that Friday has arrived. Pedro is coming tomorrow ... holy shit! I'm not sure I'm ready for this meeting, but I will meet him regardless, because I need to satisfy my curiosity. Finally, I will find out what he's hiding.

Adventure Vixen

Biting Brazil Bug

Juggling my keys, handbag and some groceries while opening the door, I manage to carry everything into the house without losing my tight grip on the bags. Once everything is on the counter I sigh in relief, glad that the end of the day is here. Saturday's appointment with the mysterious Brazilian is looming.

Pedro and I agreed on meeting in a cafe attached to the hotel he's staying in, seeing that he is carless. I'm curious enough to pay the ridiculous car-parking prices in the city to go and meet him. His accommodation is on the fringes of the city, which make things easier for parking options, but even if I like him, I don't want to be facing a hundred-dollar parking fee for the privilege of spending more hours with him.

I consult my wardrobe for something suitable to wear for our late morning meeting. A knitted dress, leggings and boots with a scarf to add extra style will do perfectly, so I lay the chosen outfit on the kitchen table ready for the morning. It is amazing how much calmer I feel now!

My peace is soon shattered by a call from Pedro, confirming our meeting time and making sure that I'm going to turn up. I check the name of the cafe with him, as I've not been to this eatery before and don't want to turn up at the wrong place. He confirms the location, and with his usual style leaves me speechless and floundering for a reply:

"Yes, perfect my sexy woman! You know, I will spot you straight away, come up behind you, and breathe softly on your neck as you wonder ... can it be? Yes, baby girl. It is I ... here for you!"

How awful it would be if he does. What if I turn around and am horrified at what I see? How bad can this date be? I have seen most of his body and face, so I'm sure Pedro in person will be fine, I tell myself.

I reply to Roshan and Krystian's messages that came through while I spoke to Pedro. Both want to make a time to see me the following week, so I agree to both meetings and feel a little happier about going on my blind date on Saturday. The next two texts waiting for me are from Billie-Rae and Lulu, both wishing me luck with the Brazilian, and reminding me to let them know what he is like as soon as possible! Of course, I told them about the Brazilian. His one-liners are too good to keep to myself, and the girls and I often amuse ourselves sharing the new lines he kept coming up with. Lulu is enthralled with them, and every time we talk on the phone, she tries to speak with a sultry Brazilian accent with a suggestive line which always has us in fits of laughter.

Saturday dawns a crisp clear day, and I'm quite calm and relaxed, until I remember that only a few hours are left until I will find out the truth about this mystery Mark. Thankful that I organised my clothes the previous night, I revel in the luxury of lazing in bed for a while before leisurely getting ready. My plan is to leave earlier than I need to, in case the city traffic is slow and chews up my precious travelling time.

Cosy in bed, I turn over lazily stretching, but stop mid-stretch when I see a faint red glow pulsing from the Book.

Oh no. My eyes widen. A shiver runs down my spine and sweat breaks out across my upper lip to compliment the extreme goose-bumpy feeling of foreboding I am experiencing. I have forgotten to consult the Book regarding the Brazilian!

Bloody hell. What should I do? It's too late to cancel the date now! For a moment I think about ignoring the warning, but I'm reminded of my disaster date with Mitch. Opening the book carefully, I search for the red glow's origin. *Just as I suspected.* The brightest red glow is centred on the Essential Criteria for Mark selection.

- *Has unobstructed clear images of his face in pictures*

Shit. That's it. I knew I should have listened to my inner voice instead of Pedro's mesmerising tones. God knows how this date will turn out, but at least I'm forewarned.

Pedro messages me at ten o'clock to say that his plane has landed and that he is on the way to his hotel. A shiver of anticipation mixed with concern rolls down my back. No turning back now. I must find out if he is all he said he is; but I need the distraction of the radio to keep my growing nerves at bay.

Parking in the closest car park to the hotel that won't rob me blind, I sit for a minute. A couple of deep breaths, a swipe of lipstick and a check of my face and hair in the mirror and I'm good to go. I surprise myself by arriving about ten minutes before the allotted time. Will I beat him to the cafe, or will he already be waiting for me? I guess the only way to know is to go and find out.

Finding the eatery is not difficult. As I cross the road and my view of the restaurant improves, I can see inside. My eyes are drawn to the back of a man sitting alone, wearing a white shirt, suit and tie with his charcoal jacket slung over the back of his seat. Can it be him?

Sweeping my eyes across the clusters of tables and chairs again, I make sure no other similar looking man is alone at a table in the cafe. He is the only one with shiny black hair, and chocolate-coloured skin. It *must* be him. With a deep breath and a slight feeling of dread I make my way through the tables towards him, scrutinising every inch of his body from behind. His shoulders are broad and lead to a narrow, toned waist, suggesting that he is a gym user. Soft ringlets brush across his shirt collar as he reaches for a menu with manicured hands. An expensive looking watch peeks from beneath his cuff.

I breathe a sigh of relief. This should be fine ... I don't know what I was worried about! He appears OK from here so far, how bad can his face be? Arriving at the table, he glances up. My smile freezes on my face, and my system goes into panic mode.

Everything falls into place and is explained as soon as I gaze into his eyes, and I curse myself for not being a thorough enough Vixen and following the rules. His brown eyes smile back at me as he stands to greet me. He gives me a welcoming hug and holds out my seat for me. The scent of his cologne lingers in the air around me. Flustered, my cheeks flame as I discreetly fan my face. I slip out of my warm jacket as a distraction and blame the difference in temperature in the cafe for my flushed cheeks.

I'm trying hard not to stare, I really am. But I'm not successful. I cannot keep my eyes off his giant *buggy* eyes! They protrude out further than normal from his eye sockets, making me want to pop them back in to place with a soft poke. At last I have discovered his secret, why he would not send a picture of his eyes to me. If I had known this before, I would not have started to talk to him. Even as I think this, I am ashamed of myself. It is not his fault that he was born with those eyes, but the fact is that I am not attracted to him now. I put aside my doubts, gather my thoughts together and smile as he hands me a menu to peruse.

"Have you had a chance to study the food choices here yet, Pedro?"

Opening the menu as I speak, my eyes are thankful for something else to focus on. What am I going to do? I will stay for lunch only, a couple of hours of chatting and that's long enough, I decide. I owe him this much at least. It's not his fault I forgot to consult the Book from the start. His reply interrupts my thoughts and makes me realize I am staring with unseeing eyes at the food descriptions without having read a word yet.

"Many things in the menu appeal to me, Kit-e-cat, but none are half as alluring as you are!"

His smile is appealing, and if those eyes could be covered, his charm might almost work. Hmmm, would he mind wearing sunglasses during the meal? Then I can at least fantasise that this delicious sounding man is also attractive to me. All the elements are present, but the eyes bug me.

Oops sorry. Had to think it ... but oh, how the wicked little part of me wanted to say it out loud! My attention safely back to the menu, I scold myself for having such mean thoughts. It's not like we can choose how we look! I resolve to be positive, and to enjoy my meal and his company as much as possible.

Pedro takes his time ordering, asking several questions about the dishes before selecting one, whereas I choose something I recognise. I envision an uncomfortable hour of avoiding too much eye contact and give an inaudible sigh. At least we're in a place I will not be recognised by anyone.

The waiter offers his suggestions on the wine, and it's like a lifeline thrown to me in the ocean to help get me through this date. I let Pedro choose after telling him the type of wine I like—the bubbly kind, not flat, as he is obviously used to overseeing the drink orders when dining out. To my surprise he orders a bottle rather than a glass, and a red for himself. When I try to protest and change the order to a glass, he will hear none of my disagreements. I just thank him and accept that I may need to either cab it home or only indulge in a couple of glasses from the bottle.

Repeating our order, the waiter bows and leaves the table. For a moment I wish he would stay as a buffer, but I know I will need to face this challenge alone and make the best of the situation. After an awkward start, our conversation becomes easier. As the attentive waiter reappears within minutes with the wine, and proceeds to pour a little into Pedro's glass for the tasting, I stifle a giggle. This is not my usual type of casual lunch cafe choice! I wave at him to continue to pour after he brandishes the bottle for my inspection and take a huge sip as soon as his back is turned.

Now I'm pleased I didn't eat before I came, so I'm hoping even a sip will work wonders at this point. I finish my first glass of bubbly in record time. Pedro raises his eyebrow as if to enquire whether I want another, and I agree.

"Kit-e-cat, you seem a little nervous. Is everything alright? I'm not going to throw you over my shoulder in the cafe. Well ... not until after we eat, of course!"

Laughing with him at the thought, I'm relaxing a little as the moment is lightened with his humour. He does have a lovely smile. We are interrupted by the first course arriving at our table, some pita bread and dips along with caramelised onion and parmesan garlic bread. Of course, not until I'm mid-bite do I remember garlic breath isn't ideal to impress a man, but on this occasion bad breath doesn't bother me! I joke about me having bad breath with Pedro, who laughs and takes a big bite himself.

"Now we will not worry about the garlic breath, sexy woman!"

Oh dear. He still thinks he is going to kiss me. Well, on the bright side, at least my eyes will be closed, and I won't be staring into his bulbous orbs! Wait, what am I thinking? Perhaps I had better slow down with the alcohol and eat, instead of picturing him kissing me.

By the time our main courses arrive, I'm a lot more relaxed and comfortable with him, and his eyes don't even seem so bad anymore. I'm unsure if I just got over the initial shock or whether my wine goggles have kicked in. Whatever the reason, what a relief! He's still the entertaining silver-tongued Brazilian in person, but not who I expected.

This physical attraction thing is a difficult one. If I come to know someone well over the internet rather than in person, and am attracted to his personality, is that attraction enough? If the pictures he posts misrepresents what he is really like, and the person is not as attractive to me in the flesh, can the relationship ever go further than friendship? Can I overcome the hurdle of my internal measuring stick?

Glad of the few minutes to myself when he excuses himself to go to the bathroom, I can now ponder these questions swirling around in my brain. No doubt that he's a gentleman with a good personality, but are these qualities enough to take the relationship with Pedro any further? From his conversations, he's well-versed in the art of making love ... but is that another thing he was not so truthful about? Should I chance a kiss to find out for myself, or should I simply thank him for the lovely lunch and conversation, and put into action my exit plan to vamoose out of this awkward situation?

Before long he is back at our table, interrupting my serious musings. Perhaps I should give him the benefit of the doubt and at least find out what he kisses like before I make my escape. He fills my glass to the brim for the third time, as I try to daintily sip my over-full drink without giggling and spilling the wine on myself.

We chat through the main course without incident after our initial shaky start, and he suggests that I might like to try one of the luscious desserts on offer ... Before he tastes the delectable dessert that is me! I almost choke on my drink when he says this, and the coughing fit that ensues brings tears to my eyes.

"Are you alright, Kit-e-cat?"

His concern is evident as I blot tears from my eyes with the linen napkin. Nodding in answer, I'm still unable to speak as I down a glass of water. If he doesn't jump up and thump me on the back, I'm fine. I give him a watery smile and laugh in embarrassment.

"Uhm, after that debacle I think I will check out the dessert menu, thanks Pedro!"

I need to stall until I decide what I'm going to do. Eating one of those delicious cheesecakes or tortes will be a pleasure to do while I think about this. I do like him as a person, but his eyes are the drawback for me. Perhaps if he's an amazing kisser or has some other fantastic hidden quality, I may be able to accept them. More so if I finish off the bottle of bubbly that is fast disappearing.

He refills my glass with the remains of the bottle as our desserts arrive; raspberry tartlets swirled with mouth-watering dark chocolate shards and mousse accompanied by a mini mountain of whipped cream drizzled in chocolate sauce. Savouring every delicious mouthful, I know decision-making time is coming. But as the wine flows through my body, my initial reasoning doesn't seem to matter as much.

After feeding me a spoonful of his dessert to sample, Pedro leans over and draws his thumb across my lower lip, sensually wiping a dash of cream from my face. He then licks the fluffy cream off his finger. Mesmerised by his tongue, and with the effects from the bubbly, I make my decision.

I'm going to chance a kiss! How much alcohol content is in one bottle of bubbly? I would check, but the ever-efficient waiter cleared the empties away as soon as the last drop was poured. Pedro insists on paying the bill while I excuse myself to visit the ladies.

I realise how drunk am when I sit on the toilet seat and almost slide off sideways. I lean forward and rest my head between my knees. No way that I'm going to be able to drive home yet! I straighten up, and zigzag out of the stall towards the mirror to view the damage my coughing fit has wreaked on my make-up. I repair the damage with only a semi-delicate swipe of a wet tissue under my eyes and a new application of lipstick.

After a final once over in the mirror, I pop a mint in my mouth and make my way back to the entrance of the restaurant where he is waiting for me. Surprisingly, I find it is easy walking in a straight line towards the door. Perhaps the drunk me thinks that I am fine but in reality, I'm stumbling in an alcohol induced fog. Pedro turns to smile at me as I approach him. He now dons his sunglasses and is so much more attractive with them on.

"Sexy woman ... that lipstick makes your lips appear so luscious I can hardly keep myself from biting them off!"

I flush, not knowing quite how to respond to his statement, as usual. He takes my hand with a confidence most Australians couldn't muster and leads me through the atrium of the hotel to the lifts. When I raise my eyebrow enquiringly at him, he laughs and tells me a visit to this beautiful city's best hotel would not be complete without getting to admire the view from his gorgeous luxury room.

Not possessing the willpower to disagree with him right now, we step into the mirrored lift which opens as if by magic. It speeds upwards in silence towards the thirty-fourth floor. As soon as the doors close, Pedro grabs me around the waist and draws me close to him. My heart is pounding, and I swear I can hear it banging in my ears.

"Mmm ... well hello, my Kit-e-cat! You're in a dangerous place now." His deep voice is almost mesmerising, and I'm powerless to move as his lips press against mine. It is a slow closed mouth kiss, which he follows up with a couple of shorter pecks before the doors slide open and I am ushered out of the lift. The hotel's hallway is lushly decorated, but I don't even have time to register more than the golden wall colour before he waves me into his room.

The room is decorated in opulence, with an amazing view. Sydney's harbour and waterways glisten magically in the afternoon sun, and with the warmth of the room I can imagine the season to be summertime, instead of the depressingly cold winter we have been experiencing.

"Can I offer you another drink, sexy woman, or would you instead like to sip from my lips?"

The thought of another drink is still more comforting than his lips on mine, so I agree to the drink and walk over to the floor to ceiling window to admire the panoramic view. This is a much nicer room than I would expect a guy who was here on business to budget for. I wonder if he upgraded with meeting me in mind. I'm a little nervous at being in alone in the room with him, but the buzzing headiness of the alcohol and the sunglasses still perched on Pedro's nose help a lot. He moves closer, leaning in for another kiss—again, a long slow closed mouthed peck, followed by several shorter ones. No open mouth. No tongues involved. What the hell?

I assume that he is warming up to the open-mouthed, passionate kiss I expect. Again, he repeats the same pattern, but this time with the added twist of admiring my dimples aloud and swooping down to bite each cheek. Hard! I recoil in surprise.

"Hey! You bit me!" Stating the obvious, I glare at him while rubbing my chomped-on cheeks. "Ahhhh, I simply could not help it Kit-e-cat ... your dimples are so delicious I cannot resist!"

I frown in response and wonder how many other girls are OK with having their cheeks bitten.

"Well that's not OK with me. Do not bite my cheeks again or I won't be responsible for my actions!"

Totally out of my comfort zone and thankful for the fresh drink, I take a larger than expected gulp. Again, I suffer a spluttering fit so bad that I almost expect the bubbly to pour back out of my nose.

"Are you OK, Kit-e-cat? Is there anything else I can do for you? Perhaps it would be wiser to sip your drink slowly, baby girl! What's with you and alcohol, woman?"

He pats my back with a grin as I regain control over my cough and dab at my face in the mirror. What is going on here? This date is going from terrible to disaster status and I'm not even taking into consideration the bulging, buggy eyes issue. I know, I know! I should have listened to the Book! Pedro is so kind and thoughtful though, that my alcohol haze insists that I give him one last chance.

He comes over to me and slides his arms around my waist, pulling me towards him.

"Let me see if I can turn your cough into a purr, my sexy woman!"

Again his lips press against mine, still closed like a ten-year-old boy. I can't stand this terrible kissing technique any longer! With the extra courage gained via alcohol infusion I grab him by the shoulders and push him back to arm's length.

"What the hell are you doing?! Why don't you move your mouth when you kiss me? Don't you ever kiss women with an open mouth and use your tongue? This time, open your mouth and follow my lead, for God's sake!"

He stares at me for a moment, surprised at what comes out of my mouth. Glaring at him, I dare him to not do what I had suggested. A look of bemusement crosses his face and annoys me even further.

"Open it!" He realizes that I am serious, and opens his mouth, more in shock than anything else. But there is nothing worse than a bad kisser. I press my lips to his, which is weird because I don't often start a kiss with an open mouth, but it seems to be the only way to get my point across to him. I move my lips, and I'm encouraged to see that he follows my lead. The tip of my tongue touches his, and I invite him to do the same. A low growl sounds from his throat as he clutches me tighter and directs me backwards towards the bed. I end the kiss as the back of my calves press against the base of the bed and look up at him enquiringly.

"Sexy woman!" He pushes me gently on to the bed. He is quick to follow, nuzzling his lips against my neck, biting. Now this is one area where I do like a guy to bite, if the bite leaves no marks! Tipping my head to the side, I allow his mouth better access to the spot that turns me on the most. His teeth graze my skin harder, and I feel a stirring of interest within. He slides his hand over my ribcage towards my breasts and squeezes one before teasing the nipple to alertness through my clothes.

I can't help but wonder what he is hiding in his pants, and whether the contents are worth finding out about or not. Perhaps he's only terrible at kissing? What if he does possess some amazing tantric ability or Karma Sutra moves like the ones he hinted at? I decide to grope at his package to discover if it is worth taking the time to unwrap or not.

I slide my hand along his thigh, and towards the area I want to feel, caressing as I go — I don't want him to realize that what I'm doing is so deliberate! Just as my hand hones in on its target, Pedro rolls his body over to face mine, effectively trapping my hand between us and preventing my fingers from travelling all the way to their destination.

Shit! Damn it, so close ... I'm going to need to try another manoeuvre and free up my hand without suspicion. I almost forget that he is kissing my neck. I am so intent on trying to cop a feel that when his lips latch onto a nipple I'm surprised and wonder how he managed to bare my breast without me noticing. Uhm ... hello alcohol!

I allow his behaviour for now while I discreetly work to free my hand trapped between us. I slide my arm away as he shifts his body, but his movement also means that my goal is too far away to reach now! Perhaps I should haul him up towards my lips and chance another kiss? Just as I wonder what the best way to do this is without raising suspicion, his teeth lock on my nipple and he bites down harder than is pleasant, which surprises me into action.

"Hey! That fucking hurt, Pedro!"

Grabbing his head, I roughly push him away from my breast. His startled expression almost makes me laugh, but I'm too annoyed to give in to the urge. God, is it really worth checking out his package or should I instead cut and run now? Perhaps the alcohol is starting to wear off and I'm coming back to my senses.

He notices that I am on the edge of giving him the boot, and is determined to try harder to coerce me to stay. He nuzzles into my neck again and works his way over to my lips. A couple of pecks on the lips preceded by a half-open mouthed mismatched kiss which holds no satisfaction, followed by yet another nip on the cheek and I know for sure that my wine goggles have slid too far down my nose to be retrieved.

The realization that Pedro just proved beyond a doubt that he is all talk in the sex department, but completely inept when it comes down to performance and skill, is quite disappointing. I was looking forward to tantric sex, orgasms for hours and a damn good workout, but all I got was a guy acting like some amateur teenager fumbling around in the dark. How is this possible? After all the build-up, and the raunchy things he said he'd do, I can't believe that he is so bad in the physical skills department. Did he learn all those lines from movies instead of with real experiences with a woman? Perhaps all previous girls he was interested in laughed at his eyes or lost all attraction to him once his sunglasses came off. I sigh, annoyed with myself for not heeding the Book's warning.

Now is the time to extract myself with an exit plan. Although he is a shocking kisser and seems to possess no idea about women, I do feel sorry for him, and want to let him down gently rather than tell him the truth. What is the point of making him feel bad? That's not what a kind human would do, and Vixens are indeed kind women, although we will not put up with less than we deserve—in any area of our lives.

I feign needing to go to the toilet which is an excellent excuse to get up and away from the bed. Kissing him briefly as I stand up, I almost want to run into the bathroom and lock the door, but I casually stroll until I shut the door behind me. I peer at myself in the mirror. A stranger's face stares back at me in the unfamiliar surroundings. The white marble tiles surrounding me are as cold and unemotional as I feel. At last the Vixen is returning to her senses, and planning her escape with a foolproof exit excuse he cannot query. Smoothing my dress, I take a deep breath and straighten my shoulders. Extraction time.

"Oh my God, I didn't realize the time, Pedro! I'm so sorry but I'm going to need to leave. A friend's engagement party is tonight, and I promised her I'd stop past and pick up their cake for her from the bakery— which closes in half an hour!"

I try to appear as genuine in my disappointment as he is when I say this, but he recovers quickly and comes out with another of his smooth lines, so I know he will be OK. I thank him for the delicious lunch and say that it had been great meeting him. These are not the words I am thinking, but this is the phrase that comes from my lips!

Pedro walks me to the door, and I insist I will be fine travelling down in the lift alone, and don't need his company, as he would only distract me and make me late to get to the cake shop in time. He takes me in his arms for a last hug and kiss goodbye, and to my displeasure finishes with a nip at my cheeks.

"Ah, I could not resist baby girl, those winking dimples are so enticing!"

I fight the urge to frown and slap him or voice what I really think. Instead I flash him a sweet smile, thank him again for the day and hotfoot it out of the door and down the hall towards the freedom of the elevators.

Not until I reach my car and sink into the driver's seat in complete privacy, can I relax. This had been the weirdest day ever, and those eyes were a surprise twist. The thing is, I could've gotten past them if he'd walked the walk as well as he could talk the talk, but in the end he proved to be talentless.

As I drive home, I make a mental note to myself: *Never* forget to consult the Book properly, and never arrange to meet a guy you have not seen a good picture of again. No matter what he says! A fit of the giggles overtakes me when I think about having to tell the girls what happened on my date.

Tonight's event is not an engagement party at all I am going to, but dinner with my girlfriends. I know they will fall off their chairs laughing at my experience with Pedro! I drive straight to the restaurant we are meeting at, looking forward to an evening of gossip and laughter— expecting quite a lot of the laughing to be at my expense ... after all, what are friends for?

Prearranged Exit Strategies

This is incredibly important, Vixens. The first meeting should ideally be able to be terminated within the first hour if it is not going well, but always in a polite and respectful manner.

You will not need to use your prearranged strategy at all should you be having a fantastic time with your Mark! But for those times you need an escape it's an invaluable thing to put in place.

You never know when you will find yourself thinking "Holy crap I've got to get away from this loser!" To leave the failing date without looking rude make sure you have one of the following suggestions of substantial exit strategies ready to go so it doesn't seem like a lie to escape his vile company and save your precious time for something else more worthwhile.

- ✓ I need to babysit my niece / friend's child earlier than first expected
- ✓ I have to return to work for a meeting / to fix an unexpected problem

- ✓ My mother/Aunt/Granny just messaged me ... I need to pick her up from hospital earlier than I thought
- ✓ My friend's car broke down so I must go now to rescue her
- ✓ I have to go bridesmaid dress shopping early ... my friend's being a bridezilla

Immediate extraction ideas (deployed in extreme cases of horror, revulsion or boredom):

- ✓ Send a signal to a friend to call with an emergency that you need to leave immediately for to help her
- ✓ Use kids (your own, relative or a friend's child) as an excuse—vomiting, broken arm, out of control allergic reactions are perfect reasons to hightail your butt out of your date
- ✓ You suffer from sudden migraines and the coffee/alcohol/ icy water you drank must have brought one on, so you can't continue with the date

Adventure Vixen

Café Play

After the Pedro disaster, I need to return to the safety of my familiar hot Marks and forget all about bitten cheeks and buggy eyes. With this in mind, and in need of some serious confidence lifting, I make dates with Krystian, Roshan and Darz all within the same week. Nothing perks my spirits up more than to see these guys and enjoy a laugh with them. I might even share my dating disaster story with them—they will appreciate the humorous side!

I'm not willing to risk another unsuitable Mark yet, so I avoid the computer's pull and concentrate on seeing my friends and going on dates with my regular Marks. I think back to Saturday night at dinner with the girls, and the horror on their faces when I told them the tale of the Brazilian disaster date. Lulu, Francesca and Billie-Rae couldn't believe I managed to stay on my date for so long, let alone endure his terrible bite-kissing technique, my description of which had them in gales of laughter begging me to stop.

My first tryst this week is with Krystian; it's been a couple of weeks since I've seen him. Always the gentleman, he greets me with a huge bear hug, and a delicious kiss that doesn't end with biting my cheeks. I sigh in relief, glad that I decided enough was enough with Pedro.

We head to the cinema after he comes to pick me up, chatting easily as we make our way towards the ticket booth. Our plan is to go to the cinema to see a movie both of us won't like on purpose. Now I know this sounds strange, but when your sole reason for going is to fool around, you don't want to be distracted by a storyline you might enjoy! Krystian left the choice to me, so I picked a horror film which is a genre I hate, so our plan should be foolproof.

The theatre is almost deserted at this time of the week, perfect for what we want. Krystian buys our tickets, drinks and even a snack. I joke that I thought we already had our snacks — each other! We both giggle and nudge each other like kids as we enter the cinema.

Trailers of other upcoming movies flash across the screen in the dimly lit theatre as we make our way up the stairs, as far as possible away from other patrons. There are only another four people in here with us, so we've got plenty of perfectly discreet locations to sit. I chose my clothes with fooling around in mind. I am wearing a long flowing skirt with side slits, and a zip front top covering a pink stretch lace camisole with black ribbon crisscrossed from the bottom to the top. I am not wearing a bra, with only crotchless black silky knickers under my skirt. Yes, I hear what you are thinking ... what a brilliant idea!

The film starts, and so do we ... Krystian lifts the armrest between us to snuggle in closer, and swoops down for a long, lingering kiss. I respond with enthusiasm, glad to be kissing in my preferred way with a guy I am attracted to.

The movie drones on in the background, but my attention is held by Krystian sliding his hand up my thigh as he kisses me, making me want to part my legs further, but we are cramped for room in the seats. I turn towards him and hook my right leg up over his knees. The slits in my skirt give easy access without looking like my skirt is out of place ... perfect.

He nibbles on my neck while I glance at the screen. A possessed porcelain doll has scribbled red crayon over the walls of an apartment, terrorising the owners. I turn my attention back to Krystian's thigh. I slide my hand across his crotch and am pleased to feel the hardness beneath his trackpants. I know he chose to wear them with easy access in mind. His fingers brush the top of my thighs and slips further down to trace the growing dampness. A low growl erupts from his throat vibrating against my neck, so I wiggle closer to him as his mouth swoops to my collarbone and shoulder to bite and kiss it.

My attention is drawn to the movie where the on-screen family has settled in a new house, and the children are playing a game of hide-and-seek. I watch with only half my attention on the scenes before me. The rest is on what Krystian's doing, and on the stiffness in his pants.

One of the little girls on the screen is sleepwalking. Suddenly a terrifying looking old hag appears on top of the girls wardrobe and scares the shit out of me! I jump in surprise and Krystian laughs at my reaction to the film.

"Stop it!" I whisper, hitting him on the arm and giggling, a little embarrassed that I reacted in such a strong way. I'm glad he can't see the red flush of embarrassment on my cheeks in the darkened theatre. Our attention is again drawn to the screen, where all sorts of strange, ghostly happenings start harassing the family.

I realize this film is based on a true story and my reluctant interest grows. The main characters are based on an American couple who investigate reports of demons and spirits. The woman is clairvoyant and can connect and communicate with spirits. Our hands still their wandering as we both become drawn in by the film's storyline and find we can't drag our eyes away from the screen. "I'm so sorry Miss Arleia, the film has caught my attention ... not quite what we came here for!" he apologises, squeezing my hand. I laugh and admit to him that I too am pulled in by the storyline. We both laugh, and I lean back on his broad chest with his arm around me, enjoying watching the true tale unfold, relaxed and comfortable with each other.

A vague thought of how nice this is, flits across my mind. It's been a long time since I've gone to the movies with a man and enjoyed the strength and protectiveness of his arm around me. We leave the cinema chattering about the movie, laughing at ourselves because the evening turned out completely different to what we originally planned. I don't mind though; the ease of friendship is growing between Krystian and me. We have a lot in common and can talk about any subject which is great. I wonder if there can ever be more than friendship in the long-term between us and laugh out loud when I remember the deal breaker points of this Mark. I realize they are too huge to overcome for any hope of a relationship together, but they're tolerable in a 'friends with benefits' situation, and I relax my guard at the internal revelation.

We head to the nearest café and soon get talking about our latest dating experiences over steaming mugs of coffee. Krystian howls with laughter at my Brazilian story. He thinks he can beat my crazy experience with one of his own stories. He tells me of a woman who suggested that he should go to her house to be restrained, while he watches her and a black guy having sex in front of him. What the heck? I can't believe someone would suggest this. "Miss Arleia, no way in hell am I going to put myself in that situation—I don't know or trust her, and who knows what would happen after they finished getting it on together! Be restrained while a big naked dude wanders the room near me? No thanks!"

He squirms in his seat as if to protect his butt from anyone touching it and I burst into laughter. I'm glad it's not just me who collects bizarre dating stories! He tells me of a girl who came over to his house and brought her girlfriend along. They all got in his spa, and after a few drinks, were getting frisky together. Krystian ended up liking the girl's friend more than her, and being drunk, lavished more attention on her friend. This caused a huge bitch fight in the hot tub. He eventually calmed them both down and convinced them that they were all on the date to have some fun and enjoy the evening, to enjoy another drink and relax.

"Will you see either of them again, do you think?" I'm curious as to whether he thought his time was worth another meeting with these two.

"Hell no! It is all too complicated, you know me—I'd rather relax and chill out in the spa, chat and play around if they want to. I'm not into drama and bitch fights, I can't be bothered seeing chicks who are hard work!"

I do agree with him. There's nothing worse than having to exert too much effort on a date trying to keep the peace or having to do most of the talking. I'm glad we can talk openly and honestly together about the other sexual experiences and the other dates we go on. It's a refreshing change from jealousy, dishonesty and sneaky behaviour between casually dating men and women.

"I can't believe we got caught up in the film instead of fooling around, Krystian! We are going to have to do better next time!"

"What do you mean ... next time? We are still out, and the night is young; and we are in a secluded corner of this quiet café. I think you should slide closer, Miss Arleia!"

With a wicked smile he pulls me closer so that my thigh is almost hooked over his. I glance around the café. There are three other couples and a small group of women seated around the café, but none are close to the high-backed booths where we are sitting. I assess the possibility of getting caught in a compromising position, and decide the chances are low.

Krystian shifts his body towards me slightly and slides his hand up my bare thigh. I grin and raise my eyebrow at him. He laughs and slides his hand up further, his finger tracing the edge of my crotchless knickers. I take a sip of my cooling coffee, pretending like nothing untoward is happening under the table as I slide my butt a little closer to the edge of the seat.

He smiles knowingly and traces the juncture between my thighs before slowly pressing his fingers against me. I gasp and writhe in my seat as his fingers caress the right place.

"Shhhh Miss Arleia, you'll cause a scene! Sit still ... that's it. Good girl."

I can do nothing but bite my tongue and grin at the control he has over me. With one slight movement he can make me gasp or moan involuntarily. I don't want to alert other patrons as to what's going on at our table. I stay silent. Excited energy builds inside me, wondering what he will do next.

Krystian moves his fingers slowly. He makes me gasp softly against his neck, but not loud enough to draw attention. I can feel the dampness between my thighs growing as he works his magic. His thumb circles, hitting the exact spot that makes me moan.

Horrified that I just moaned aloud, I try to cover it with a cough to avoid raising suspicion. To my relief no-one seems to notice. He laughs at my attempt to be discreet, so I punch him gently in the arm for teasing me.

"Stop that! Someone might have heard me then, Krystian! You're so naughty I should spank your ... Ahhhhhh!"

To stop me mid-sentence he flicks his thumb firmly across my clit. The effect is immediate, as an involuntary moan of pleasure erupts from my lips.

His lips capture mine halfway through the moan, so the sound is swallowed up by his throat. We kiss again slowly, and I pull away smiling in satisfaction; until I see a waiter fast approaching our booth.

"Shit Krystian, a waiter's coming! Act natural!" I whisper in his ear moments before the waiter arrives. In an attempt to do so, I pick up my mug and drain the last of the now cold liquid as he asks if we are finished with our cups. Krystian's fingers twitch slightly, and I jump in my seat as I reply to the waiter's question and slide the empty cups towards him. His quiet laughter is drowned out by the waiter asking if there is anything else we need?

"No, thank you! I think we have had enough for the evening!" My double meaning isn't lost on Krystian, and he roars with laughter.

The waiter gives him a puzzled look and moves to the next table that needs clearing. Alone again now, Krystian withdraws his wandering fingers from beneath the table. He licks them slowly, his eyes locked with mine. Damn that's sexy! He runs his thumb over my lips so I can taste myself, then flicks his tongue across my lips.

"Time to go, Miss Arleia." It was a statement rather than a question, but I agree. It is time to go. If he turns me on any more, I might demand that he takes me on the table then and there, regardless of who is watching!

We finish our evening with a long lingering kiss and a promise to catch-up soon, and as I drift off to sleep that night, I have a smile on my face. We had an enjoyable evening, even though it was not quite what I expected.

Soon I will see the delicious Roshan again ... I love my life!

Adventure Vixen

Sexy Spaghetti

Roshan and I are meeting up straight after work, so I put extra thought into what I am wearing to the office, as well as the heel height of my shoes, seeing that he is only slightly taller than me. He arrives at the hotel before me and is easy to find at this early time of evening as the restaurant section is still quiet. His handsome face lights up with a welcoming smile and he stands up to give me a hug.

"Let's head into the bar for a drink first, Arleia!"

I smile in agreement and we pick a cosy booth. As he walks away to get drinks, I can't help but admire his peach-shaped butt and delicious broad shoulders. Perhaps we should enjoy a quick dinner and head to my place, so I can rake my fingers down his muscled back and over his well-developed biceps. This thought pattern leads to a twinge of desire through my body. I'm already hornier than usual after the café play date with Krystian, so it's no surprise that my thoughts are drawn in this direction. We chat over our drinks, then move to the restaurant area to order our food. I manage to refrain from drooling over his delicious body, so I am hoping that the service is fast here tonight.

Over another glass of wine and entrees, Roshan entertains me with stories about his second job as a stripper for hens' nights. Regaling me with tales of drunken bridesmaids and being groped by the brides-to-be makes me think of ripping his clothes off myself and copping a feel of his body next to mine right now. I wonder if my thoughts are obvious as I lick my lips, hoping he thinks I am showing my enjoyment of the meal, not anticipating seeing him naked. Vixens don't like to appear too eager in front of their Marks.

My shoe slips off easily under the table and I stifle a naughty smile. My eyes sparkle in mischief as I stretch my foot out towards him. His muscled thighs are wide open, as he lounges back in his chair, engrossed in our conversation. Perfect. My stockinged foot connects dead on target, and he jumps in surprise. A low laugh of satisfaction erupts from me as I wiggle my toes against his crotch. He slams his thighs shut, trapping my foot between them. I try to twist my foot free, but his thighs are like rods of steel.

"So that's how you want to play it tonight, Vixen?"

"What do you mean, Roshy?" Pretending to be the innocent maiden, I try to convince him my shoe flew off my foot by itself, and that I was merely looking for a place to warm my toes.

"Rather than telling me little white sexy lies, your lips should replace your foot ... and be wrapped around my cock instead."

A flare of internal heat jumps at his words, and a clear picture of this image appears in my mind. If there were long tablecloths in this restaurant, I may have considered his suggestion. I squirm in my chair. Damn! Why did we order entrées as well as main courses?

Just as this thought occurs, a waiter arrives at our table laden with delicious smelling dishes. My stomach growls in appreciation as the aroma of fresh pasta drenched in a garlic and tomato sauce permeates my nostrils. I inhale deeply. I need to eat this first before any tomfoolery! The waiter offers us parmesan, ground pepper and a drizzle of olive oil. I nod in agreement to all, but my mind is occupied with chocolate sauce instead of oil, being drizzled all over Roshan.

We start eating in silence. Staring at each other, we speak volumes with our eyes as we devour our pasta. My foot is still held prisoner between his thighs, pressed against the growing hardness there.

Winding the pasta slowly around my fork, I lift it to my lips. I suck in the slippery pasta slowly, letting the sauce spread over my lips, and drip on my chin. His thighs squeeze tighter against my calf. I wiggle my toes and lick my lips slowly, daring him to break eye contact.

Roshan can't help himself. His eyes dart to my tongue, my mouth. The sauce is dribbling further down my chin. I raise my hand as if to wipe the sauce from my chin. He grabs my wrist forcefully, stopping me. Reaching forward with his other hand, he traces his thumb over my chin; wiping away the trail of red sauce there. Leaning back, he trails his thumb across his own lips licking it clean.

My heart beats faster as I watch his tongue flick over the remaining sauce. Who knew eating could be this sensual? He still has hold of my other wrist, and I wonder if he can feel my pulse jumping in excitement under his fingers. Grabbing a hunk of bread, he makes an animalistic sound in his throat and tears off a piece with his teeth. Tossing his head back, he sucks the last of the sauce from his thumb and chews on the bread like a cave man.

I have forgotten we are in a restaurant. I have no idea who is around us. I can't drag my eyes away from this erotic food dance happening between us. With my free hand I pick up my fork and stab it into a steaming meatball. I raise it to my lips, licking the sauce off underneath before a drop can escape. Roshan stares intently at my tongue and the meatball. He moans his approval softly as I open my mouth wide and it disappears inside; reappearing in my cheek for a moment before I swallow it.

A flare of warmth invades my cheeks as he stares at me. Picking up a fork with his free hand he twirls on some pasta. He leans forward, indicating that I should open my mouth. I open it without thought, and as I close my mouth over the saucy pasta he withdraws the fork, still holding a few strands attached to my mouth.

He lifts the fork to his mouth, transferring the pasta so that we are connected by the strands. Pulling me closer across the table by my imprisoned wrist, he sucks in the sauce covered strands then covers my lips. The sensation of his tongue and the slippery pasta in my mouth is surprisingly sensual. We break our kiss for a moment to swallow our food before he recaptures my lips again in a hard kiss.

"Let's get out of here woman ... But give me a minute!" The words come from his throat like a low growl. I grin, understand his meaning. He releases my wrist and foot at last, so I can feel around for my shoe under the table. I vaguely wonder if anyone was watching our sexy food dance, but I don't really care. That was mild compared to the café with Krystian!

The restaurant is fast becoming crowded as we leave. Perfect timing, I think, while desire zings through my body and my fingers itch to touch his muscled chest! We head back to my place which is our only viable option, seeing that Roshan still lives in the family home with his parents. That's a massive deal breaker for me!

This can be a problem with dating men in their late twenties. Many still live with their families these days, rather than wanting to be independent as early as they can. I guess I can understand still living in your parent's home if you are still saving up for your own place or for cultural reasons. I couldn't wait to start my own life path and moved out at nineteen; so to be still living with parents in my late twenties like Roshan was never going to happen!

I race inside and light some candles and incense to set the mood to amorous and seductive.

Roshan arrives at my door with a loud knock, letting himself in as I walk towards the door. He embraces me in a warm tight hug with a cheeky grin, forcefully pushing me up against the wall as he lifts my chin and swoops down upon my mouth. His kiss is deep, tongue entwining and desire stirring, and I gasp as he presses his body closer to mine, so the full length of his hard body is against me.

He leads me backwards down my hallway and into the bedroom, still kissing as we go. His strong arms encircle me until we are safely in my room, and he pushes me back, playing with me so I bounce a couple of times. A twinkle of desire flashes across his intense brown eyes. I know I will be satisfied tonight.

The next morning, I wake before my alarm with a smile on my face. Roshan did not disappoint! A few stiff muscles protest as I stretch out, then snuggle back deeper into my cocoon. He demonstrated some good moves in the love making department, but I did note he was happier to receive than give when it came to oral sex. As enjoyable and sexy as he is, his lack of enthusiasm for performing oral sex is something to make a negative note of in my spreadsheet I think ... for future reference!

Adventure Vixen

Home Run

My mind turns to Darz and our date set for the following night. I'm glad I gave myself tonight off, as I am going to need the time to soak away the stiffness from last night in a bubble bath.

I invited him over to my place for drinks this time, rather than going out to a bar or café. He is bringing over a selection of movies to choose from, so I'm looking forward to an easy, relaxed night with him to conclude my busy dating week.

Work is a bit slower by the end of this week, so I manage to leave a couple of hours earlier than usual. I stop at the supermarket and bottle shop for supplies for our movie night. I even have plenty of time for a shower and to get everything ready before my evening's date. I glance at the Book as I get dressed. The last two successful dates with my regular Marks were great, but

I'm still a little rattled after the Pedro episode. A golden glow reassures me that Darz is a good guy, and that tonight's adventure will be a positive one.

Darz arrives about fifteen-minutes after the designated time, which is fine when we are meeting at my place, but I hope he will not be so tardy when on future dates ... another note to add to my spreadsheet, I think! He arrives laden with movies and alcohol which he sets down before giving me a warm bear hug and kiss. He gathers me up tighter and twirls me around before setting me back down with a grin.

"It's great to see you, Arleia! It feels like ages since we last caught up. I've been looking forward to a cosy night with you on the couch snuggling together!"

I laugh at his infectious enthusiasm and offer him a drink, while asking him what our choices of movies are for tonight. He starts reeling off the titles to me, and I hate to admit I'm not familiar with any of them.

Finally, there is one I have heard of ... Pirates. I'm sure that's the film set in the Caribbean with Johnny Depp as the star, so I suggest that we start with this one. A fit man onscreen is always a good start for a romantic movie evening. He tells me that this one stars Jessie Jane. I guess guys always note the hot chicks starring in movies, and women only notice the hot men.

We catch-up on each other's lives over our drinks. Darz offers to set up the DVD player while I prepare us some movie nibbles. I leave him to do that while I arrange three different cheeses, carrots, grapes and crackers on a plate. Brandishing my impressive cheese platter, I balance the tray on the coffee table along with my wine glass and sink down next to him on the lounge.

"Ready for me to start the movie now, woman?"

I laugh and hit him with a cushion in response, calling him a cheeky shit as I do.

"Oooooh ... pillow attacks now, huh? I'd rather you put me over your knee and spank me!"

Was he joking or is he turned on by the idea of a girl spanking his bare bottom? I don't know him well enough yet to have the answer, but I'm curious to find out. I picture him lying face down on the couch, his round, edible bare ass draped over my knees, and me caressing his smooth cheeks before giving one a sharp slap and leaving a red mark. Something appeals to me about this vision, and I'm turned on thinking about him sprawled over my thighs.

"You better watch out, Mr Smart Mouth, or I will haul you over my knee for a spanking!"

I retort, pretending that I am going to drag him across my knees this very second. A blaze of desire flashes across his eyes, and I have my answer. I feel powerful knowing that I have control. I wonder if there is a right and wrong way to spank someone. I wouldn't want to hurt him, and I'd want the spanking to be a pleasurable and sensual experience, not the kind of punishment you would run away from as a child. Oh my God, something else I'm going to need to research!

My mind is diverted by him turning the movie on, and the lingering kiss he gives me as the opening credits flash across the screen. We part reluctantly as the film starts, and I'm determined to view at least some of the movie without being distracted by his hand caressing my thigh.

A lot of good-looking pirates and wenches with massive breasts prance across the television, but so far there is no sign of Johnny Depp. I muse that maybe I've got my wires crossed, when I am surprised to see a *very* hot and heavy plundering sex scene steam up my vision. What? This doesn't look like the 'M' rated cinema version of Pirates I expected! I can sense Darz shaking in mirth next to me at my puzzled expression.

"What sort of pirate movie is this, Darz? I was expecting Johnny Depp!"

He explodes in laughter and can't talk for a minute. Tears stream down his face as he struggles to regain control. Once he calms down he explains that, yes indeed Johnny Depp is the star in the *Pirates of the Caribbean*, but the star of this film Jessie Jane, is a porn star. Oh. *Ohhhhhh.* Now I feel a bit silly! It's been so many years since I watched a porn movie, and they have obviously improved so much since then that I didn't pick up that I was viewing one! "Well shit, I was wondering why the actresses all seemed to have massive breasts and wear skimpier outfits than I expected!"

Laughing, we clink our glasses together as he confesses that all the movies he brought are porn, but in his defence, they are all recent ones of the best quality. No wonder I didn't recognise any of the other titles he listed. Personally, I prefer to be having sex in real life with a hot guy than observing other people having sex on the screen, but now I'm curious. I may as well keep watching this graphic movie and increase my education!

The buxom blonde is naked now and her body writhes beneath the muscled pirate as he holds her hands without effort, using only one of his. He suckles noisily on her pink nipple, and she moans and cries out as he slides his fingers into her wetness. The camera swoops in to focus on the pirate's huge cock and I almost want to lick my lips. No wonder he is starring in a porn film—if I was a guy with a penis that impressive I'd want everyone to see it too!

He adjusts his position, so that the head of his penis is poised above her mouth, then the greedy pirate wench swallows the monster almost whole. Geez! Where the hell did she put that log? She must be akin to a sword swallower or something ... there is no way that thing could fit in her mouth! Is that a special talent she's always had, or did she develop the ability through sheer perseverance and hard work? How far exactly did it go down her throat with no visible gag reflex?

The scene moves on to a close-up of his cock sliding into her, as they both let out what I think are ridiculously exaggerated moans. I can't help but be turned on a bit by the sight but wonder how intrusive being filmed with the camera almost right in the way of the action is for the actors. The pirate flips the wench over onto her knees, and almost in horror I realize he is going to screw her up the arse with his massive tree trunk.

Holy shit! My own butt cheeks clench in response and I must turn away from the scene that is too graphic for me to watch. I leave the room with the excuse of refilling our drinks, and take a break from the steaming hot screen of my massive television. I think it is worse watching porn on a big screen, because of the incredible close-up shots they favour, making cocks look bigger than my arm, and breasts appear the size of small mountains.

The painful-looking section I wanted to avoid has passed by the time I re-enter the lounge room. I also gulped down an extra glass of wine in the kitchen in readiness for the remainder of the film. After a few more raunchy scenes, Darz and I almost abandon watching the movie, and instead are entwined on the couch involved in our own X-rated version of the evening, and fast becoming frustrated at the restrictive clothing between us.

I suggest that we would be more comfortable in the bedroom and we make our way down the hall, half-undressed and locked together. The music of seduction from the film is still playing in the background as we fall onto the bed shedding the rest of our clothes. Our breathing becomes heavier and small moans of pleasure between kisses erupt from us both. This is much more interesting than watching two actors on the screen!

He slides his body down further and wraps his arms around my thighs, burying his face into my warmth, spreading me wider with his tongue. My thighs sink lower, as his fingers join his tongue in the sensual trip he is taking me on. I arch my back, urging him on. He doesn't disappoint. Stars burst behind my eyes as he flips me over the edge.

I grab for him, pulling him up against my body, wanting to feel him inside me. Out of all my Marks his cock is the best size for me. Long, thick and veiny, it fills me entirely and presses on all the right spots. I can feel his hard cock throbbing beneath my hand. He withdraws from my greedy hand for a moment, before driving himself in so deep that it feels like he will poke through my stomach. We both groan in pleasure. Sensations wash over me. His hands pinch my nipples, mouths locked, tongues dancing. Our rhythmic motion increases, I can think of nothing but him. My entire being is focussed on these amazing feelings. Our movements culminate in a crescendo of satisfied cries as we tumble back down the mountain together.

Sated afterwards, we lie in each other's arms, comfortable enough with each other now that we can chat about all sorts of things. The conversation moves to spanking, and he confesses that he would love a woman to spank him. He also admits to being turned on by being tied up, and the thought of a woman dominating him. Who could have guessed that this would be a fantasy of his? I'm a bit intrigued, and because I feel safe and at ease with him, I agree that we might need to try the spanking idea one day.

I almost shock myself by agreeing with the idea. Yet I shielded away from dominant/submissive suggestions when the delectable dreadlocked Sean proposed them.

Perhaps I am more curious than I thought about this area, and having spanking suggested to me by Darz doesn't seem as big of a deal as it did when Sean mentioned his fetish tastes. Maybe I'm becoming desensitised to the idea and the bit of research I have been doing demystified the subject matter for me?

After Darz leaves, I lie in bed alone thinking about our conversation. I decided to spend more time looking into the fetish world, and to investigate spanking methods online—if there is any such thing! Falling asleep with the image of me wielding a hairbrush over Darz's naked bottom somehow turns into a dream where I have a long line up of men waiting to be spanked over my knees ... How bizarre!

Spanking Guidelines

- ✓ Only spank or be spanked in a Mark relationship of absolute trust
- ✓ Ensure both participants are comfortable in their chosen positions
- ✓ Spank only in the safe zone: Swat mainly on the cheeks
- ✓ Start with lighter swats to warm-up the cheeks first
- ✓ Alternate between swats, gentle caresses and rubbing for maximum pleasure
- ✓ Build the anticipation between each swat
- ✓ Finish with an affectionate cuddle to discuss the session

Adventure Vixen

To Spank, or Not to Spank

I'm becoming obsessed with the idea of peachy round cheeks begging me to slap them. Since Darz told me that he would love a woman to spank him, that's all I have been able to think about. The amount of information online about this subject is staggering, and the more I read, the more it interests me. Educational YouTube clips, step-by-step instructions, stories and blogs crowd my screen begging for my attention.

Darz possesses the perfect round backside; perfect for spanking, I decide. A hand will be my preferred choice of weapon, and I have told him via text already that because he was so rude to suggest this to me, I think that he really *does* need a spanking now. And I'm the woman to wield this punishment!

Had I wished to ask I'm sure Sean would have been happy to demonstrate his spanking skills. But he is a little too far out of my league in the fetish department. At least I know all Darz wants is to play with spanking. *That* I can do.

We already have a play date set up for this Saturday night. I'm a bit nervous, but I think it will be fun. It's just taking the playful butt slap a bit further—nothing too weird about that, surely. Perhaps that's why there are so many sexy schoolgirl costumes available to buy online—there are a lot of sneaky spankers out there! Of course, it will be me that's spanking Darz, not the other way around, so there's no need for me to get a costume … yet. But I might keep it in mind for future adventures.

Saturday arrives, and heralds the start of spring at last with a few blossoms bursting forth in the warmer sun. This is the perfect time for a new adventure into the unknown! This time I will consult the Book, though. Although my Mark is familiar, this spanking business isn't! I reach for the Handbook hidden in a bottom drawer, looking for guidance.

As I pull it from the drawer, a grunt of surprise escapes me and I drop it. A strong purple glow outshines the reassuring golden light of approval for Darz. Frowning, I pick it up and leaf through the pages, looking for the source of the sparkling purple. Oh my God! An entire new section glows at me from the once blank pages for me to read ... *On spanking!* I lie back on the bed in a fit of disbelieving laughter. I love this Book! I wonder what other surprises it may have in store for me in future.

Since I am early and Darz seems to be running late, I reach for my Goddess cards for further guidance on my tiny foray into the fetish world. Shuffling the cards, I see one flip from the deck for me.

Freyja: Bold

Don't play it safe right now. Instead, take bold action in the direction of your desires. Success comes not from timidity but from committing yourself fully. Enjoy the excitement of taking risks and of being bold.

Flirt. Take risks and be daring. Unleash your adventurous side!

While I laugh at the direct message from the card, a shiver of delight washes through me. I'm even more excited about tonight's spanking session now.

Darz arrives about twenty-minutes late. I am exceedingly happy about this, as I was struggling to think of a way to start the spanking conversation. Now I can admonish him for his tardiness, and demand that each minute he kept me waiting be branded with red marks across his butt by my hand. Power and control are the feelings that course through me when he knocks at the door. I am prepared and ready. In fact, I am eagerly anticipating giving the spanking!

His sexy grin greets me as he steps in the door and enfolds me in a bear hug. I breathe in his appetising scent and want to bite his neck. Instead, I pull back and frown sternly at him.

"Just what time do you call this, young man?" I demand with a straight face. Surprise, then desire crosses his handsome face.

"Ohh, you are right … I am *really* late. I'm so sorry, Mistress!" Managing to look contrite, he stares back at me hopefully, willing me to continue the charade.

"Such bad behaviour—I cannot abide this! There will have to be a punishment administered so that you do not again keep a Vixen waiting!" A smile threatens to break free, but I suppress it. To be honest, it really is not OK to keep a Vixen waiting. He hangs his head, waiting for my next words, hoping I will say what he really wants to hear.

"You will be spanked for this mistake, mere mortal. One butt wobbling stinging smack for each minute you kept me waiting. Do not repeat this tardiness again."

I gesture for him to follow me into the lounge, allowing myself one small smile while my back is turned—but when I turn around again, I am controlled and emotionless.

"Take your jeans off. *Now!* How can you expect me to spank you with those on? I think you've just earned yourself an extra ten butt slaps Mister, for the slowness you exhibited then. Now hurry up!"

Part of me is laughing. Another part serious, and yet another part of me is turned on. He stands almost naked before me, waiting for my next command. My eyes travel slowly down his chest, appreciating the muscular contours of his body. He really does have the perfect form. Hard and muscular, broad shoulders, with a beautifully curved butt. Not to mention something hard peeking from the top of his underwear. I realise it will be pressed against my bare thigh and feel my desire for this idea grow even more.

I sit on the couch and pat my thighs, indicating that he should lie across my lap with his cheeks in the perfect spot for me to reach easily. He obeys with a murmured, 'Yes Mistress' and positions himself across my thighs as requested.

I stroke my hands across the curves of his cheeks softly, before administering the first stinging slap to his right cheek. He jumps in surprise but says nothing. I pull the top of his underwear down to expose the redness slowly appearing in the affected area. I rub it gently to take the sting out of the slap, as suggested on the instructional video clip I liked the best.

Trailing my fingers down the valley between his cheeks, I brush the tops of his thighs and balls. This makes him squirm in my lap, and I can feel his hardness growing against my thigh. Another slap to the left cheek covered in silky fabric, and another quick two to the right cheek. Again I slide down his underwear, and caress the hot stinging skin beneath my fingers, and squeeze it gently. A small groan of pleasure escapes him, and I feel my sense of confidence grow.

I lose count of the slaps, as I'm mesmerised by the perfect roundness of his cheeks, the pink marks I've left, and his hardness against my thigh. I strip his underwear right down over his thighs, fully exposing the marks across both cheeks and the tops of his thighs. He shifts position slightly, and his nakedness rubs against me, turning me on even more. I boldly stroke my fingers downward between his cheeks and cup his balls, caressing them as they brush the base of his cock.

His groan of desire is louder this time, and I feel my own body echoing his sentiments. I slap his cheeks hard again, sternly admonishing him aloud for enjoying his punishment. He jumps, and he's pushed between my thighs, the head touching my damp inner thighs. My breath catches in my throat as I feel my body respond to him. I continue my pattern of slaps, caresses, fondling and squeezing ... slowly increasing the desire in both of us. He moans and I feel dampness from his tip on my thigh.

Enough of this teasing—I want satisfaction, and I want it *now*. With one last slap and caress of his cheeks, I let him know in no uncertain terms that I thought he was enjoying the spanking far too much, and I would have to think of another punishment for him instead.

"I'm sorry Mistress, Vixen. I will do whatever you want! Anything!"

Mmmm, I like the sound of that. *A lot*. What can I ask of him? The tingling between my thighs responds for me with an excellent idea. His tongue. There. Right now.

I verbalise my request, and he kneels on the ground before me, smiling. He pushes me gently to lie further back on the couch, parting my legs with his knee. The first lick of his tongue is divine. The smooth texture against my lips melts me and makes my thighs want to part wider. His lips and fingers move expertly over me, coaxing me to reach the place I want to fly to.

Before long he has achieved his goal, and I am parachuting downwards back to earth again. A satisfied grin spreads across my face as I try to blow a strand of hair from my face that's stuck to my forehead. He slides his body up along mine to deliver a kiss to my mouth instead, and I taste the faint sweetness of myself on his lips.

"Are you satisfied now, Mistress Vixen?" he laughs and indicates that he's going to need to go to the bathroom and clean himself up. Only then do I realise he had been touching himself too and that we had both reached the pinnacle at the same time.

"Mmm, yes I would have to say that I am extremely satisfied, Mister Naughty!"

We laugh as he heads up the hallway to the bathroom while I sprint to the kitchen for water and a fast hair and face check in the mirror. Startled at my reflection, I stare for long minutes at this stranger in front of me. This sexy, powerful confident woman surely is not me? I know that following the Book can change a woman; this face staring back at me seems different to mine. I can't quite put my finger on exactly what I see … but I know I have changed. A different Me has emerged.

I feel the power; the control over my life and the yearning for adventure growing within. Society's boundaries are nothing but blurred distant shapes on the horizon, ineffectual and forgotten, with no relevant meaning. I recall the words uttered long ago on that day at the psychic fair, by the mysterious gypsy woman who had pressed the pulsing Vixen's Secret Handbook into my palm.

She spoke of power, and both physical and mental changes within. Warned me that with a different path comes change—and that I could not always know what this would be. The Book would guide me, she said. And I believe her.

So far, I've learnt a golden glow from the book shows approval for the Mark I will meet next. A red glow is a warning that all is not well, though the Book does not always expand on what the problem with each Mark is. I must do some of the thinking myself!

She also told me the Book has the power to update itself when required heralded by a purple glow, which I have now also experienced. She warned of blinding blue flashes and a few other vague instructions, but she would say no more than this to me. I have no idea what she means, *yet*. But my intuition is on high alert, and I have the feeling I am going to find out what she meant very soon.

The shower is running in the distance; Darz must have decided on a full body wash. I know he will be back - I'm not fully satisfied yet! But my attention cannot be drawn from my face, as I see tiny new flecks of gold twinkle within my irises. A flickering golden glow radiates from my body, as if shining through from the depths of my soul. Excitement fills my being, as I realise that I have had a glimpse into the unknown. My inner light shines brighter, and my confidence grows.

My skin feels smoother, softer, younger. I even feel lighter. I shake my head at my fanciful musings. That's all they are, aren't they?

Unbidden, my thoughts turn to Dreads, and his fetish like suggestions. If spanking was this easy and enjoyable; perhaps he *does* know something I don't about pleasure. My curiosity is running wild. Should I add him to my list of Marks? What would a play session with him be like?

The water shuts off and I hear Darz call me to get him a towel. I smile and reply that I'm coming, as I watch the last of the golden glow of my body shimmer into nothingness. What *was* that? I look closer into my eyes to see if the new golden flecks remain, or whether I just imagined them too.

The gold specks are still there. And I do feel different. Blinking rapidly, I smile a greeting to Darz as he emerges from the bathroom wrapped only in a towel. I have the feeling that there's going to be more surprises in store for me in the near future.

But exactly what that will be for this Vixen, I can only guess … for now. It seems that *anything* is possible!

Adventure Vixen

Thank you so much for purchasing this book!

If you enjoyed the story, I would be eternally grateful if you'd let the world know! If you loved Adventure Vixen and want to help the series grow, tell a friend about the book. Also tell other readers why you liked the book by leaving a review on Amazon, or sharing the Adventure Vixen book link on Amazon to social media.

If you love the books or if you leave a review, let me know at contact@karinachapman.com so I can thank you with a personal email.

Your support means more than you'll ever know! Thank you!

ABOUT THE AUTHOR

Karina Chapman is a Soul Journey Adventure Writer who has always loved connecting with others through both the spoken and written word.

Born in country South Australia, this Adelaide-based author, speaker and facilitators goal is to inspire others with her words by sharing the wisdom gained during her life so far.

Writing under the name KM Chapman, Karina's fictional books are based on real life experiences and the knowledge acquired on her journey.

Her intention is to entertain, uplift and help others by sharing her stories to encourage soul growth and connection.

The inspiration that she writes with comes from the many different lives she has already lived within this lifetime ... and from the Universe.